TWENTY TWO:THIRTEEN

ECHOES OF THE BLACK ROOM

JOSIAH BYJU GEORGE

BLUEROSE PUBLISHERS
India | U.K.

Copyright © Josiah Byju George 2025

All rights reserved by author. No part of this publication may be reproduced, stored in a retrieval system or transmitted in any form or by any means, electronic, mechanical, photocopying, recording or otherwise, without the prior permission of the author. Although every precaution has been taken to verify the accuracy of the information contained herein, the publisher assumes no responsibility for any errors or omissions. No liability is assumed for damages that may result from the use of information contained within.

BlueRose Publishers takes no responsibility for any damages, losses, or liabilities that may arise from the use or misuse of the information, products, or services provided in this publication.

For permissions requests or inquiries regarding this publication, please contact:

BLUEROSE PUBLISHERS
www.BlueRoseONE.com
info@bluerosepublishers.com
+91 8882 898 898
+4407342408967

ISBN: 978-93-5989-434-8

Cover Design: Shubham
Typesetting: Sagar

First Edition: January 2025

"To the ones who've had faith"

Roots

When I was nine years old, I wrote my first story. It was called *Josiah in Chocolate Land*. I can't even recall where the idea came from, but I remember scribbling it down during a free period in class. I pulled out my rough notebook and wrote two pages about Josiah's journey to a magical place made entirely of chocolate. That story wasn't great—in fact, it was terrible—but it became a defining moment in my life. A classmate noticed me writing and decided to report me to our teacher, Miss Archana Gonsalves, accusing me of wasting time. When Miss Archana took my notebook, I was certain I was doomed. I packed my bag, bracing myself for a scolding and possibly a call to my parents. Instead, something extraordinary happened. After reading the story, Miss Archana stood before the entire class and said, *"I just read a story written by one of our students, and I must say, I really liked it."* Then she asked everyone to give me a round of applause. To this day, that moment is etched in my memory. For the first time, someone recognized and appreciated my creativity, no matter how raw it was. I'll always be grateful to Miss Archana for that. That applause wasn't just for a story—it was for thinking differently, for daring to create. It's a memory that fuels me even now. No matter how my book is received, I'll always be proud that I've stayed true to the dreams of my nine-year-old self.

There's something else I want you to know. Whatever proceeds this book generates—be it ten rupees or ten crores—will go directly to charity, with a focus on education for underprivileged children. This isn't a marketing gimmick; it's a promise. Writing has always been my passion, a way to express the stories playing out in my mind. I've never written with the intention of making money. But if my words can help a child get closer to their dreams, then that's a driving force I'm happy to embrace. Passion should never be driven by greed. Because when it is, the passion fades, and all that's left is emptiness. For me, writing is about connection, creation, and purpose—and I hope that spirit comes through in my work.

Juxtapose

Will this work?

Taps the ashes of the cigar, eyes fixed on the dim light ahead.

It should.

Voice steady, he leans back, exhaling slowly.
Put 5 years of work into this.

Inhales a puff, letting the smoke curl upwards.

How do you think he'll react to this?

A brief pause, uncertainty flickering in his gaze.

Uncertain.

Reaches for the phone, dialling quickly.

What's the progress of Project Jenesis?

A voice crackles through the receiver.

Voice on Phone: 86%, sir. Should be done by tomorrow. I had informed sir, JAMES.

Looks at the man sitting across and mouths 'Did she?'

JAMES nods YES.

And the vitals?

Concern deepens.

Another pause.

Voice on Phone: Not constant, sir.

Hangs up, the line going dead, tension thick in the air.

Stress getting to you? *Asks JAMES*

Brushes it off.

The sequence doing fine?

Looks like it.

A knowing look.

Yes, you are stressed.

A slow exhale, eyes narrowing.

JESUS CHRIST has stopped funding. They want to see the results now, *continues JAMES*

Can't blame them.

Leans in, voice dropping to a murmur.

Worried about the subject?

Looks him in the eye, the smoke swirling between them.

No.

Coughs softly, clearing his throat.

How's the team looking?

Brief hesitation.

Stressed.

Smirks.

Side effects of an undercover operation. How much longer?

Checks his watch, calculating.

18 more hours. And when this works out?

Eyes narrow slightly, the weight of the moment pressing down.

JESUS CHRIST takes the credit.

A cold, distant look.

What if tomorrow's a code RED?

Gets up slowly, the man with black balaclava labelled PETER, walks away, the echo of footsteps lingering in the silence.

I

As the moonlight seeps into the room through a gap in the curtains, J lies there in the midst of a deep slumber, oblivious to the world around him. His senses detached from the realm of reality, while he is soaked into the cozy blanket in a state of tranquillity. The temperature of the room is pleasantly cool. The silence of the night amplifies every tick and tock of the clock hanging on the wall behind.

Yet in this calm setting, reality appeared to distort, making room for an unexplainable change. A towering, ominous creature stepped out of the darkness. With a strong physique and a height of six feet, he seemed almost ghostly in the moonlight, his features somewhat hidden but definitely human. He stood perfectly still for what seemed like an eternity, as though he was caught between worlds. Then, as if a machine had gone silent, he moved slightly, stirring with deliberate, exact movements. His eyes lingered on the street lamp-lit world below. He moved around the space with intention, moving as though he was reestablishing contact with a world that had been lost. His eyes lingered on the clock, its hands frozen at two, betraying a familiarity with the room's every detail.

02:10

Turning his attention to the softly humming laptop on the desk beside his favourite book **Small Arms of the World by Edward Clinton Ezell**, he paused, his gaze fixed on the screen, as if contemplating a decision. And then, with a resolve that seemed to echo through the night, he directed his gaze toward the bed, where J lay in peaceful oblivion. With a sense of purpose, he closed the distance, his intentions veiled in the mystery of the night. With careful steps, he moved towards where J lay, each motion carrying the weight of familiarity. Every corner seemed to whisper a story he knew by heart, from the slight imperfections on the walls to the way the moonlight danced on the floor. It was as if he had walked these paths countless times, guided by a deep-seated understanding that transcended mere recognition. As he traversed the space, there was a sense of ease in his movements, a certainty that bordered on instinct. It was as though the room itself had woven its essence into his being. But as he moved closer, his steps began to slow down as if understanding and learning from the sight entering his eyes. He stopped. He stayed motionless by the bed, as if in a deep state of shock, as if somebody had hit the pause button. All of a sudden, his back hit the wall on his right, as if somebody pushed him hard, or more like the sight of what he was seeing pushed him hard. The silhouette leaning against the wall, didn't take its eyes off the bed, he continued staring in horror as he witnessed his lifeless body lying on the bed undisturbed.

As J hovers over the body, his spectral form trembling with disbelief, he scrutinizes every detail, searching for any sign that this is all just a cruel trick of the mind. With every beat of his heart, dread consumes him, each pulse echoing the desperate plea in his mind: *'Please be a nightmare, please be a nightmare.'* With thorough care, he inches closer, afraid any sudden movement might shatter the fragile illusion. The similarities become impossible to ignore—the contours of the jawline, the curve of the lips—all too familiar, all too real. Cold dread settles in his stomach as he realizes the horrifying truth: it is indeed him lying there, lifeless. And yet, even as the evidence mounts before him, J refuses to accept the grim reality staring him in the face. He needs more than just visual confirmation; he needs tangible proof.

Anxiety grips him as he extends his hand, but instead of touching solid reality, he's met with a void, heightening his fear. His spectral form lacks the ability to interact with the physical world, leaving him adrift in despair. In that moment, the full weight of his predicament crashes down upon him, trapping him in a nightmare from which there is no waking.

As J hangs in the space between consciousness and the afterlife, his subconscious mind begins to whisper unsettling truths he'd rather not confront. *You're dead*, it murmurs, each word a chilling echo in the silence of his mind. Despite the relentless pounding of his heart, his outward expression remains blank. It's as if he's forgotten how to feel, how to react to this situation that confronts him. In denial, J resists the truth that lies before him. *This has to be a nightmare*, he whispers to himself, clinging desperately to the hope that he'll awaken in his physical body, safe from the horrors of the unknown. Without hesitation, he lowers himself to the cold, unforgiving floor. To his surprise, he does not pass through the floor as he might have expected in his spectral form. Instead, he lies there, in contact with the solid ground, a curious sensation that leaves him pondering the limits of his newfound existence. Could he pass through at will, or was he bound by some unseen force to the physical realm? As he lies there, eyes shut tight against the oppressive darkness, J clings to the fleeting hope that this is all just a dream from which he'll soon awaken. With each passing moment, he waits for the relief of consciousness to wash over him, to banish the nightmare that has consumed his reality.

After a while, J slowly opened his eyes. Deep down, he was almost certain nothing had changed, but a sliver of hope lingered in his mind. To his despair, he was still there, lying on the cold floor while his lifeless body lay on the bed above him. Tears welled up in his eyes as the harsh reality began to sink in. It felt as though his heart would burst from his chest; the agony too immense to contain. He started sobbing uncontrollably as thoughts flooded his mind. His life was over, just like that. There had been no warning, no last chance to be with his loved ones, to savor those final moments. Life had been snatched away in an instant. J sat up, leaning against the wall, his head resting against the cool surface. He folded his hands on his thighs and crossed his legs, his body shaking with sobs. Inside his head, he screamed for it all to be a dream, a cruel nightmare from which he could awaken. The realization of his untimely end overwhelmed him, and he continued to weep, the grief consuming him.

This is unbelievable. I don't know what to do. Who's going to help me? How did I even die? J's mind raced with questions, his thoughts a whirlwind of confusion and desperation. *I just want to get back. I haven't lived my life. I'm only 23. There's so much more to experience, so much more to see. I have dreams and goals... and what's left of them now? I'll never get to talk to Mum, Dad, and Meow again.*

The thought of his love, Meow, broke something inside him. The sobs he had tried to control erupted into wailing, the pain of never being able to speak to his loved ones again piercing his heart with unbearable pain. Distracted by the faint rattling of cars outside, J forced himself up, tears dripping onto his hands as he moved. He walked towards the window and stood there, staring out into the night. The street below glowed with an eerie orange hue under the street lamps, casting long shadows on the empty road. A few dogs lay asleep here and there, undisturbed by the world around them. One car sped by, taking advantage of the deserted streets, its headlights briefly illuminating the surrounding darkness. Across the street stood another building with numerous windows, all darkened. It seemed everyone else was enjoying a deep, peaceful slumber, oblivious to the turmoil J was enduring. He envied them, their ability to escape into dreams while he remained trapped in this nightmare, unable to find solace. His glance shifted to the sky; it was a new moon night. The absence of the moon made the sky seem even more desolate. J missed the comforting presence of the moon; it felt as though even the celestial body had abandoned him in his time of need. As he stood there, the weight of his predicament pressed down on him like a physical burden. The silent streets, the darkened windows, and the moonless sky all seemed to reflect his own sense of isolation and despair. He felt utterly alone, cut off from everything and everyone he had ever known.

As he continued to stay there, his head leaning against the window, he questioned himself: Where did it all go wrong? What did he do to deserve something like this? What sins had he committed, and of what magnitude, that he ended up dying? *So, is this the afterlife then?* he asked himself. *Is this what happens after death? Do you just roam around your lifeless body, reflecting and questioning yourself? And I'll have to watch my parents discover my dead body? Isn't this painful enough?* Despite his despair, a strange feeling arose within him. It was a curiosity, a keenness to see how people would react to his death. Deep inside, as this feeling continued to grow, he suppressed it because allowing it to surface would make him question if this was something he had wanted to see. Had he somehow manifested this earlier on? J turned back and looked at his dead body on the bed, nestled under the covers, motionless. The thought of getting to watch everyone react to his death was, in some unsettling way, going to be pleasant for him.

Out of nowhere, a quick thought surfaces: 'What if I just call out to someone? My dead body won't hear me, but what if someone else can?' Even the worst-case scenarios seem like a glimmer of hope. It's always better to try than do nothing. With that, J decides to go to his parents' room to see if he can call out to them, despite how absurd the idea seems. He rushes to leave the room, expecting to pass through the door. To his dismay, he collides with the solid wood. Taken aback, J realizes he can interact with some objects but not others. He pushes the door handle and pulls it open, expecting to find the hallway leading to his parents' bedroom. Instead, he's met with an abyss. The door opens into a black room, a void that swallows all light and sound. For a moment, he stands at the threshold, the darkness whispering secrets he cannot grasp. Fear grips him, but curiosity compels him forward. What lies beyond this darkness? As he steps into the void, the world as he knows it dissolves behind him, leaving only uncertainty ahead.

II

03:15

For a second, it seemed like it was probably dark because there was no light in the hallway. J even ignored the fact that usually the hallways would be dimly lit by the moonlight coming in from the west window. Tonight, it was pitch dark. J stepped across the threshold, trying to find the switchboard to his right. He was well-versed with this routine, having done it before when he used to stroll after midnight for water or a snack. Muscle memory guided him as he moved his hand to the right, trying to locate the switch he wanted to flick, but he found nothing. Immediately, panic set in, and he became restless trying to find the switch. Sooner rather than later, he realized there was nothing there. Finding the switch became a secondary concern when he realized he couldn't feel the walls either.

Eager to check whether he could feel any of the other walls, he walked a little further with both arms raised sideways, desperately trying to grasp something. He moved left and right, ran his hands over what, on an ordinary day, would have been the door to the bathroom on the right, or the kitchen counter on the left. This night, he felt the same on both sides: nothingness. When he first entered the room, he had hoped his pupils would adjust to the darkness, but his vision remained useless. The pitch-black void seemed to swallow everything, heightening his sense of dread. The darkness swallowed him whole, surrounding him in an eerie void. It felt like he had stepped into a shadowy abyss. With a mix of anticipation and fear, he couldn't resist calling out. His voice echoed through the emptiness, a solitary cry into the unknown. *Is anyone there?* he shouted, his voice shaking in the oppressive darkness, hoping for a sign or presence to break the silence and offer guidance. As J's voice faded, no response came. The silence lingered undisturbed, and the darkness continued to envelop him, offering no clues, answers, or comfort. A deep sense of isolation settled over him as he stood in the abyss, realizing he was truly alone in this mysterious place. It was a disheartening moment, and left him feeling lost.

It was emptiness all around him. Nothing to see, nothing to feel, nothing to hear. It was as if his basic senses were rendered useless. Slowly, J felt the urgent need to get out. He realized it was better to stay in his room by his lifeless body than to wander in this void. He quickly stepped backward, hands reaching behind him to find the doorknob and fall back into his room. The thought of never finding the doorknob and being stuck in the emptiness hit him hard, causing his anxiety to spike. He hastily searched for the knob, the fear of being trapped growing stronger with every step back. Just as he was about to give up, he felt a cold sensation on his palm. He twisted the knob and the door opened.

J is the kind of person whose faith was as weak as a whisper. He only called out to God when he was obliged to. But tonight, when emptiness and silence are his only companions, he called out to God, as an act of duty. He was probably doing it to satisfy himself that he did ask and God didn't respond. To look like he called out for help, but God didn't. J's voice quivered with desperation as he called out, *God, please help me!* His plea echoed through the darkness, a heartfelt cry for guidance and understanding in this strange and bewildering realm. As he waited, his heart heavy with uncertainty, he hoped for a sign, a glimmer of light, or some form of divine intervention to light his path. In this surreal space, he sought solace and direction from a higher power.

With no response to his plea and the oppressive darkness pressing in on all sides, fear and panic began to claw at J's chest. His breath quickened, and his heart pounded in his spectral chest. The realization that he was lost in this unfathomable void, separated from the world he once knew, gripped him like a vise. Panic surged through him, and a cold sweat formed on his brow, despite his lack of a physical body. Every shadow seemed to conceal unseen horrors, and the silence of this emptiness became an unbearable presence, suffocating him. His thoughts raced as he felt trapped in a nightmare with no escape. Amid his fear and panic, J's longing for answers and a way out intensified, driving him to search frantically for an exit. As the disorienting darkness threatened to overwhelm him, J's frantic eyes scanned his surroundings, desperately seeking any glimmer of hope. It was emptiness all around him. He realized it was better to stay in his room by his lifeless body than to wander in this void. He quickly stepped backward, hands reaching behind him to find the doorknob and fall back into his room.

In a sudden shift of reality, J found himself no longer standing but lying down on what seemed like satin bed sheets, feeling comfortable under the satin blanket in a well-conditioned room. The sound of the ticking clock once again filled the air. He blinked his eyes open to see the room bathed in soft moonlight. He was lying on his bed in his room. It must've indeed been a nightmare, he thought. He sat up in bed, as if to confirm he was in his physical body again despite the obvious cues. He looked at the clock.

03:17

Funny, he thought, the time seemed to be moving in sync with his nightmare. The last time he checked the clock, it was ten minutes past two. Or maybe he was overthinking it, he mused. Just one last time before going to bed, he checked his surroundings to ensure everything was normal and nothing stood out. Sure enough, it was his room, and he was in his own physical body. Everything seemed normal, confirming that what he had experienced was indeed a nightmare. Sincerely relieved, he lay back down, covered himself, and grinned at how silly it all seemed.

J lay in peaceful slumber, gripping the blanket up to his face. The room's temperature was perfect, creating a balance between warmth and cold. Even in deep sleep, one thought lingered in his mind: *I would like this night to go on forever.* As the clock ticked on the wall and the laptop hummed on the desk, J suddenly felt a change in gravity. He felt a weight on his legs, his body crouching forward, almost about to fall. He struggled to stabilize himself. Opening his eyes, he found himself standing in the corner of the room again. In the darkness, with the little light from the moon, his slouched silhouette looked like an old man. Frightened, he straightened up, wondering what was happening. Experiencing the same nightmare for a second time felt strange.

If I turn around, am I going to see my lifeless body again?

He didn't want to turn and check, but his body seemed to think otherwise. It took control and spun him toward the bed, where his lifeless body lay in the exact same position as before. He glanced at the clock above.

03:27

It had been exactly ten minutes since he last checked. The uncanny synchronization of his nightmares unsettled him. As the night continued, this nightmare was starting to feel less like a nightmare. He examined himself and confirmed he was in his spectral form again. Not particularly curious about the night's mysterious events, J decided to head to the door of his room, hoping that repeating the same action as before would help him return. He was caught between wondering if this was a nightmare or not. Regardless, he didn't want to be in this nightmare anymore. He would've preferred any other nightmare — even a more terrifying one. At least then, he'd know for certain it was just a dream.

Before anxiety and panic gripped him, J sped up to the door, opened it, and stepped over the threshold to enter the vast room of emptiness. This time, the aura felt different from the last. Despite having been there once before, the sight before him never ceased to intrigue him. *What was so darn attractive about nothingness?* His pupils, fully dilated, couldn't see anything in the dark void. He fought the urge to go exploring again but was reminded of the panic that had gripped him the last time when he was unable to find the door. He remained close to the door, with his back leaning against it as if to make sure it didn't disappear. For some reason, he thought to himself, if I step out too soon, I might not have changed anything, regardless of how absurd it sounded to him. Without wasting any more time, having spent about 10 seconds in the room, he turned the knob to get out. As he opened the door, in another snap, he was back in his bed. J flashed open his eyes, sat up, and looked at the clock.

03:27

The clock showed the same time as it did a moment ago when he was caught in the nightmare just 10 seconds earlier when he opened his eyes into the spectral realm. When the exact same thing happens a second time, it can't be dismissed as just a nightmare. Something about this night was way off. The only difference between this and the last transition was the time. This time, the time hadn't changed much, giving him all the more reason to think something was amiss.

He lay back down, now wide awake. The slumber he craved was unattainable. Every time he drifted into deep sleep, the nightmare recurred. He lay there, pondering the room he had just seen. Had he encountered something earlier that day which manifested in his dreams? What was that room anyway? It was the most dreadful thing he had ever seen, despite being completely empty. As he continued to contemplate the nightmares—or perhaps visions, he thought—he couldn't help but fall asleep again.

Mere moments later, to his horror, he cried inside his head,

Not again, please not again, please be on the bed, please be on the bed...

In the midst of the nap, J felt a weight on his legs and the cold tiles beneath his feet. He slowly opened his eyes, hoping, wishing, maybe even praying, that he was still in bed. But there he was, standing away from his bed, in the same spot he had found himself twice already that night.

03:28

He was overwhelmed by frustration and sorrow. He wanted to cry and lash out simultaneously. In frustration, he marched to the door, flung it open, and stepped inside. Barely two seconds passed before he opened the door to exit. As expected, with a quick change, he was back in his bed. He jolted upright, as if deciding not to sleep anymore that night. The night he had wished for peaceful rest had betrayed him. He thought perhaps the only way out was to stay awake. He sat up, his back against the headboard, heart pounding.

I am having a nightmare within a nightmare, he thought.

Even after it had happened three times, J struggled — or perhaps he was forcing his subconscious — to believe it was just a nightmare. But how much longer could he keep that up?

III

J gripped the blanket tightly in his hands like a frightened child. His situation tonight was becoming increasingly dire and frightening with each passing moment. Dreading another transition, he sat there motionless, hoping it wouldn't happen again. Not only did he dread experiencing it, but he also feared that it would confirm the enigmatic events of the night were not just a nightmare. In a flash, it happened again. Panic-stricken, J stood with his back turned to the bed. He stared at the wall, consumed with dread. For the fourth time tonight, he found himself in this form: a ghost, a soul, a spectral assailant. At this point, he was certain this was no nightmare. It was something far more sinister. Once again, his body took over. He didn't want to see it, yet he turned towards the bed, compelled to witness himself soulless. As he slowly pivoted, shivers ran down his spine at the sight before him. His lifeless body, unlike the last three times, was now seated with its back against the headboard. But that wasn't the most terrifying part. What made his skin crawl was the position of his body's head—tilted back against the wall, mouth agape, eyes rolled back. It looked as if someone had violently torn the soul from him. In the previous instances, his body had shown no such signs, but this time was different. There was no room for curiosity, only sheer terror. J was overwhelmed with fear, realizing that the way out of this predicament was nowhere in sight.

03:29

He could hear his own raspy breathing, his head pounding with his heartbeats. Despite the situation he was in, he discovered that his spectral form could interact with the window, the pane, and the little platform by the window where he chose to sit. Thoughts were running wild inside his head:

What's happening? Why?

How long will I keep going in and out of that door?

What is that room?

Am I dead? Will I be this way forever?

Amidst these questions, he desperately tried to avoid thinking about his loved ones. However, he could fight it no longer when Meow's face surfaced. It was a memory, or maybe not. He saw himself going to get her from work, listening to her talk about her day, hearing all the gossip about her co-workers, eating out together, and watching her laugh after teasing him. Every little thing that had seemed insignificant when he was alive now felt poignant in this moment. No matter how much he tried, the thought of never getting to do any of that again pained him. There was a feeling in his stomach, best described as unpleasant. One thought led to another, and soon he was imagining how Mum and Dad would react to his lifeless body sitting there in a very unsettling manner. Mum would scream at the top of her lungs; Dad would have no choice but to stay strong for her. The more he thought about it, the more he panicked.

Tears started to well up in his eyes. He knew that if he started crying, the thoughts that followed would only deepen his sorrow. He crouched down on the floor, controlled tears dropping onto the tile one after another. He thought about the life he had lost—all those moments, the fights with his parents, the arguments with friends—that now seemed precious. He longed to hear their voices, to feel their warmth. Tonight, the value of each of those moments had skyrocketed. J didn't know what it would take to reclaim his life; he would give anything, but he had nothing left. Despite this, he was willing to pay any price. The more he thought about what he was leaving behind, the more desperately he wanted it back. The determination growing within him acknowledged the difficulty of his situation, but when weighed on a balance, the need to regain his life outweighed the challenge ahead.

J then sits back, his legs folded beneath him, and gazes at the door. He thought to himself, every time he's entered the black room, the time he got back in the living world became shorter and shorter. The least amount of time was during his latest visit to the room, where he had barely 10 to 11 seconds back in the mortal realm.

So, he wondered:

Is there any way I can end this, or is there a way to somehow prolong my life in the living world?

But the time I get back has decreased significantly. How do I reclaim my life?

Would he come back if he stepped into the room this time, given that he's down to 10 or 11 seconds? What if the next transition halves it to 5 or 6 seconds? And after that, will the next transition be the last, leaving him stuck forever? Yet, he contemplated, there might be one more chance to figure it out. One more chance to study and understand the nature of the black room. This time, he would have to optimally utilize his time in the black room, gathering whatever information he could to escape this enigma.

Determined, J got up on his feet and walked towards the door. He reached the door, placed his spectral hand on the knob, and took a deep breath. He turned the knob and pulled the door open to the vast emptiness, the dark void, the endless room, the nothingness... to The Black Room, as he now coined it. J took in the view as if it were his first time. Despite having visited the room three times already, something about the atmosphere in the emptiness always seemed a little different. He stood at the threshold, taking it all in, then stepped inside, shutting the door behind him.

03:33

He stood near the door, turning his neck in all directions. His determination seemed to waver in comparison to the sight of endless emptiness. He moved a little further, carefully taking four steps, and turned around. There was no way to tell the door apart from the darkness, as there were no discernible features like light creeping in from the gaps around it. It looked no different from the one he had in his room. J worried that the deeper he went into this room or chamber, the harder it might become to find the door again. But at this point, it was now or never; he had to figure something out before he stepped back into his physical self. He needed to find a way to get to the exit if he went into the depths of The Black Room. He looked around again, this time to see if he could use anything to his advantage to trace back his steps. He couldn't see anything; he was as good as blind. He figured he needed an alternate solution,

I need to count my steps and only turn at right angles, he thought.

That seemed like the way to go. In this oppressing darkness, it was his best chance. But he felt the need to test this idea before going any further.

J moved a little from where he was, changed direction, moved for a short while, changed direction once more, took four steps, and halted. Now it was time to retrace his path. He recited the steps in his head, turned 180 degrees, took four steps forward, then took a left. He walked eight steps in that direction, turned right, took three steps, and halted. If he had returned to exactly where he had started, taking four more steps to his left would bring him face-to-face with the door. Carefully, he turned left, walked four steps, and came to a halt. He reached out to feel the knob, and there it was—the exit, right in front of him. He was certain he would have to use this method to find his way back. With this in mind, J set off into the expanse of The Black Room. As he walked, it made no difference whether his eyes were open or closed; both looked the same. He kept his arms up to avoid running into anything—or, to his horror, anyone. He made sure to take a fixed number of steps so that he wouldn't forget the count and only took turns at right angles. He decided to go left first, hoping to eventually come across a wall. J carefully walked the calculated number of steps, his arms stretched out in front of him.

After what felt like several minutes of walking and trying to feel or grab hold of something—anything—J gave up. The room seemed endless, boundless. It would have continued indefinitely if J had kept searching, but he stopped. Tracing his steps back to the exit door was easy since he hadn't taken any turns and had gone straight in the left direction. He reached the exit door, now on his right, and contemplated whether he should explore the other way as well. What if he found something in that direction? Reminding himself that this was probably his last chance to find anything before he ran out of time and was out of his body forever, he hesitated.

He stood there for a few seconds, trying to come to a decision. If the other side was the exact same as this one, crossing would be pointless. However, it would be foolish to leave stones unturned. So, he decided to go further—not as far as he did on the previous side, but at least some distance.

He went straight ahead without turning, walked for over a minute, and halted when it felt like he was getting nowhere. One thing he noticed was that his senses were useless in the black room. There was no smell, no sound; the silence seemed to make him nauseous, and there was obviously no sight. Feeling a little disappointed that he hadn't figured anything out, he turned to leave. As he slowly walked back, he couldn't shake the feeling of being watched. He shrugged it off, thinking it was just the darkness and the result of watching too many horror films with Mum. He continued walking, but a bit faster this time. After another four or five steps, he could no longer resist and turned to look. A pair of glowing green eyes stared back, sending shivers down his spine. He jolted, ran as fast as he could, and occasionally turned to see if he was being chased. The eyes shrank with distance as he ran. The spine-chilling sight caused him to lose count of his steps. He stopped immediately when the eyes were no longer visible but panicked, knowing he couldn't find the exit door. His pounding heart was the only sound in the room. With trembling hands, he reached out blindly, unsure if the door was within reach or agonizingly far away.

At irregular intervals, he looked back for the eyes while searching for the door. He felt a jolt of pain when his hand hit a spherical object—the doorknob. He yanked it open and looked around one last time to see if he was being followed before stepping out of the Black Room.

IV

According to the assumptions made by J, if indeed the time was being halved after every visit to the black room, this time he might have only 5 to 6 seconds to spare until he dies again. J shot up in bed, sitting straight with his heart hammering in his chest. He looked around frantically to see if the pair of glowing green eyes had followed him into the living world. Immediately, after confirming the eyes were not in the room with him, he looked back up at the clock.

...3......4......5......6...

Six seconds had passed, and J didn't die. This meant his assumptions were wrong. But now a more pressing question gnawed at him: how long until he dies? What if this was it—what if he had escaped the black room once and for all? He desperately wanted to believe it, but something didn't add up. The dread lingered, tightening around his chest like a vise.

03:53

It had been 20 minutes since J had entered the room. He decided to wait a few more minutes before taking any action. Sitting on the bed, he anticipated the next transition might occur at any moment. As he waited, he pondered: if he did escape, what had he done differently? Retracing his steps, he realized he had only gone in and out of the black room, just as he had done three times before. What had changed this time? The only difference he could identify was that he had stayed much longer than in his previous visits. Glancing at the clock again, he saw that it had been 20 minutes—longer than all three visits combined. What could this mean? Did it suggest that the longer he stayed in the room, the more time he gained back in the real world? He quickly reviewed his visits. The last two stood out because they were the shortest, while this visit was the longest. For the first two, he couldn't quite remember much about them, but he recalled that the first visit had resulted in about 10 minutes gained. If his theory was correct, then spending more time in the room would indeed result in a longer life. But what was the exact amount of time needed? He'd have to wait to find out. So far, 9 minutes had passed, and with the passing of the 10th minute, his assumption would be confirmed.

04:03

He sat there, pondering the events of the night, wondering if anyone would believe him if he shared his story. They'd probably think he was going crazy. Even if the events continued, there was no one he could confide in without sounding absurd. Despite this, a tiny glimmer of hope flickered inside him, suggesting he had regained control of his life, though logic argued otherwise. He felt a surge of excitement at the thought of meeting Meow the next day, of seeing Mum, and reconnecting with his friends. Was it because he had come so close to death that night, so close to losing his loved ones forever? Regardless, the thought of seeing them filled him with warmth. Slowly, without realizing it, this warm sensation lulled him to sleep as he sat on the bed, leaning against the headboard. The position looked uncomfortable, but it had been a long time since he had gotten any rest.

As time passed and J continued to sleep, the world beyond carried on, unbothered and unyielding. The soft hum of distant traffic and the occasional bark of a dog marked the early morning hours. A faint breeze rustled the leaves of the trees lining the street, carrying the scent of damp earth. J's theory had just been confirmed, but he wasn't awake to realize it.

After having been in a deep slumber for a while, the loud and heavy sound of the milk truck disrupted his sleep. Every morning at thirty minutes past five, the truck arrived with gallons of milk for the store. The truck was so old that its exhaust system made noises so loud it acted as an alarm for most of the people in the neighbourhood. As usual, J woke from his sleep to the sound of it and headed to the washroom to relieve himself. Still groggy and moving on muscle memory alone, he seemed to have forgotten what had happened earlier and mindlessly opened the door to the washroom. As he returned, his body ached to reach the bed. He was so lost in his desire to sleep that he missed the sound of a thud from behind him. But as he opened the door to his bedroom, something was amiss. It took a few seconds for him to become fully conscious and realize he was standing at the threshold to The Black Room. In utter shock, J stumbled back, leaving the door open.

How had it happened? I thought... I thought it was over. Wha-?

He turned back to face the sight that greeted him. His body, again lifeless, lay on the cold floor, face down. This time, fear gripped him so hard that the closer he seemed to get to ending it, the further away the end seemed. He spun around, realizing he had left the door open, and fearing the pair of glowing green eyes, he jolted and closed the door.

05:33

His heart felt like it was going to break out of his chest. He looked at the time and realized Mum might wake up any moment now and see his body lying on the floor.

Even if I can get back, that's going to be a lot of explaining to do, he thought. I can't let her see me like this—not just because of the explanation, but because of the mental impact of seeing me face down on the floor, not moving. If she gets close enough to realize I'm not breathing, I can't face her reaction. J checked the time again. Two minutes had passed since the transition, which meant it had happened exactly at thirty-three minutes past five. Now, if he could establish a relationship between the time spent in the black room and the time, he regained consciousness, he might find a way around this predicament. He calculated: it had been an hour and forty minutes since he exited the black room, which was 100 minutes. He had spent 20 minutes in the black room, and the relationship between these two figures was that the greater one was five times the smaller one.

Does this mean for every amount of time spent in the black room, he regains five times that amount back in the real world?

There was only one way to find out, he thought. To have enough time to return to his physical body and get back to his room before Mum came out of hers, he'd need at least five minutes in the real world. If his calculation was correct, he'd get those five minutes by spending one minute inside the dark void. With a plan in mind, J strode towards the door and opened it. As he stood there, about to enter, the fear of being in that room with those eyes watching him from some corner filled him with dread. But, determined, he stepped in and closed the door.

He clung to the door, afraid to step out any further and risk encountering the pair of eyes again. For now, his only goal was to stay inside for a minute and then leave. He wasn't sure if his calculation was correct, but it was all he had.

Better than nothing, he thought.

The immediate problem was tracking the time. He quickly started counting from ten, assuming about ten seconds had passed since he entered. J didn't realize it, but his counting quickened to match his racing heartbeat. Despite the pitch darkness, he kept looking around for any sign of the glowing eyes. As before, the aura within the void seemed to shift slightly, but it was almost impossible to discern what was changing each time he was in there.

32... 33... 34... 35... 36...

He leaned his head back against the door, listening for any sound of Mum approaching or any indication that she was out of her room. J felt the need to write down his equation when he got out of the room. He wondered, what were the odds that he was trapped in a nightmare within a nightmare? But everything felt too real to dismiss as just a dream.

51... 52... 53... 54... 55...

With five seconds remaining, he still heard no signs of Mum. He told himself he needed to finish quickly. Even if Mum saw him, she shouldn't see him lying on the floor.

SIXTY!

He turned the knob and, in a flash of shifting reality, woke up with pain searing across his face from the fall he had taken a few minutes ago. He got up, holding his face, almost silently wincing in pain. Most of the pain was coming from his nose and forehead; the rest of his body seemed alright.

Are you alright, J? Mum asked, having witnessed everything from behind him.

Yes, yes. Just returning to bed, J replied, startled.

I just saw you get up off the floor. Did you fall?

Yes, I slipped.

Let me see...

No, Mum, I'm alright. I'm going to bed now.

You better be alright, J.

J wanted to rush back to his room, but to avoid arousing suspicion, he moved slowly, like someone who had just woken from a deep sleep. He made his way to his room and gently closed the door behind him. He looked at the clock, he had five minutes till the next transition.

05:34

He latched the lock on the door and sat at his desk, taking out a paper and a pen. He recollected the relationship between the times he had calculated earlier and penned it down. With the relationship clearly in front of him, he decided to simplify it into an equation. According to his deduction, the amount of life regained is equal to five times the amount of time spent in the black room. He created a simplified equation for this code breaker: $[y = 5x]$, where y is the amount of life regained and x is the time spent in the black room. If J spends 2 minutes in the black room, he regains 10 minutes of life. Just as he had calculated, when he spent 20 minutes in the black room, it resulted in 100 minutes of life regained. He carefully folded the piece of paper, placed it neatly on the keyboard of his laptop, and closed it.

Earlier, his mind was racing with thoughts of being trapped in a nightmare within a nightmare. If that was the case, he needed to do something that would stand out in the real world—something odd and unmistakable. After considering a few options, he came up with an idea. He got off the chair at the desk, walked to the door, and pressed his ear against it to listen for sounds on the other side. A quick glance at the clock told him he had two more minutes. Whatever he planned to do, it had to be done within that time. From the sound of it, Mum had walked towards her bedroom at the other end of the house, as she normally would every morning, with her cup of tea. She would sit on her chair by the window and enjoy her tea. Seizing the opportunity, J stepped out and headed to the kitchen. It wasn't as dark as before. The sun was beginning to rise, casting a faint, bluish light. He walked through the dining room to the kitchen, went to the counter with the cutlery tray, grabbed an old silver spoon, and rushed to the washroom. Before entering, he checked to make sure

Mum wasn't around. He hid the spoon in the cabinet beneath the washbasin, then hurried back to his bedroom and shut the door behind him. Relieved, he stood by the door.

Everything changed when he saw his body fall from within him and hit the floor face-first. J, now in his spectral form, remained standing against the door. It had happened again—his body crashed to the floor. He looked at the clock and realized he still had a minute left, but then it occurred to him that he might have miscounted the seconds. He needed just a few more seconds to get up and into bed. Without further hesitation, J opened the door to the black room again. He counted to five and exited the room. This was the sixth time he had transitioned in and out of the spectral realm. He woke up on the cold floor, pain soaring through his jaw this time. Grunting, J got into bed. He lay down as he would while sleeping, awaiting the transition in about 15 to 17 seconds. He ran his fingers across the regions where he experienced pain, feeling his lips and forehead swollen. In the next moment, a surprising change of events occurred: he found himself, for the seventh time, in his spectral form, standing by the window. Did the transition happen too soon? he wondered. Was he overthinking? Even when he had at least 10 seconds left, how did he end up in the spectral form so quickly again? Did he miscount the seconds again? he thought. Having experienced this several times, J seemed on the brink of losing hope. He didn't look anything like before; he appeared tired and hopeless, painfully aware of his helplessness. Without even glancing at his body lying on the bed with its mouth agape and eyes rolled back, he turned then walked despondently towards the door. As he placed his hand on the knob, he shuddered slightly at the thought of what awaited him inside. Would the pair of glowing green eyes finally confront him? And if they did, what would he do? He opened the door and stepped inside slowly, like a prisoner being led to his cell, then closed the door behind him.

V

05:41

He leaned against the door and slid down to sit there. Before he thought about anything else, he realized he needs to figure out at what time he needs to leave the black room in order to regain sufficient time to live in the real world without raising any suspicion. He thought about the equation he had written down, **y=5x**. On an ordinary day, J would wake up at around 8:30 or 9 latest. So even today, he'll have to do the same, at least till Mum will have to wake him up. If Mum did go and wake J up, she'll see the open mouth and eyes rolled back and that will cause her pressure levels to drop and God knows what will follow. He decides he'll have to wake up at 8:30, which must be around two hours and fifty minutes from now, he thought. That should give him somewhere around 14 hours or so. He further calculated, according to the amount of time in the mortal realm regained, the next transition should occur at around 11:30 pm at night.

The plan seemed fine, but nevertheless all of this dreaded him because there looked like there was no way out of this, and if he did want to confide, whom would he confide in?

J sat there, feeling hopeless, searching for a light at the end of the tunnel. In his case, any visible light seemed to be blocked by huge boulders.

What's next? he wondered. *I can't spend the next few years of my life based on precise calculations! I want to be out there, not in this dark room of nothingness.* If this was a nightmare, he pleaded silently, someone needed to wake him up.

Suddenly, a thought occurred to him: how was he supposed to keep track of time? He definitely wasn't going to count up to the 180th minute. If he messed up, the consequences might not be as severe, but he wasn't willing to risk it. He needed to find a way to track time easily. The only likely solution seemed to be guessing time based on the noises outside. Around 6:30 a.m., the sound of school buses could be heard, sometimes even the chatter of children. Between 7:15 and 7:30, the milkman delivered a litre of milk. Now, he just needed one more sign before 8:30. J got to his feet and began pacing back and forth, a habit he had whenever he needed to think. He considered the garbage man, Sam, a nice guy he'd known for almost

15 years. But in all that time, J also knew that Sam didn't come on Tuesdays. Sam would have been an easy marker—he came at 8:30 every morning, except Tuesdays. The next reliable sound came at 9:30, when his mum's alarm went off as a reminder to take her morning medicine. If only it were at 8:30, things would be so much easier.

But as he continued to think, he couldn't ignore the fact that, for the seventh time, the aura inside the black room seemed to have shifted again. The change was indescribable yet evident and unsettling. He carefully scanned the room, looking for the pair of glowing eyes, but found nothing. One thing was certain: the air in the room felt denser. Sliding down against the door, he sat down.

I've figured out the first two signs. Hopefully, the third will come to me naturally, he thought. But instead, he procrastinated, choosing to sit and sulk, probably.

He continued to sit there, and memories started rushing into his head. Memories of Meow. It came out of nowhere, but in times of despair, he often thought of her. Somehow, thinking of Meow always helped to calm his racing heart. He was immediately transported back to the time they first met. They had arranged to meet on a Sunday evening after cancelling their plans the day before. J vividly remembered making a U-turn in his car, and as he did, he saw Meow approaching on her scooter, wearing a pink hoodie. In that moment, unlike any other first meet-up, J suddenly felt the urge to turn around and go back home. Meow looked mad about something. Though he had known her for a long time, he hadn't seen her in years. So, for him to speculate that she might be angry didn't seem far off. But then he thought,

Why not give it a shot?

He picked her up, and she sat in the car. Surprisingly, the vibe started off well. As it turned out, they had a lot to chat about. Meow was now working, unlike the last time he'd seen her, and she had plenty to say about the corporate world. The immediate thought that crossed J's mind was,

This chick seems very ambitious...

On the same note, J didn't have much to add, as he was still a student. Yet, unlike every other awkward first date J had experienced, this one felt remarkably comfortable. There was plenty to talk about. He wondered if it was because, as Schrödinger might say, the cat was alive—or if it was because he felt some pressure, given the high expectations Meow had set through their texts before meeting. Whatever the reason, they hit it off well. Unfortunately, J had to cut the date short because of a sparring practice. Both of them went home that evening feeling content. They decided to meet the next day, and as luck would have it, the very next day was Valentine's Day!

06:34

The chatter of kids and the hum of the bus engine brought him back to reality, signaling that it was around 6:30 AM. Nothing had changed in the black room; the air was still dense, his dilated pupils still adjusting to the lack of light, and the only thing adding color to his life was the memory of Meow. The sounds of the clinking of utensils could be heard from the other side. It was Mum doing the dishes probably.

J, annoyed that the sounds had disrupted his thoughts, leaned his head against the door and closed his eyes, hoping to pick up right where he left off. Instead, his mind wandered to a different memory with Meow. This time, it was around her birthday. J had spent the entire week planning it. On the evening of her birthday, Meow was blindfolded and led to the bedroom. When the blindfold was removed, she was greeted by a breathtaking sight: a room filled with flowers, chocolates, and soft toys. For someone unaccustomed to receiving gifts, she was overwhelmed by the scene before her. Later that night, J felt a warmth in his chest—it was one of the best nights he'd ever spent with Meow, if not the best.

Later that night... later that night... what happened after we cut the cake?

For some reason, he couldn't recall the rest of the evening. It was a strange sensation. No matter how hard he tried, the memory eluded him. He could feel the joy of that night, but why couldn't he remember it? The absence of such a significant memory puzzled him. To reassure himself, he began to fabricate memories, convincing himself that they were real.

Yes, yes, then we had dinner and went for a drive! That's right, he thought.

But deep down, something was gnawing at him, something he chose to ignore.

Time seemed to be moving faster. Being lost in his thoughts made the minutes slip by more quickly than usual. Surprisingly, his mind then drifted to a memory of his grandfather—or GP, as he fondly called him. J had been very close to his grandfather, but in recent years, the angels had taken him.

J used to eagerly await the end of his exams, knowing he'd be heading to his GP's. His holidays there were always full of adventure. GP always had something planned, no matter what. Among GP's prized treasures was a vintage bicycle from the early

1900s, lovingly fitted with a small seat, perfect for little J. They would ride it together, running errands and exploring their surroundings, as though that old bicycle could carry them across the entire world.

GP was incredibly loving — he cared for J in ways that made him feel cherished. He bathed him, dressed him, sang him lullabies… everything a child dreams of when they think of love. As J grew older, he came to realize that no one could ever love him the way GP had. GP always shared his hopes and excitement for J's future, dreaming of the day he'd see J graduate and rise to great heights. But sadly, GP had to say goodbye too soon.

This memory, however, was one that J cherished. He was nine years old, during his summer holidays. His parents used to send him to GP's house during the break. J remembers this vividly because something about that one evening stayed with him through the years. It had started like every other evening at GP's house. It was 4:30 in the afternoon. GP's house was perched on a hilltop, part of a Military Colony designated for army officials like him. The scenic view from the patio was breathtaking—the golden glare of the setting sun, plants and trees all around, everything was silent and peaceful. After a post-lunch nap, both J and GP sat on chairs on the patio, enjoying the view. The smell of chips wafted from the kitchen. The steam from their tea danced lazily in the sunlight, like a fleeting ghost. GP pushed his reading glasses down to the tip of his nose and continued reading the remaining articles of the morning newspaper. Just then, Gramma (his grandmother) brought out a bowl of crispy, hot banana chips, filling the air with their irresistible aroma. J was overjoyed when she placed them on the small, round table between him and GP. He put down his book and eagerly dove into the chips. GP watched happily and joined in, while Gramma sat on J's right. What made that evening so special to J was the simplicity of it: the three of them sitting on the patio, enjoying hot chips and tea in comfortable silence. The atmosphere was so serene that words were unnecessary—they were probably conversing in silence. The peace he felt that evening was unmatchable.

Just as J felt that same peace settle within him, the sound of a doorbell abruptly startled him back to reality.

07:19

He figured the time was somewhere between 7:15 and 7:30 AM. Now, he realized he needed to find a way to track 8:30 AM. Fortunately, he had two signs to tell him that two hours had passed. But what next? He started brainstorming again, knowing that if he didn't figure out a way and missed his slot to step out, his mother would find him dead, and everything that would follow...

No more vehicles to signal 8:30 or even 8 for that matter, he thought.

After several minutes of thinking, J still hadn't come up with a solution. He was proud of himself for figuring out how to track time the first two times, but now he felt foolish for being stuck. It was as if the universe was playing with his life. The only option left seemed to be counting. If the time was 7:30, or *WORST-CASE SCENARIO*, as he would say in life, 7:20, he would need to count for approximately 70 minutes—4,200 seconds. Without wasting any more time, J began counting.

1...2...3...4...5...6...

He felt absurd doing this. Even as he counted, he knew his pace wasn't constant—sometimes too fast, sometimes too slow—but he hoped the overall result would be somewhere near 8:30 AM, if not exactly on point. As he counted, his thoughts drifted to another memory.

21...22...23...

It was a memory of Dan, his beloved dark-brown Great Dane, whom he used to call his brother. J got Dan when he was 13. Those were some of the happiest months for J, until Dan was sent away as a guard dog. But during those months, Dan brought so much joy to the house. On an ordinary day, their apartment felt gloomy, but after Dan arrived, the atmosphere changed. J had so much fun and laughter playing with Dan every day. As soon as he got off the school bus, Dan would poke his head through the apartment window and bark, as if saying, *come home, bro, let's play!*

Excited, J would run home, and Dan would jump on him, licking his face. J didn't even bother changing out of his school clothes; they'd start playing right away. J would face the wall and start counting to 10 while Dan would hide behind the couch, unaware that his tail was poking out from the other end.

582...583...584...

After counting, J would pretend not to see Dan and look around. As soon as he got near the couch, Dan would jump out, and J would act surprised. But after Dan was sent as a guard dog to Dad's factory, their time together dwindled to once or twice a week, and as J got older and busier, it eventually became once or twice a month. The growing gap always gnawed at J, and even now, he often felt guilty for not being a good brother. The thought of Dan completely occupied his mind, and J swore to himself that he'd spend time with Dan as soon as he got out of this.

Time was flying by now, and J mindlessly counted past 2,000 seconds. Short memories of Dan kept playing in his head. Dan grabbing a food packet from a plastic bag and running, with J chasing after him to get it back. Dan jumping onto the couch, biting open the packet, and pulling out his favorite chew sticks. J laughed at the sight but had to take the packet away because too many chew sticks weren't good for Dan. Another time, J saw Dan carrying his 'Blankie' across the room, searching for the perfect spot to nap. As a pup, Dan was so smart; he'd fetch his blankie whenever it was time to sleep. As soon as he saw J heading to the bedroom, Dan would grab his blankie from the balcony and excitedly run to J's room, carefully spreading it on the floor before lying down. J missed those moments but was grateful to have experienced them.

3061...3062...3063...

08:10

He realized he was roughly 1,000 seconds—16 minutes, or a quarter of an hour—away from 8:30 AM, assuming his calculations were right. Time should be 8:14 then, he thought to himself. Suddenly, something caught his attention from the other side. J got off the floor and pressed his ear against the door. It was the man who sang in the morning. J had completely missed this. Every morning, around 8 AM, the man would start singing and continue until 10. J had never been so glad that the man sang every day and so loudly. It indicated that time had passed 8 AM but hadn't yet reached 8:14 AM because the man always started before then. J figured he might be off by a few minutes but thought, *It must be around 8:05 or something.*

The man continued singing louder and louder. On an ordinary day, it would've been annoying, but today J was more than glad to hear him. J remembered waking up to him singing some days as J lay in bed, eyes partially open, and would try to locate the source of the sound through the window and see this man, topless and wrapped in a cloth around his lower half, screaming songs at the top of his lungs.

The thought of lying in bed reminded J of the state his physical body was in at that moment. Before Mum witnesses the horrifying sight of his mouth agape and eyes rolled back, he needed to get back. He recalled that it was usually around this time that Mum came into the room to throw open the curtains. J immediately scrambled to his feet and prepared to get out.

3348... 3349... 3350...

J figured there was no point in counting anymore; he was almost 90% sure he was there. He needed to get out right now. With a deep breath, J twisted the doorknob and stepped out of the void.

VI

08:16

His eyes snapped open, and a jolt of pain shot through his jaw from having been agape for so long. The sunlight poured in, forcing his pupils to adjust to the brightness. The once-muffled sound of a man singing now resonated clearly in the room. The sudden noise of footsteps made him flinch, his mind racing with the thought that the pair of glowing green eyes had returned. But it was only Mum, opening the windows.

Wake up, sleepyhead!

Despite everything, a glimmer of hope sparked within him. Maybe it had all been an elaborate nightmare. That thought brought a small measure of relief, settling uneasily in his stomach. Determined to confirm if it was indeed a new day, he got out of bed. Fully awake now, he grabbed opened his laptop from the desk and his heart sank as he saw the piece of paper on the keyboard.

Could it really be just any paper?

He unfolded it carefully, revealing the equation written in neat script:

$y = 5x$

This sight crushed his fleeting hope. The nightmare from the previous night seemed all too real now. His hope oscillated wildly—sometimes rising, only to plummet deeper than before. Disheartened, J folded it back and placed it inside the laptop and closed it.

While brushing his teeth, J's mind was consumed by the events of the previous night. His body moved on autopilot, guided by muscle memory. He barely registered his actions until he found himself halfway through his shower. As he stepped out and caught his reflection in the mirror, the sight of his bruised face brought a jolt of reality. His lips were swollen, and his forehead was a patchwork of bruises. Pain radiated from these areas, along with his jaw and body, sore from the falls.

After dressing, he sat down for breakfast, his thoughts still mired in disbelief over the night's intensity. How had he experienced what felt like an afterlife and returned? He realized he needed to search for answers.

Has anyone else gone through something like this?

He was about to head back to his room when Mum appeared with a plate of bread and scrambled eggs. Her eyes immediately caught the bruises.

Is that a bruise, J? Oh, dear Lord, your lips are swollen! Did you get into a fight? You were fine last night before bed! What happened? Did you fall this morning when I saw you?

Yes, Ma. I slipped near the bathroom and fell face-first. Nothing to worry about, okay?

She insisted he sit down while she fetched a warm compress. *Be careful when you're walking. How tough is it to walk anyway? I've been walking for 45 years and only fallen twice.*

Okay, Ma. It happens. I was in deep sleep, and the floor was wet.

Your feet were wet, you idiot! You didn't dry them properly. (She started dabbing the warm compress on his face) *How many times have I told you to dry your feet properly? You never listen!*

Despite her scolding, J felt a flicker of contentment. It was comforting to hear her concern, a stark contrast to the fear he felt last night when he thought he might have said goodbye to everything dear. The warm compress provided some relief, and he resolved to get to his phone as soon as possible.

IS THERE AN AFTER-LIFE?

- **Wikipedia: Afterlife**
  - *Summary:* Explains the afterlife as a state where consciousness or identity might continue after death.
  - *Link:* Read more

- **Britannica: Afterlife - Definition, Belief, Religion**
  - *Summary:* Discusses various religious and philosophical views on continued existence after death.
  - *Link:* Read more

- **Quora: What Happens in the Afterlife?**
  - *Summary:* Personal opinions and near-death experiences shared by users.
  - *Link:* Read more

J tapped on the Wikipedia link first, hoping for a general overview of the concept. He read about different cultural beliefs and theories regarding the afterlife, intrigued by the variety of perspectives. The Britannica entry provided a more detailed analysis of religious and philosophical views, which added depth to his understanding. The Quora results offered a range of personal experiences and opinions, which felt more subjective but still insightful. Finally, the rest of the articles presented a spiritual perspective on what happens after death, aligning with some of J's own contemplations. As J continued to search, he was met with increasingly mixed and conflicting answers. The variety of perspectives only seemed to deepen his confusion and erode his hope for a clear answer. Each new source added to his growing sense of uncertainty, making him feel as though he was spiraling further away from the answers he desperately sought. Feeling both overwhelmed and enlightened, J closed his phone, realizing that the search had only scratched the surface.

J decided to search further with different keywords, but nothing reaped of benefit. It was the one and the same results over and over till J typed something odd into the search bar and tapped GO.

THE BLACK ROOM

1. **"The Black Room: A Mysterious Phenomenon"**
    - *Summary:* An article exploring various accounts of a phenomenon known as "The Black Room," where people report experiencing a pitch-black space during intense or near-death experiences.
    - *Link:* Read more
2. **"The Black Room: Psychological and Paranormal Perspectives"**
    - *Summary:* Discusses psychological explanations and paranormal theories related to the concept of "The Black Room." Examines how it might relate to the brain's response to extreme stress or spiritual experiences.
    - *Link:* Read more
3. **"What is The Black Room? Personal Stories and Theories"**
    - *Summary:* A collection of personal stories and theories from people who have encountered or dreamt about "The Black Room."
    - *Link:* Read more

J tapped on the first link, eager to learn more about this intriguing concept. The article delved into accounts from people who had experienced a sensation of being in a black, void-like space during critical moments, which seemed eerily familiar to what he had felt. As he read on, he wondered if there was a connection between his own experience and these accounts.

But nothing he read matched what he was experiencing. These articles described dreams of being in a dark void or an empty space, but none spoke of drifting between realms. One thought kept coming back to him—he needed to talk. Someone who could understand the depth of his situation, someone who would sincerely listen. He needed to confide in Meow. Despite his earlier hesitation, he knew this predicament was too overwhelming to handle alone.

He opened their chat to message her, only to realize he had left her on seen after their argument last night.

MEOW (Last Seen at 1:15AM)

YESTERDAY

Meow: It feels like you're not putting any effort into this relationship, J. **[11:53 PM]**

TODAY

J: Hey, sorry about last night, but can we meet in the morning please? I really need to talk to you about something. **[08:50 AM]**

Meanwhile, J sat back in his seat at the dining table, nervously waiting for his phone to buzz, desperately hoping to see a "YES" from Meow. He put the phone down and decided to eat. Maybe the events of last night had built up an appetite.

Are you okay, J?

Yes, why?

It's strange that you didn't notice I forgot to toss some salt into the eggs.

Oh... umm... I think they taste fine.

Oh, please, daydreamer. Here's some salt. And seriously, you can admit it's your fault sometimes.

Yeah... yeah...

As J continued to chew, his taste buds were working, but the flavours weren't reaching his brain.

He was too caught up in calculations. According to the spectral equation, as he termed it, the next transition—the eighth—should happen at 10:30 PM. Unfortunately, everyone knew J didn't go to bed at 10:30. He usually hit the sack around 1 or 2 AM, calling that time the "chillax period" of the day—his time to randomly scroll through Instagram, watch videos, or read. Convincing anyone that he'd go to bed early was going to be tricky, but procrastination always wins. He decided to plan for that later. For now, he desperately needed to talk to Meow and kept checking his phone. That's when he noticed a notification from his beer-buddy, Smo.

SMO (Last Seen 4:03 AM)

TODAY

S: Bro!! Wer you at? I got some green, you down? [03:30 AM]

J: Nah bro. Let me know if you are free for a beer in the evening. Having a shit day today. [09:01 AM]

J and Smo had been friends since childhood. Smo was two years younger than him but seemed two years older when it came to intoxication. Not intoxication in a bad sense, but in a decent way—if there's such a standard at all. Three years ago, their childhood group shattered due to cracks forming in their friendships. J and Smo were the only ones to survive the fallout. Since then, they had become beer buddies, but their meet-ups were more about exchanging life lessons than just drinking. They would grab two bottles of Budweiser Magnum, head to a secluded spot deep within the woods, and park their vehicle. The beer bottles, wrapped in newspapers, were carefully unwrapped as they waited for their eyes to adjust to the darkness. The surroundings would soon transform into a beautiful sight—trees everywhere, even overhead, with a small clearing left open to watch the sky, and sometimes, the stars. After a couple of sips, they would start talking about life.

They called this their shrine. Every visit to the shrine was fun and enlightening. They would leave with a bottle of beer down and a fresh perspective on life. Today, more than any other day, J felt the need for it.

MEOW (Online)

Meow: No, let's end this. I cannot waste my time like this. **[09:30 AM]**

J: Babe, I am really sorry about last night, but I really need someone to talk to right now, I need you, please!! **[09:31 AM]**

Meow: Say it on chat. **[09:31 AM]**

J: If I could, I would, but I can't so I won't. Please understand. **[09:31 AM]**

Meow: Meet @5 **[09:32 AM]**

J: OK, great! Thank you so much. **[09:32 AM]**

She didn't reply to J's last text, but he was relieved that she was willing to meet. Now, J began to piece together how he would describe the events of last night. How could he explain it in a way that sounded real and not like a desperate attempt to get back together?

Let's just get there first, he thought.

VII

Having spent most of the morning and afternoon fighting off panic attacks, J tried to distract himself with some light-hearted activities. But as the day wore on, it was finally time to meet Meow.

16:30

J headed to his room to change. Today, the goal wasn't to look good, but just to show up and try to open up to Meow, hoping she'd understand. He grabbed the first clothes he could reach and put on an old, worn watch with a leather strap. This watch held a significance only a loving eye could recognize—it had once belonged to GP, who passed it to J before his death last year, along with a copy of **Small Arms of the World by Edward Clinton Ezell**, knowing J's fascination with firearms. The watch wasn't just an heirloom; it had been GP's during his military days.

Mum was napping in her room, enjoying a post-lunch rest. J had informed her of his evening plans during lunch, so he quietly left the house. They had decided to meet at a nearby café, but first, J had to pick up Meow. Under the bright red skies, as the fresh air hit his face while he maneuvered the motorcycle, he felt a rare surge of positivity. He was looking forward to seeing Meow today. As he reached the main lane, he took a left turn and joined the main road. A little further ahead, he spotted Meow standing on the curbside. Meow didn't look thrilled—in fact, her expression was clouded with concern. The smile that had formed on J's face began to fade. He slowed down and moved to the left, but something felt wrong.

16:45

As he glanced at Meow again, her expression had morphed from unhappy to outright scared. She opened her mouth wide, as if to shout, but J couldn't understand what was happening. Suddenly, Meow started screaming. A deep fear gripped J. In the following seconds, everything became painfully clear—he was no longer in control of the motorcycle, nor of his own body. The transition had occurred. Spectral J came to a halt, floating, as he saw his physical body crash into a light post on the left. He turned to see Meow, who had dropped her bags and was now running towards his body, screaming. Tears streamed down Meow's face as she collapsed beside J's body, which lay in a growing pool of blood, that matched the color of the scarlet skies. A crowd began to gather around the accident. She screamed for help, and fortunately, a white Skoda Kodiaq stopped. Three strangers lifted J's body and placed it in the back seat of the car, with Meow getting in as well, cradling his head in her lap. The vehicle sped away, leaving spectral J behind, watching helplessly.

The white dot of the car disappeared from view, leaving J standing alone, trying to figure out what to do next. It wasn't like he could just ask for a ride—no one could even see him. Panic began to rise within him again, and tears welled up in his eyes, Meow's screams echoing in his mind like a broken record. Before, when the transitions occurred, there was always his bedroom door to enter in and out of— where was he going to find a door on the road this time? Frantically, J looked around. No door in sight, no way out, until he spotted a kid entering an ice-cream parlour. Clinging to a thread of hope, he marched toward it, praying that this would be the door— otherwise, he was screwed. His hand managed to grip the handle, and he opened the door, stepping into the vast emptiness... The Black Room, once again.

Meanwhile, the car sped through the streets toward the nearest hospital, each passing moment amplifying Meow's anxiety. She kept talking to J, pleading for any sign of life, but he remained unresponsive. J, from his spectral side, prayed she wouldn't check his pulse—the absence of it would shatter her. Yet, he was more perplexed by something else: his calculations didn't work. It wasn't a mistake, because if it was, it wouldn't have worked the first seven times. Something had changed. Instead of getting 14 hours and 15 minutes, he had barely 7-8 hours, if that.

As he struggled to make sense of it all, something caught his eye—his watch. Somehow, it had crossed over with him into the spectral realm, and what was even more surprising, it was still ticking.

17:06

The watch's surface was cracked, yet it continued to function. Standing near the door in The Black Room, J could hear faint sounds from the other side. It was from inside the car—Meow's unmistakable sobs echoed through the silence.

J, you are with me, right? You are going to be alright, okay?

Meow's voice was fragile, trembling as she fought to keep herself from breaking down completely. The sight of J's blood, still trickling from his head, terrified and devastated her. On the other side, J's heart ached knowing he couldn't console her, couldn't tell her he was fine, just trapped on this side. J fought the overwhelming urge to leave The Black Room, to return to the mortal realm and his physical body, but he knew he needed time. With the change in the spectral equation, he couldn't afford to act impulsively. He had to wait, to choose the right moment to step back into his body, or risk losing everything.

The car sped through the crowded streets, honking incessantly as the driver weaved through traffic. He kept glancing at the rear-view mirror, his eyes filled with concern for the bleeding man in the backseat. This wasn't how he'd imagined his road trip with friends would turn out—he hadn't expected to be thrust into a life-or-death situation. Yet, he felt an overwhelming sense of responsibility for J's life. In The Black Room, J leaned his head against the door, tears streaming down his cheeks. He could only hope and pray that Meow found the strength to endure this ordeal. It was far too much for anyone to bear. The hospital was just 3 kilometres away, but the congested streets made the journey feel like a marathon. The two other men in the car leaned out of the windows, shouting and gesturing to clear the way, making the frantic drive a bit smoother. Meow's hand gently caressed J's chest, but she hadn't noticed the missing heartbeat. As J stood in The Black Room, a horrifying realization struck him—once his body reached the hospital, the doctors and nurses would immediately check his pulse and declare him dead. He didn't know exactly how these procedures worked, but he knew it was only a matter of time before the worst happened. Earlier, when the ticking of his watch caught his attention, he'd noticed the time. But now, he wondered why it even mattered. If the transition could happen at any moment, what was the point of keeping track? Still, his mind couldn't help but start calculating, searching for a pattern, a revised spectral equation.

Suddenly, a memory surfaced, vivid and clear. J was on a road trip with his dad, and the speedometer in their car had stopped working. His dad, with a mix of curiosity and amusement, had challenged him: *Can you calculate our current speed, J?* Rising to the challenge, J had used the time it took to cover a known distance to calculate their speed with impressive accuracy. It had been a moment of triumph, a testament to his problem-solving skills and a bonding moment with his father. But J hadn't stopped there. He'd figured out a clever way to maintain a particular speed using landmarks and a simple timer—a demonstration of his resourcefulness and ingenuity. J had always been good at calculations, solving complex problems in his head without needing a piece of paper.

Back in The Black Room, J's mind raced, and after a moment of thought, he figured it out—the revised spectral equation was two times shorter. If he spent 3 hours in the void, he'd get 9 hours in real time. It wasn't perfect, but it was a start. He just hoped he was right, and that he could make it back in time. Based on his previous visits to the area, J estimated that it would take about 10 to 12 minutes for the car to reach the hospital. With the revised equation in mind, 10 minutes in The Black Room should grant him roughly 30 minutes in the real world. But as before, his primary concern was to stretch that time as much as possible in the void.

He factored in the distance to the hospital, the traffic conditions, and the time it would take for the medical staff to attend to him once they arrived. Every second counted, and J knew he had to make the most of the time he had left, both in The Black Room and in the physical world.

VIII

Back in the physical world, the hospital staff rushed J's body into the emergency room. The medical team quickly went to work, assessing his condition and trying to stabilize him. Meow stood by, anxiety and fear etched across her face as she watched them work diligently to save J's life. The medical team in the emergency room immediately sprang into action as they received J's unconscious body on the stretcher. Their primary concern was to assess his condition and provide the necessary medical attention to save his life.

Meanwhile, inside the black room, J's watch showed that he had been in the spectral state for nearly 10 minutes. He could feel the seconds slipping away, and anxiety gnawed at him. Every moment counted, and he needed to transition back to his physical form soon, or the doctors might declare him dead. Inside the emergency room, the medical team's frantic efforts continued.

The trainee nurse checked J's pulse as part of her new routine. Having never played this role before, she seemed confused by the absence of a pulse—was it because she didn't press her thumb on the right spot, or was the man already dead? She doubted herself. Since the nurse was a trainee, the doctor, however, wanted to confirm this critical detail for himself. He placed his fingers on J's wrist, searching for any sign of life, but the absence of a pulse confirmed the nurse's earlier observation. With a sense of urgency hanging in the air, the doctor swiftly assessed the situation. He knew that every second counted when a life was at stake.

The doctor didn't waste a moment. His years of training had prepared him for situations like this. He calmly and quickly confirmed the absence of a pulse, and the gravity of the situation was crystal clear. He shouted out orders to his team, *Nurse, we need an IV line and adrenaline, stat!* His voice was firm and commanding, ensuring everyone knew their role.

Meanwhile, Meow, who had been asked to wait outside, heard the commotion inside, including someone yelling, *Pulse is missing!* She crumbled at those words. Despite trying to fight the thought, it kept creeping in—J might have died. She had never felt so much pain in her chest. Feeling helpless and clueless, she somehow managed to carry herself to a chair opposite the emergency room. She buried her face in her arms, just like J had the previous night, hoping desperately that this was all just a nightmare. Her sobs filled her ears, drowning out every other sound around her. She created a shell around herself, wanting to be alone, wishing to hear the words, *It was just a small wound, he's alright!*

The doctor sprang into action, his hands steady but his eyes betraying the urgency of the moment. He tilted J's head back, sealing his lips over J's to deliver life-saving breaths. Each breath was a plea, each chest compression a command for J's heart to beat again. The nurse beside him quickly handed over a syringe of adrenaline, which the doctor injected with practiced swiftness. Another nurse wheeled in the defibrillator, her face pale but determined. *Clear!* The doctor's voice cut through the chaos as he pressed the paddles to J's chest. J's body jolted violently from the electric shock, but the heart monitor remained an unyielding flatline. They didn't stop. The team moved with desperate coordination—compressions, oxygen, medication, shock. The doctor's hands pressed into J's chest with rhythmic precision, sweat lining his brow. Meanwhile, another nurse pressed gauze to the gash on J's forehead, staunching the steady flow of blood. Someone else worked to secure J's airway, connecting him to a ventilator to keep oxygen flowing to his brain.

Minutes felt like hours. The room buzzed with the sound of beeping monitors and the quiet murmurs of commands exchanged between team members. Every second was a battle, every motion a declaration of defiance against the cold grip of death. The doctor paused briefly, scanning the monitor for a flicker of life, his face a mix of hope and exhaustion. *Clear!* Another jolt surged through J's body. They pressed on, tireless, their collective will unwavering. Every eye was fixed on J, every hand working to pull him back from the brink. The tension in the room was palpable, but so was their determination. They refused to let go of the thread that tethered him to life.

Meow, who had been a helpless spectator throughout this, stood up in the corner of the emergency room, her heart heavy with fear and anxiety. Her eyes welled up with tears as she watched the medical team's frantic efforts to revive J. The beeping monitors, the hushed voices of the medical staff, and the sterile scent of the hospital created an overwhelming atmosphere of uncertainty. She clutched her fists, her knuckles turning white, praying silently for J's recovery. Meow had never felt so powerless in her life, and the sight of someone she cared about on the verge of life and death was almost unbearable. The tension in the emergency room was palpable as the medical team tirelessly worked to revive J.

Meanwhile, in the black room, J's anxiety was at its peak. Time seemed to crawl as he paced back and forth, his eyes locked on the watch's minute hand. His mind raced, trying to formulate a plan to manage his transitions with the newly altered spectral equation. The question that haunted him was whether he would be conscious when he returned to his physical body or remain unconscious. The uncertainty gnawed at him, and he dreaded what state he might find himself in when he finally made it back to the mortal realm.

As in every movie related to reviving an almost-dead patient, the hero wakes up at the third delivery of shock, and so the entire room went silent, maybe hoping that was what would happen as the doctor prepared for the third shock. J braced himself to exit, his hand gripping the doorknob, waiting to hear that third shock, ready to make an unwillingly dramatic entrance back to life.

17:22

The beeping of the monitors and the rhythmic thumps of chest compressions filled the air and like a miracle, J's heart began to beat on its own once more, achieving Return of Spontaneous Circulation (ROSC). He could sense the palpable relief among the medical team as they realized they had successfully revived him. His chest throbbed with pain, a searing reminder of the injuries his body had sustained in the crash. Every breath was a battle, each heartbeat a reminder of his fragile mortality. J tried to move, but the pain was overwhelming. The crash had left him battered and bruised, and it was a struggle to regain control over his body. He could feel the tightness of bandages and the presence of tubes and wires, evidence of the medical procedures that had been performed to stabilize him. A collective sigh of relief swept through the room as the medical staff observed the returning signs of life. The doctor quickly checked J's vitals, and though he was still unconscious, it was a glimmer of hope amidst the darkness. The medical team continued to stabilize J, ensuring his airway was secured, the bleeding was controlled, and monitoring his vital signs closely. In the midst of the chaos, Meow sent her silent gratitude to whatever forces had intervened to give J another chance.

The room buzzed with excitement — not just because J's return felt like a miracle, but because it also carried a touch of drama as well. A lot of questions lingered in J's mind as he lay there and felt so many hands working over him but it was strangely a calming experience knowing that he won't be having to move a muscle. For now, rest was the priority. He had been through a traumatic experience, both in the black room and in the accident that brought him to the hospital. The physical and emotional toll was heavy, and he needed time to heal. As he lay in his hospital bed, the pain medication eased his injuries. The rhythmic beeping of the machines and the quiet sounds of the hospital offered a strange comfort, reminding him of the real world, so different from the black room. He took slow, deep breaths, trying to find peace. He took slow, deep breaths, trying to find peace amid the chaos, knowing he would need his strength for whatever came next.

Juxtapose II

KA-BOOM!

Kra'thuun, crashes down, his massive, crystalline form casting jagged shadows.

Kra'thuun:
I am Kra'thuun, the Shardbound Keeper of Virethos and the protector of Virethos. That seed is mine, and I'll take it if I must.

Above, a shimmering figure descends, wreathed in mist.

Vy'laash:
I am Vy'laash, Mist Weaver of Aethyra. My world needs that seed, Keeper. I won't let you starve my people for it.

Kra'thuun:
And I won't see Virethos go hungry for your sake!

Vy'laash hovers, mist swirling around him.

Vy'laash:

Then prepare yourself.

They clash, powers colliding with an earth-shaking force.

BOOM! BOOM! BOOM!

Explosions ripple through the air, shaking the worlds of both Virethos and Aethyra.

He jolted awake, startled! He must have been in a deep sleep, he thought.

BOOM! BOOM! BOOM!

Someone was really furious, pounding on the door. He wondered why. Glancing at the alarm on his nightstand, he saw he still had 30 minutes before he needed to be at the lab. He scrambled for his glasses, buried somewhere under the mess of papers on his bed. With a swipe of his hand, papers went flying—along with Kra'thuun and Vy'laash, who were just about to clash in their epic battle. Finally, he found his glasses and made his way to the door.

THAD, dude! Where are you?? You're late, and Sir PETER's pissed. BART's voice was urgent.

Late? It's only 6:30, man. Go back to sleep.

Dude, there was an announcement this morning to assemble at 6.

Huh? What announcement...

Of course, replied Thad knowingly.

What? Just get dressed and get to the lab now!

Even after nine months, THAD still couldn't wrap his head around how a local comic strip competition had landed him in a secret facility, part of a highly classified project. He dressed faster than usual, not bothering to check how he looked. Even as he stared into the mirror, all he could think about was whether Kra'thuun would get the last bit of seed or if the people of Aethyra would starve to death.

He briskly walked into the super lab, finding only a few people there—none of them from his team. It was the engineering division, already working hard. PETER turned as the lab door shut behind him.

You do realize, PETER said sharply, *when one person falls behind, it exponentially slows down everyone who's shown up on time?*

Sir, I didn't hear any announcements. The speaker in my room is not working.

Really? You've got an excuse?

No, sir. Actually, it's been out for a while.

...And you chose this moment to mention it? Not when you first figured it out?

THAD remained silent.

Kid, get it together. I'm not even going to ask why you're dressed so shabby, because I'm sure you've got some excuse that'll just set me off.

PETER sighs

The reason you were called in early was because the engineering division could use an extra hand. So, get to the equipment bay, grab what you're told, and start working.

THAD felt the pressure to prove himself. He knew he had to make up for the time he'd wasted. He walked quickly to the equipment bay, where BART asked him to pick up the headphones and microphone. But in his clumsy rush, he dropped the set.

PETER closed his eyes, taking a deep breath to calm himself.

THAD, dear, go to the inventory. He tossed him the keys, which THAD somehow managed to drop again. *You'll find a section labelled 'spares.' Get the spares for the ones you've dropped.*

Ashamed, THAD hurried out and headed toward the inventory, situated between the rooms and the super lab. As he returned to work, he constantly reminded himself to stay focused, to be careful, to stay in the present. Normally, his mind would drift to the next scene in his comic, but today, an overwhelming urge to prove himself to the higher-ups consumed him.

What the hell do you mean by 50?

The progress is at 91%.

Stop beating around the bush and tell me what the problem is.

The progress has crossed 91%, but we've only written and fed 50% of the memory sequence.

The man jolts to his feet, eyes wide with disbelief. The lady stands frozen, her mouth dry, searching for words.

So, when the progress hits 100%, we'll have only fed half the memories? Who's going to write the rest?

They're writing, sir PETER...

They're writing? They're writing? Why on God's green earth did we start the project with only half the sequence completed?

We had to meet the deadline, sir... **she stammers, her voice trembling.**

Shit!

The man storms past her, flinging the door open, marching into the vast lab. He bears down on the group of five huddled around a table, the empty chair glaring at him.

Sorry, did I interrupt something? Did I disturb you while you were finishing the goddamn sequence?

The five men spring to their feet, startled. The shortest one fumbles, dropping his coffee cup with a crash.

How hard is this to understand?

The project's on track, sir. We can feed the rest once this part is complete, the boldest of them ventures, his voice unsteady.

What does deadline mean to you? For heaven's sake JESUS CHRIST is coming tomorrow!

At the mention of "JESUS CHRIST," the shortest man, let out an involuntary chuckle. The room instantly went quiet, every eye locking onto him in stunned horror.

Son of a bitch.

Without a second thought, the man draws a gun from his back pocket and fires. The shortest man crumples, a bullet in his head.

THAD had died.

Nine people gasp, their faces pale with shock.

Clean this up and get back to work.

With that, the man turns and strides out of the hangar, leaving them in stunned silence.

What the hell was that?

He lights a cigar, the flame flickering in the cool monsoon breeze. *We hired a bunch of idiots.*

Why the hell did you kill the kid?

The man says nothing, his eyes fixed on the runway and the encircling trees, the monsoon air heavy with the scent of rain. He exhales a long plume of smoke.

They're all worried. Some are even talking about wrapping up.

They step out, I shoot... **He flicks ash to the ground.** *Let them know that.*

NO! Absolutely not! Have you lost your bloody mind? We hired the smartest, youngest minds, and you kill one of them!? A freaking kid?

The kid wasn't cut out for this.

He has a family!

Oh, trust me, he sneered, foster parents don't count as family. The kid was dead weight, dragging us all down, slowing the process.

And now? We're faster? **came the sharp retort.**

Silence.

That's a weak excuse... What were you really aiming for?

He sighed, holding the other man's gaze steadily. *I'm in charge of every dollar THO sends for Pro-Jenesis. Wiring funds, signing checks, keeping this place running—it all goes through me. I calculated* *that if we wrapped up on time, there'd be a surplus. So, I used... the surplus, assuming no one would notice. But THO caught on......They gave me two days to recover the funds, but that money is long gone.*

So, what happens when you don't?

They told me one thing "A farmer doesn't waste feed fattening every hog when times are lean. Instead, he cuts the ones that eat the most but bring little in return, keeping the strongest to see the winter through." **He paused, letting the words hang in the air.**

They were either saying they'd kill me, or...

IX

It was just a small wound, he's going to be alright!

Said the doctor as he stepped out of the room. The medical team had managed to successfully revive J, and the doctor took a moment to reassure her about his condition. With a calm and reassuring tone, the doctor began to explain the situation. He said that the bleeding from J's head was due to a minor cut he had sustained during the crash. Thankfully, most of the impact had been taken by the motorcycle, which had prevented more severe injuries. The doctor went on to clarify that J's loss of pulse was a result of a cardiac arrest brought on by the shock of the accident. While it had been a frightening experience, the medical team had swiftly taken action to revive him, and his heart was now beating again on its own. He assured Meow that despite the initial appearance, J's condition was not as severe as it might have seemed. The primary concern was the minor head wound, which would heal with time. J was stable and, with proper care and observation, he would be okay. The doctor's words were a relief to Meow, who had been through a whirlwind of emotions during the entire ordeal. As the doctor left to attend to other patients, Meow was finally able to let out a sigh of relief. J was on the path to recovery, and her fear and anxiety began to subside. She knew that it might take some time for J to fully heal, but this was a promising start.

J was then moved to a more comfortable room in the hospital. It was a sterile and well-lit space designed for both patient comfort and medical functionality. Its white walls and tiled floors created a clean and clinical atmosphere, while large windows allowed natural light to filter in. Thin, pale blue curtains provided privacy and a touch of color to the room. At the centre of the room was a hospital bed with clean, white sheets and a green privacy curtain drawn around it. The bed was adjustable, allowing the patient to find the most comfortable position. An ECG monitor was connected to J, displaying vital signs and heart rate on a screen. Beside the bed was a rolling tray table with a glass of water and medication. Against one wall, there was a comfortable visitor's chair for Meow or other guests, with a side table nearby for placing personal items or reading materials. A wall-mounted teLEVIsion was opposite the bed, offering entertainment for patients during their stay. The room was meticulously clean and organized, with medical equipment neatly arranged, emphasizing the hospital's commitment to maintaining a sterile and welcoming environment for patients like J.

17:30

J lay in the hospital bed, conscious, since it was just a minor injury. But his body wracked with pain from the accident, the aching in his head seemingly unbearable. But the physical pain wasn't the only torment he was enduring; it was the relentless ticking of the clock, counting down the minutes until he would transition back and into the black room for the 9th time. As he stared at the ECG monitor, dread gnawed at him. He knew that in mere 40 minutes, he'd transition again and the electric signals from his heart would diminish, causing the monitor to flatline. This, in turn, would trigger an alarm, alerting the medical staff that he is dead, once again.

As his mind raced, searching for a solution, Meow entered the hospital room, her eyes carrying the weight of the harrowing experience they'd just been through. When their gazes met, it was as if an unspoken understanding passed between them. There was a sense of relief, a silent acknowledgment of their shared triumph over the dire situation. Her presence was a soothing balm to J's tortured mind. Their eyes locked for a brief moment, and in that silent exchange, a small, tired smile played at the corners of their lips. J looked at Meow with a heavy heart as he noticed the bloodstains on her clothes, evidence of the tumultuous events of the day. He knew that he had put her through a lot, and he felt a strong sense of guilt. He began by apologizing for the chaos and unpredictability of the past few days. Meow, with a reassuring smile, gently said,

J, it's okay. We'll talk about everything later. Right now, I'm more concerned about how you're doing and the pain you must be in.

J winced slightly, acknowledging the discomfort that radiated through his body.

The pain is pretty bad, but it's manageable. I went blank for a moment, lost control, and crashed into the lamppost.

Meow nodded, her worry evident in her eyes. She reached out and held his hand.

I'm just grateful you're here and that the doctors managed to help you.

With concern, Meow decided to call J's mother to inform her about the accident and his current condition. She explained the situation, reassuring her that J was stable and receiving medical attention. They shared a moment of support as Meow promised to keep her updated. In the dimly lit hospital room, J reflected on a conversation he and Meow had about life, family, and their differing viewpoints. He remembered the day he had shared his perspective with Meow, expressing his wish to shield his parents from unnecessary worry. J knew how sensitive his mother could be and wanted to spare her from anguish. Meow, always compassionate and reasonable, had countered that his parents would be concerned regardless of his efforts to protect them. She argued that keeping them in the dark might only heighten their anxiety, as their imaginations could run wild with worst-case scenarios. As they debated, J recognized the validity in her argument. He understood that in times of uncertainty, open communication was crucial. Grateful for Meow's insight, he appreciated her perspective and the profound impact it had on his approach to family and communication.

In many ways, Meow helped J become a better man. She didn't expect him to be the best; she simply wanted him to be a better person than he was yesterday. As he lay there, he wondered what his life would have been like without her. The changes he had experienced over the past year were remarkable. Instead of just finding someone to show the world, he had found someone who showed him the world.

As the call ended, Meow returned to J's side. *Your mom knows now. She's on her way here.*

J smiled faintly, appreciating Meow's support in the midst of this chaos. It was clear to him that he was not alone in this journey, and he felt fortunate to have Meow by his side. J wrestled with his desire to share the baffling events of the previous night with her as he had originally planned. But he knew that opening up to her might burden her with concerns and questions, and he didn't want to add to her worries. With a heavy heart, he decided to keep the peculiar occurrences to himself, at least for now.

17:41

Meow sat in the chair beside the bed.

How are you feeling?

Never been better.

Shut up, J, she laughed.

How did Mum react?

She was really scared; I could hear her breathing get heavy. I told her you were completely alright, and that seemed to calm her down a bit.

Okay.

You feeling alright?

Yes. You're better now, so I'm alright.

J gave Meow a warm smile.

Don't tell anyone else, alright?

Like who? We don't have that many friends! (She joked)

J and Meow often laughed about their preference for a small circle of friends. They were both content with the minimal number of people in their lives, unlike many others they knew. For Meow, who had been well-known and had large circles, the fame had become irritating, and she began to crave smaller, more trustworthy friendships. On the other hand, J, an introvert by nature, was perfectly comfortable with his small group of friends, whom he proudly called his inner circle—or as Meow jokingly put it, *The Only Circle.*

18:05

Time flew by as J and Meow were immersed in conversation about gossips from work. They often had fun sharing gossips and they would also deem that the only reason they have been together for so long. As the minutes ticked away, J glanced at the wall clock, realizing that he had just five minutes left before his next transition would occur. The urgency of his situation weighed heavily on his mind. He knew he needed to act quickly to avoid any complications when the ECG flatlined and the alarms went off. With a sense of determination, J decided to buy himself some time.

Have you gotten my painkillers love?

Yes, I have. You want anything?

Seemed like the right time to ask for something. *Can you get me something to drink? Feeling a little light headed...*

Yes sweets, right away! (With a heartwarming smile)

Meanwhile I'll take short nap.

Once Meow left the room, J seized his opportunity. With careful yet hurried movements, he unplugged the ECG machine from its power source. The device, which had been monitoring his heartbeat and vital signs, was now temporarily disabled. This gave him the minutes he needed to spend in the black room without any alarms or medical staff rushing to his side. With a sense of relief that he had gained some control over his situation, J laid back on the hospital bed hoping Meow wouldn't notice the ECG switched off. He closed his eyes, prepared to enter the black room once more. With the increasing weight of the problem, he continued to ponder if he should confide in Meow or not, is it going to be a little too much burden for her to bear?

X

18:10

Yet again, for the ninth time, J found himself in the emptiness. Meow had left, and he knew she wouldn't be back for at least 5 to 10 minutes. He had taken a calculated risk by unplugging the ECG machine, hoping to buy more time in the spectral realm. But as he considered the ticking clock—both figuratively and on his wrist—terror struck him. His watch was missing. The realization hit him: the nurses must have removed it when they changed him into the hospital gown. Anger bubbled up, replacing his initial frustration. Without his watch, how would he calculate the time?

Unlike before, there were no cues he could use—no truck, no milkman. He knew Meow would return soon, and she might instinctively check the ECG monitor. He prayed she wouldn't. On the other hand, his mum was expected at the hospital within half an hour. The possible outcomes raced through his mind.

He thought,

The best plan is to stick to the basics—stay as long as possible and face what comes next.

One possibility was that Meow would realize the monitor was off as soon as she entered the room and call for help. That would give him time until the attendant arrived to plug it back in. The second possibility was that his mum would notice the monitor was off when she came in, allowing him to prolong his stay in the black room. The third, and least likely, possibility was that neither of them would notice, and he could get the most out of it.

The unplugged ECG machine was a potential giveaway, and he needed to remain vigilant for any signs of approaching footsteps. In his spectral form, J positioned himself close to the door, straining his senses to detect even the faintest sounds emanating from the hospital room beyond. Again, he slid down and sat with his back against the wall.

What had gone wrong? he wondered.

The calculations couldn't have been wrong; they worked the first seven times. So, what changed? Why did the time shrink all of a sudden?

Did my knowledge about it cause it to change, so that I struggle to adapt?

Considering everything that had happened so far, it was hard to ignore the possibility.

J was surrounded by a cacophony of thoughts and unanswered questions. The abrupt reshaping of the spectral equation had caught him off guard, adding new complexities to an already bewildering situation. He pondered the possibility of a set of enigmatic rules governing this enigmatic realm. It seemed likely that he had inadvertently transgressed one of these rules, resulting in the immediate alteration of the spectral equation.

As J thought about the day's events, he couldn't shake the feeling that he was missing something important. The idea that had crossed his mind earlier, though it seemed unlikely, kept nagging at him. He was convinced that something during the day had triggered the change in the spectral equation.

He recalled the emotional ups and downs he'd gone through since morning. The room had caused him a lot of pain at first, but over time, that pain had shifted into something more bearable. He realized he'd learned to handle it, to endure the room's challenges.

This made him wonder: *Was the black room designed to cause emotional pain, or was it worse than that? Was it adapting to make him suffer more as he got used to it? Why was it changing the spectral equation to add more pain?*

J's mind was in turmoil, filled with questions and fears about the black room. The thought that the room might be adjusting to his emotions, making his suffering worse as he learned to cope, left him feeling vulnerable and exposed.

As he dwelled on these thoughts, footsteps approaching the door startled him out of his contemplation. It could be Meow returning with the hydration drinks, or medical staff checking in on him. The urgency to exit the black room and return to his physical body grew stronger with each passing moment. Pressing his ear against the door, he strained to catch any sound from the other side, hoping for the slightest hint of conversation or movement. Then, the rustling of plastic bags confirmed it was Meow. She had entered the room and was busy near a table. J had no idea how much time had passed since he entered the black room. His time in the spectral realm was limited, and he needed to act quickly to avoid complications. The absence of the watch was imminent, if J was going to step out now, he would be doing so without any clear indication as to how long has it been.

Am I going to step out too early?

If so, he'd have to come up with another explanation for his nap.

J's mind raced as he stood near the door, waiting for Meow to notice the unplugged ECG monitor. Time was precious in the black room, and he couldn't afford to lose any. He also recognized that he needed a more sustainable solution, as repeatedly unplugging the ECG was not a viable long-term strategy. J was aware that he couldn't rely on this tactic every time he entered the black room. He needed to come up with a way to prevent the flatlining of the ECG when it was reconnected and ensure that his transition back to the real world went smoothly. It was becoming clearer to him that the more he tried to cope with the room's enigmatic nature, the harder and more complex the challenges became. As J thought about his situation, he couldn't shake the idea that he might be paying for past actions or choices. If this was a punishment, he knew the only escape might be through realization and repentance. But what he needed to realize or repent for was still a mystery. The lack of answers and the black room's cryptic nature only made him feel more desperate.

J's mind was a labyrinth of memories and emotions, and in the midst of his turbulent thoughts, a cherished recollection from his past emerged. Just like every other day during his summer break at GP's, even this evening, he sat on the patio with his GP, sipping tea and gazing at the serene beauty of nature. While Gramma brought hot and crispy chips, but made of jackfruit this time. J's grandfather had led an intriguing life as an army mechanic, traveling the world to repair and maintain heavy machinery, including the war machines of his time. Their conversations often revolved around their shared passion for engines, whether it was the intricacies of car engines or the latest advancements in engine technology. Grandpa had a particular fascination with V engines, and he was genuinely surprised when J introduced him to the concept of W engines. The simple act of sharing tea had the magical ability to unlock the deeper levels of their wisdom, and they engaged in profound discussions about life itself, despite the significant age gap between them. Amidst the discussions, Grandpa had offered a piece of wisdom that, at the time, had seemed cryptic to young J. He had said, *Little one, sometimes complicated problems have complicated solutions*. Perplexed, J couldn't quite fathom the deeper meaning of this statement. Grandpa, ever the loving mentor, then simplified it by stating, *Complicated questions have complicated answers*. It was evident in his grandfather's countenance that these words carried a weight of experience and hard-earned wisdom, born from the challenges and trials of his own life. Now, as J revisited this significant memory, he couldn't help but wonder why this particular moment from his past was coming back to him at this critical juncture.

As J pondered the memory of his wise grandfather's words, he was abruptly jolted back to the present by the sounds of approaching footsteps and conversation. The voices were those of Meow and his mother, who had entered the room. Meow had kindly gone downstairs to fetch J's mother. Time was of the essence, and J knew he needed to exit the black room soon to avoid complications. He knew his time inside the room was up. However, J made a calculated decision to delay his exit until the ECG was reconnected, providing him with more time in the physical world. As he waited in the black room, he strained to hear snippets of the conversation between Meow and his mother. Meow conveyed the information provided by the doctor regarding J's recovery status and the expectation of him being discharged the following morning.

As J continued to strain to hear the conversation, he was able to pick up on the sudden shift in Meow's tone. She noticed the blank ECG Monitor and burst out. J had not considered that Meow might approach him to check on his condition first, knowing that the ECG was not currently monitoring his heart. Thus, limiting the time, he thought he had until the ECG was reconnected.

18:48

Without wasting any more time, J made the decision to exit the black room before the situation escalated.

XI

In the hospital room, as Meow approached J to check on his well-being, he slowly opened his eyes. His mother, standing nearby, wore a look of profound relief and gratitude. She had clearly been through a harrowing experience, imagining her son's life hang in the balance. It seemed like she was silently thanking any divine forces for watching over him. Confusion clouded Meow's drowsy mind as she peered at the blank ECG screen. Meow, was not one to tolerate any disruptions. A furrow formed on her brow, and a low growl escaped her lips. *What's wrong with this thing?* she muttered to herself; the concern evident in her eyes. Without hesitation, Meow strode into the hallway, her determined voice echoing through the sterile corridor. *Hey, someone! We need help with the ECG machine in here. It's not working!* Her urgency reached the ears of an attentive attendant who immediately abandoned his duties and hurried towards them. In the room, Meow gestured towards the silent machine, frustration etched across her face.

The attentive attendant, a man with a quick stride and a no-nonsense demeanor, approached the ECG apparatus. His eyes widened with surprise as he discovered the root of the problem – the machine was unplugged. He swiftly reconnected the wires and powered up the device, making the room come alive with the familiar electronic hum. Turning to face Meow, J, and his mother, the attendant couldn't hide his astonishment. *It was unplugged,* he announced, pointing at the socket. *Someone must've stepped on the wire, and it got disconnected.* Mum and Meow exchanged incredulous glances, their minds grappling with the absurdity of the situation. J, feigning surprise but consumed by his own thoughts, observed the unfolding scene. The attendant, sensing the collective confusion, decided to shed light on the mysterious incident. *Accidents happen, you know,* he explained, a half-apologetic smile on his face. *Probably someone passing by didn't notice and accidentally kicked the wire. It's all fixed now, though.* He checked the ECG to confirm its functionality, the reassuring beeps returning to the room. As he prepared to leave, he offered a final apology. *I'm sorry for the inconvenience. If you need anything else, just let us know.* With that, the attendant departed, leaving the room in a state of bewilderment.

Meow gently allowed J's mother to take a seat beside him, and she began to unpack some home-cooked food that she had brought for J.

How's the pain son?

I'm alright Ma, it is just a minor wound. My baby took all the impact, I'm more worried to see the state she might be in. (Covering up head and body discomfort due to the crash)

Haven't I always asked you to ride carefully (concern evident in her eyes as she welled up)

Meow sensed the need to step in...

He was riding alright, an old man switched lanes without indicating.

Mum somehow seemed comforted knowing it wasn't her son's rash manoeuvring.

19:01

The aroma of a freshly prepared homemade meal filled the room, bringing comfort and familiarity. Meow unfolded the hospital bed's table and placed the meal in front of J, who shifted on the bed to find a comfortable spot for eating. Meow served some food to his mother as well, then sat beside her. The meal had a special kind of healing power – it soothed both body and soul. J's mother, reassured by his condition, chatted with Meow, while J quietly enjoyed the food and the comforting presence of his two favorite people. As he ate, their conversation faded into the background. J found himself lost in thought, contemplating the challenge ahead. Earlier after exiting the black room, the first thing he checked while he resurrected on the bed was the time on the wall clock. He realized he had spent 38 minutes in the void, which should result in roughly two hours. So, he should be transitioning for the 10th time at 20:42, to be precise. Amidst his thoughts, J suddenly realized that his mother had asked him something, and she was waiting for a response, a small chuckle on her face. To avoid arousing suspicion, he simply nodded in agreement and forced a smile. However, the haunting questions about the nature of the black room and how this situation would ultimately resolve continued to trouble him at the back of his mind.

J made a conscious effort to shift his focus to the problem at hand. He needed to devise a plan that would ensure a safe transition back to the spectral realm without causing any alarm. It was clear that simply unplugging the ECG monitor was no longer an option. As he contemplated a solution, J wondered if there was a way to display vitals on the monitor without actually having a real pulse. He felt the need to consult the internet for possible solutions. J asked Meow to hand him his phone from the table, and as he received it, he began typing his query into the search bar:

Is it possible to fake a pulse in an ECG?

To his disappointment, the search results did not yield the answers he was hoping for. The articles he found explained that tampering with an ECG was not only impossible but would also trigger an instant alarm. J kept his phone aside and lay back, feeling the weight of the situation pressing down on him. He couldn't shake the sense of impending doom and the need to share his concerns with Meow was growing stronger. J contemplated whether he should discuss the predicament with Meow or if he should bear the burden on his own. He knew that she had a remarkable ability to think in multiple dimensions and might provide a fresh perspective on the problem. However, the thought of her being dragged into this troublesome situation made him hesitate. Just as he was mulling over his options, a nurse entered the room, carrying a stethoscope, penlight, a watch with a second hand, a notepad, and a pencil. It was the trainee nurse who had previously discovered the missing pulse on J's ECG monitor.

The trainee nurse was a young lady in her early 20s, full of enthusiasm and passion for her work, as also anxious and inexperienced. Her nervousness was evident in her interactions, especially as she was still learning the ropes of her profession. She was very talkative and enjoyed engaging in conversations with anyone who showed interest in what she did. Her innocent and kind nature shone through as she eagerly shared her knowledge and experiences with others. Her love for her profession was evident in her cheerful demeanor and her willingness to help and connect with people. She was there to perform a routine check on J's vital signs, which included measuring temperature, blood pressure, heart rate, and respiratory rate. As a trainee nurse, it was part of her training schedule to monitor and care for the assigned patients. The nurse inquired about how J was feeling, and he replied that he was doing better. She then turned her attention to the ECG monitor, which had piqued J's interest. He watched her closely, knowing that he might learn something valuable during her examination. The nurse appeared somewhat anxious and inexperienced, which wasn't surprising given her status as a trainee. J noticed her trainee badge and decided to engage in a conversation. He asked her how long she had been working at the hospital, and she informed him that it had been just a month. Taking this opportunity, J decided to ask her if she knew how to operate the ECG monitor. She revealed that their training program included an ECG training day, which encompassed instructional lessons, hands-on practice, interpretation training, and clinical rotations. She expressed her enthusiasm for learning and how every day at the hospital was a new opportunity to gain valuable experience.

The trainee nurse appeared to be open and eager to engage in conversation, making J feel that he might find a solution to his ECG problem by asking her enough questions. He wanted to understand how their training sessions worked, hoping it might provide insights on how to manipulate the ECG monitor effectively. J proceeded to ask whether their training sessions involved connecting real patients to the ECG to monitor their vital signs. The trainee nurse was delighted by J's interest in her work, as it was rare for someone to engage in such a conversation with her, especially about her training. She responded enthusiastically, explaining that during their training, they used ECG simulation hardware that mimicked the electrical activity of the heart. Real patients were not connected to the ECG during training, and instead, the trainees learned from a senior nurse and a doctor. This information seemed to hold the key to resolving J's current dilemma. He was relieved to learn that the training didn't involve real patients but worried about how he could access the ECG simulation hardware and bring it to his room without raising any alarms.

As the trainee nurse wrapped up her routine check she politely proceeds to leave the room to check on other patients. Meow's observant nature picked up on J's unusual behavior. His inclination to engage in a conversation, especially with a stranger, was a departure from his usual introverted self. The questions he posed to the nurse and the genuine interest he showed in the details of her training raised Meow's curiosity. Meow's concern deepened as she observed J's silence and introspection. She knew him well enough to recognize the signs of him grappling with something significant. Meow had always encouraged him to share his thoughts and concerns, emphasizing the importance of open communication in their relationship. Seeing J lost in thought, Meow decided to approach him with a gentle inquiry.

Hey, is everything okay? Her voice carried a mix of care and concern.

Yes, why?

Just checking. So, what did you want to talk about earlier today?

Umm, I just wanted to see you and talk after our fight last night, J said, realizing he'd decided to open up. But he thought now didn't seem like the right time.

Okay.

She hoped that J would open up and share whatever was weighing on his mind, knowing that sometimes verbalizing one's worries could alLEVIate the burden. Meow, sensing that J was not ready to open up at the moment, respected his decision. She knew that J had a tendency to keep things to himself, especially when he believed it might cause concern or worry. Though she wished he would confide in her, Meow understood that sometimes he needed his space to process things. Opting not to press further, Meow continued with her meal, maintaining a supportive presence beside J. She hoped that when he felt ready, he would share whatever was on his mind.

19:18

J finished the last bite of his meal, the clink of the fork against the plate signaling the end of his brief respite. He set the plate aside, his mind refocusing on the pressing matter at hand—the acquisition of the ECG simulation hardware. The room was bathed in a soft glow from the lamp on the bedside table, casting shadows that danced along the walls. As he sat there, a flood of thoughts surged through his mind. He couldn't help but reflect on how the unforeseen circumstances had led him to undertake tasks he never imagined himself doing. The world had a strange way of pushing people beyond their comfort zones, forcing them into roles they hadn't anticipated. In the dimly lit room, J's brow furrowed with determination. The clock on the wall reminded him of the ticking seconds, emphasizing the urgency of his mission. The ECG hardware needed to be in his possession before 20:42, a deadline that seemed to hang over him like a looming storm.

But one question remained: where would he find it? In a sprawling hospital with multiple floors and rooms, where would he locate the ECG hardware? He wasn't going to ask the trainee, no matter how talkative she might be. Tonight, he was sticking to the rule of discretion. It felt like he was planning a bomb planting. He picked up his phone from the bedside and searched again. Luckily, this time the search results were useful. According to the information, equipment for teaching purposes could be found in the MEC (Medical Education Centre), a room dedicated to holding teaching tools and equipment, which might also include a hall for lectures.

The search results further stated:

Not every hospital has a dedicated Medical Education Centre. Larger hospitals, especially academic medical centers or those affiliated with medical schools, are more likely to have comprehensive medical education facilities.

J reasoned that if there was a trainee, there had to be a Medical Education Centre, but the question remained: WHERE? With the clock ticking and roughly an hour and a half left, J knew he had to act swiftly to secure the ECG hardware. There was no chance he could ask someone to get it for him, so he needed to find the MEC and get it himself. Crafting an excuse, he approached his mum with a reassuring smile, assuring her that everything would be fine.

Hey, Mum, I'm in good hands here. Meow's with me, and there's really no need to worry. I think it'd be best if you head home for the night. I'll be back first thing in the morning.

The sincerity in his eyes calmed her concerns. Reluctantly, his mum agreed, trusting that Meow would look after him. J seized the opportunity and suggested,

Meow, could you walk Mum out? I'll be okay, and it would mean a lot to me.

Meow, always caring and considerate, agreed without hesitation. As they left the room, J's mind raced with the urgency of the task at hand. However, his plans took an unexpected turn when his mum insisted that Meow stay with him, emphasizing that she would be fine on her own. Thinking on his feet, J quickly improvised,

Meow, did you get the protein bars the doctor asked for?

He did? (Surprised that she hadn't heard and the doctor hadn't told her.)

Yes, he mentioned that consuming protein is essential for such injuries.

Um... alright, I'll get them. Do you need anything else?

J decided to improvise, knowing he needed as much time as possible to locate the MEC and procure the ECG hardware.

You know what? Why don't you go home and freshen up? You've still got stains on your clothes.

Realizing she still had the stains; she had no choice but to agree.

Okay, I'll be back within an hour or two.

Yes, be safe and go slow.

As they left and closed the door behind them, J noticed a laminated piece of paper glued to the back of the door. It was an exit plan. Excited, J jolted off the bed, ignoring the pain radiating from his body, and leaned closer to examine the sheet. To his relief, he found that the MEC was on the same floor. Now, he just needed to figure out how to get there and secure the ECG hardware.

He waited long enough till the floor was clear of Mum and Meow. He carried his phone along, to keep track of time. His heart raced as he studied the layout. The map revealed a promising location: the Medical Education Centre (MEC). A small smile crept across his face as he realized this was likely where he'd find the ECG hardware. He glanced around to ensure no one was watching, then slipped out of the room, silently closing the door behind him. Following the map's guidance, J weaved through the labyrinthine corridors of the hospital. Knowing that the training centre emptied out by 6 in the evening, J's task became easier.

As of now he didn't have a backup plan, he didn't want to think about the possibility of not finding it. Just like the other times he thought,

Will see to it when I get there. (As he walked briskly, hoping no one would see him and doubt)

With determination in his stride, J reached the entrance of the Medical Education Centre and swung open the door. The Medical Education Centre (MEC) room welcomed J with a spacious and well-lit environment, contrasting the subdued ambiance of the hospital corridors. The sterile scent of antiseptic lingered faintly in the air, indicating the professional setting that the room held. Upon entering, J found himself in a large, open area that served as a multifunctional space for medical training and education. The walls were adorned with anatomical charts and diagrams, showcasing the intricacies of the human body. A row of neatly arranged desks and chairs suggested a classroom setup, where medical professionals and trainees likely gathered for lectures and discussions. The centrepiece of the room was a sophisticated simulation station. The ECG hardware, the object of J's quest, lay on a clean, organized table near the simulation station. The equipment gleamed under the bright overhead lights, its cables neatly coiled and ready for use. Several medical mannequins, used for hands-on training, were strategically placed around the room. Their lifelike features and articulation hinted at the realism required for effective medical simulations. Cabinets lined the walls, storing additional medical equipment and supplies, contributing to the room's clinical yet purposeful atmosphere. Large, soundproof windows allowed muted daylight to filter into the MEC, creating a calm and focused environment. The quietude of the room, punctuated only by the hum of electronic equipment, amplified the sense of solitude, considering the training had concluded earlier in the evening.

Luckily, J didn't have to worry about learning how to use it. Earlier, he had planned to look it up on the internet or YouTube, but now, as he stood in the MEC, he noticed three standees placed around a table. Each displayed a presentation on how to use and read an ECG monitor. The ECG simulation hardware rested on the table, a compact and smart device meant for practicing electrocardiography. According to the standees and it's various pictures, its central unit had a clear display screen lit in a gentle blue light. The buttons on the front allowed users to navigate through different settings for training. Connected to the main unit were color-coded leads and adhesive electrodes. These attachments were ready to be placed on a training mannequin or a simulated patient, mimicking a real ECG procedure. The simulation hardware aimed for realism, replicating human cardiac activity with various simulated heart rhythms. The screen displayed ECG waveforms, offering hands-on experience in interpreting different heart conditions. Quickly, he snapped some pictures of the presentation for future reference. As J picked up the ECG simulation hardware, he felt its solid build and recognized the responsibility it held. With the equipment in hand, J prepared to head back.

Juxtapose III

You don't think they're serious, right?

About what?

They conversed in hushed tones.

You know... about killing us if we try to leave.

The body we helped clear earlier says otherwise.

But they need us, man. Without us, this whole ship sinks!

No response.

It's been nine months, dude. Nine months since we are on lockdown.

The man stared at his computer screen, fingers flying over the keyboard.

And the food? It's getting worse day by day.

Still no response.

We can't even interact with anybody here.

No reaction.

If I find a way out, will you come with me?

Woah, woah, dude! No! Are you out of your mind?

What if I have a foolproof plan?

Hell no! Just because we don't know who's under each other's masks doesn't mean they don't know us. They've got our friggin' resumes!

The man continued; voice steady.

Didn't you know all this? Didn't you read the instructions? It said we'd be cut off from the outside world for 9 months. That we'd have to sever ties with our loved ones. That we're not supposed to discuss personal lives or stay in touch after this project ends.

Tell me, why exactly are you here?

We all are here for the same reasons, money, experience, and if this thing succeeds—money and job security.

I don't know about the rest, but I am not here for the same reason as you are!

Whatever...

And you're fine with working for 14 hours?

Yes.

And now, with one person down—one of us—we'll have to work even more.

Silence...

He continued, I wanna feel some fresh air. They don't even let us out of the compound. Can't access the internet. I'm so frustrated. How is this any different from being in a prison?

CAUSE YOU GET PAID! Now, please get back to your work, for heaven's sake, I don't want a bullet in my head.

The fat man continued to speak under his voice,

I personally believe, people here would've been more productive if at least we could've seen each other's faces than wearing balaclavas with voice modulators and a stupid initial of our aliases slapped on our bloody forehead!

We need to prepare reports for tomorrow, said the woman in the balaclava labeled JUDAS, who had just walked in.

She continued,

They need the report to be as detailed as possible. It should include every action you've taken, every step executed, every problem faced, and the counteraction for each problem, if any. Also, the pace of progress, the vitals at each stage, temperature, and finally, the results. Another thing they've asked for is to attach your daily reports for further reference.

What are they gonna do with that? the fat man asked.

It doesn't concern you. Do as you're told. This applies to the engineers as well. As the head of the writers, it's my duty to inform you. So, get it done. I'm pretty sure I don't have to tell you what could happen if you don't adhere to the rules.

He looked like he was finding it hard to comply.

Problem, LEVI?

No Ma'am.

Also, I asked the engineers if it was possible to speed-run through the rest of the memory sequence within 12 hours. They say we might end up losing the progress we've made so far. So, just continue working on it as we have been.

XII

As Meow collected some protein bars from the vending machine downstairs, she cradled them in her arms, conscious of the urgency J had expressed. The hum of the vending machine and the distant sounds of the hospital created a backdrop to her quick descent. With the bars secured, Meow briskly made her way back to the floor above. Meanwhile, J paced anxiously, the weight of the ECG simulation hardware in his hands reminding him of the critical task at hand. Despite the injuries that slowed his pace, his determination propelled him forward. Parallel to Meow, they both headed back towards the room, their paths converging on the quiet hospital floor. J's mind raced with thoughts, formulating a plan and a backup strategy. He considered the best way was to either hide the hardware or, if time permitted, to connect it to the monitor without raising suspicions. The room was just around the corner, and he knew that every second counted. The weight of the ECG simulation hardware in his hands became a metaphor for the gravity of the decisions he was about to make. Meow reached the top of the stairs, protein bars in hand, ready to hand them over to J. She approached his room, anticipation in her eyes, only to find the door slightly ajar. With a curious glance, she reached out and pushed it open, expecting to see J inside. To her surprise, the room was empty. Meow furrowed her brow, a hint of confusion and concern colouring her expression. She leaned back, looking out into the hallway, searching for any sign of J nearby. Failing to spot him, she hesitated for a moment before deciding to walk into the room. Placing the cans on the table, Meow couldn't help but wonder. *J's been acting a little strange lately*, she thought to herself. She couldn't shake the feeling that something was going on. Hoping to find an explanation, she decided to check the washroom. As she approached the door, her hand poised to knock, the unmistakable sound of a flush reached her ears. Startled, Meow looked up just as J opened the door, rubbing his hands against a towel. Their eyes met, and a mixture of surprise and curiosity played on J's face.

Hey, how come you're back so early?

I went home, got what I needed, and thought I'd freshen up here. I didn't want you to be alone for so long.

Thank you, babe. That's very thoughtful of you.

I'll just drop these here.

The air held a moment of unspoken understanding, as both of them sensed a subtle shift in the dynamics of their interaction. Meow's suspicions lingered, but for now, she chose to keep them at bay. As J continued to dry his hands, the room held a quiet tension, a silent dance between the unspoken and the unexplored.

19:50

Earlier, in a hasty manoeuvre, he had hidden the ECG hardware behind the bed. The original intention was to connect it to the computer and run the simulation before Meow returned, but the constraints of time had dashed that possibility. With Meow's imminent return looming, J decided to postpone connecting the simulation hardware to the computer for now. It seemed like the only time he'd have to connect the simulation hardware to the monitor was when Meow stepped in for a shower. Based on his previous experiences, she took about 10 to 15 minutes.

The plan would only work if J managed to capitalize on that time slot. His mind raced, formulating a new plan on the fly. Connecting the hardware was just the first step; he needed to run the software to mimic a normal heartbeat, and 15 minutes wouldn't suffice. Contemplating the options, he weighed the idea of asking Meow to go out and get more items. However, he discarded the idea swiftly, fearing it might raise suspicion. Instead, the primary goal now was to create an opportunity to enter the black room, granting him the time needed to return, connect the hardware, and run the program seamlessly. Knowing he had unplugged the leads from his body earlier, he acknowledged that he didn't have to reconnect them unless prompted. Meanwhile the monitor showed no signal.

J was running out of ideas now. Even if he did initiate trying to get the ECG simulation hardware to connect the monitor, it can't be done in under 15minutes as this is not something he does on an everyday basis. He will have to learn step by step without making any mistake.

However, the potential risk lay in Meow asking him to reconnect, a situation that could derail his plan. As he pondered the dilemma, he understood that the only option to execute his plan flawlessly was to get it done somehow within the time slot. Unplugging again was not an option, and time was of the essence. With a determined yet slightly anxious expression, J waited patiently for Meow step in as a car racer hovering his foot over the pedal.

J, I'll go take a shower alright? And why are you not lying down? Please take ample rest. You want me to get you anything to eat before I step in?

No, I'm good we'll eat together.

In a quick second of reflection as he watched her step into the shower, a bittersweet emotion enveloped him. J wasn't very fond having to keep this from her, but at the same time didn't want to bother her with something as enigmatic as this. Just as she was about to step in, Meow turned back, her gaze meeting J's in a poignant exchange of unspoken understanding. In that brief moment of locked eyes, a wave of relief washed over J. Meow's small smile became a beacon of joy and happiness, filling him with a sense of contentment. Their silent exchange spoke volumes, a shared acknowledgment of the depth of their connection. J couldn't help but reciprocate with a genuine smile, the unspoken *I love you* passing between them like a whispered promise. J stood there, momentarily lost in the emotion of the moment. The love he felt for her reverberated in his heart, making him yearn for a future where he could be with her openly and without the shadows of his mysterious experiences. In that quiet room, he wished for the day when everything would be over, and he could embrace Meow with a peace that transcended the complexities of his current reality.

Reeling back to the current predicament, with about 10-15 minutes in hand, J decides, it is now or never. He can't sit there waiting for an idea to arrive, he had to move now and face whatever may come. He then plugs in the hardware to the computer with the remaining time left. J's hands trembled slightly as he unpacked the ECG simulation hardware. He glanced nervously at the instruction manual. With a deep breath, J tentatively connected the hardware to the computer, the USB cable feeling foreign in his hands. It clicked into place with a satisfying snugness, and for a moment, he marvelled at the simple act of connecting a cable. The power button on the simulation hardware stared back at him, an invitation to unlock the mysteries within. Swallowing his nerves, J pressed it, and the device came to life with a soft whir. The blinking lights on the hardware seemed to wink knowingly at him, as if reassuring him that he was on the right track. Next up, the software. J fumbled with the mouse, opening the ECG simulation program with cautious optimism. The screen transformed into a canvas of unfamiliar buttons and sliders. He felt a bit like an explorer in uncharted territory. As he navigated through the software, J's eyes widened with each menu he uncovered. Heart rate, rhythm, leads – terms that seemed to belong to a foreign language. With a mix of uncertainty and curiosity, J selected what seemed like reasonable parameters for his first attempt. Heart rate? Let's go with a steady 60 beats per minute. Leads? He chose a combination that felt right, hoping it was akin to assembling the pieces of a jigsaw puzzle without the picture on the box for reference.

Taking a shaky breath, J whispered to himself,

Here goes nothing.

The cursor hovered over the **Start** button, a moment pregnant with the potential of success or failure. With a cautious click, the simulation commenced. The room seemed to hold its breath as the hardware responded, generating electronic pulses that danced on the screen. J watched the simulated heartbeat unfold before him, each waveform a testament to the connection between the hardware and the human heart. The blinking lights on the simulation device seemed to cheer him on, a digital pep talk that whispered,

You're doing it.

As the simulation played out, J adjusted settings with a mix of intuition and trial-and-error. The simulated heartbeat evolved on the screen, mirroring the imagined rhythm of a living, breathing heart. In that moment, the uncertainty gave way to a sense of accomplishment.

20:12

Surprisingly, J managed to complete the setup in around 12 minutes, leaving him with a sense of relief. Now, he faced a choice: either connect the leads to his body and lie down or wait until 20:40, two minutes before the next transition. The decision hinged on the unpredictable nature of the black room, which made him ponder what might have gone wrong—and more importantly, whether there was an underlying pattern to the altering spectral equation. If he needed to figure this out, he'd need a piece of paper and a pen, preferably the parchment placed neatly in his laptop.

You seem to be in deep thought, said Meow as she stepped out, dabbing her hair dry.

Yes, I was wondering if there was any way I could get my laptop. I should have asked you to bring it.

Oh, I'm not going out again now.

Yes, yes, it's alright.

Do you want me to?

No, it can wait.

J began scribbling equations in his mind while he stared at his phone screen, where the revised spectral equation was typed out. No matter how much he focused on the equation floating before him, he couldn't identify a pattern. It felt as if a higher power was altering it at will. Realizing that there was no way he could wrap his head around it, he put down his phone, still involuntarily reciting the equation—**$y = 3x$**.

J, as usual, couldn't just sit and think; he got off the bed, pacing as if to stretch and walk.

Feeling a little stiff.

I can imagine. But don't stay up for too long.

J continued to brainstorm, pretending to take small steps while his mind raced with equations, memories of his past visits to the room, and questions about consistency. What was the inconsistency that caused the shrinkage? Or, as he'd contemplated before, was it all occurring at free will?

J!!! Meow screamed, startling him.

20:20

He spun around to see his body lying on the floor. It wouldn't have mattered so much if Meow hadn't been there to witness it—but she was, and she saw everything. In the next second, J had to decide: should he quickly transition back, pretend he fainted, say he lost his balance, his sugar levels dropped, or he slipped? Or should he just tell the truth? None of it would be believable. Should he fabricate a more convincing lie?

Meow rushed to his side, realizing he was unconscious. Panic-stricken, she dashed to the door and screamed for help, her worry evident, her breath heavy. Somewhere in her mind, she feared J might be gone.

Without wasting any more time, J rushed to the bathroom door, the one that had led him to the black room before.

1... 2... 3... 4... 5... 6... 7... 8... 9... 10... 11... 12... 13... 14... 15..

J, now back in his physical self, quickly jumped to his feet.

J!! Are you alright???

Yes, but I don't have much time...

J pulled her toward the bed he had been lying on.

Here's my phone. Open the browser and check my search history.

What? I don't...

Just do as I say. I'll explain everything when I wake up. Please, trust me on this, okay?

Meow was speechless as J abruptly handed her his phone from the bedside into her trembling hands.

Don't worry, I'll be alright, J said, noticing her trembling hands.

J knew time was of the essence. Quickly, he picked up the ECG leads, connected them to his body, and turned on the simulation. The monitor came to life, mimicking a normal human heart rate. He lay down and looked at Meow. She stood there, watching in confusion, as if she hadn't moved a muscle.

I'll be okay, J assured her.

Meow watched as J closed his eyes.

J?

...

J, are you asleep?

...

She looked at the monitor, which indicated he was resting well. But little did she know, the 11th transition had taken place. And, to J's dismay, Meow had witnessed it, while the spectral equation changed once more.

XIII

RECENT SEARCHES:

- **Is there any after-life?**
  - She pauses, her eyes lingering on the words. A simple question, but one that carries the weight of desperation.

- **What happens when you die?**
  - Her heart skips a beat. Why would he search for this? What was he hoping to find?

- **Can the soul leave the body?**
  - A cold shiver runs down her spine. The implications of this question are too disturbing to consider.

- **Death and Resurrection**
  - She feels a lump form in her throat, the starkness of the query almost too much to

bear. What was going through his mind when he typed this?

- **The Black Room**
  - Her breath catches. This isn't just curiosity—this is a red flag, a signal that something is very, very wrong.

Meow struggled for words.

What was going on? she thought.

What she saw seemed far too absurd to be true, and the thought that lingered in her mind was something she refused to believe. Reluctantly, she strode to J and roughly began trying to wake him up.

J! Wake up, please tell me what's going on... Her voice cracked as she started sobbing.

Oh God... The sobs turned uncontrollable as she rocked J, her tears falling and traveling down her arm, eventually resting on his. She knew she should call someone, but her faith in J held her back.

Meanwhile, in The Black Room, J stood close to the door, as if ready to embrace Meow and tell her everything was alright—but that would be another lie. He heard her sobs; he heard her trying to wake his physical self. But J knew he had to wait. More importantly, he needed to figure out the new spectral equation.

What was the point of calculating, he thought, *when the equation kept changing?*

Despite his pondering, he was certain there was no underlying pattern, no matter how many different angles he considered. He began pacing back and forth, deep in thought.

I was supposed to get 114 minutes, until 8:42 pm. The time was 8:20 when I transitioned, which means I died almost 22 minutes before the estimated time. That means I only got 92 minutes, out of the 38 minutes I spent earlier. So, if I'm not wrong, the new spectral equation should be $y = 2.4x$.

It occurred to J that each spectral equation might have a validity period, the parameters of which were still undetermined. Eleven transitions down, two changes—or expiries—and still unable to decode the true nature of The Black Room. He lifted his wrist to read the radium glow emitting from the cracked glass of his watch.

20:30.

After the transition dropped him to the floor, the first thing he managed to grab from the main table was his watch. Unaware of the validity of the third spectral equation, J calculated he'd need at least an hour to console and explain his ordeal to Meow. He would have to spend about 15 minutes more in The Black Room to get an hour out of it.

J stayed against the door with his ears pressed, wondering if it was the right thing to do? He asked himself if he had done it impulsively or was it destiny to tell her.

20:45

I didn't tell you anything because I was afraid, you'd think I'm crazy. All of this would seem absurd if I just sprung it on you. Plus, it was already weighing heavily on me; I couldn't bear to see you burdened with it too.

J turned towards Meow, gently taking her hand.

Meow, you have no idea how hard I've tried to shield you from all of this. All I wanted was to confide in you, to share what I'm going through. You've always been my rock, the one who helps me make sense of things. I was hoping for your support, but the thought of seeing your reaction... I couldn't bear it.

Regardless, J! I don't care how it sounds! We face whatever comes our way together. Keeping things from me because you're worried about my reaction isn't how we do things. How can I find peace knowing you're holding back, no matter how dire the situation? How can I not worry when you're keeping such weighty secrets from me? Things like near-death experiences, J!

Meow's voice cracked as she fought back tears. What's happening, J? She pleaded; her distress palpable.

Okay......

As J recounted the events of the previous night to Meow, his voice trembled with a mix of fear and urgency. He began with the chilling moment when he found himself hovering over his own lifeless body, a ghostly observer in his own bedroom. With each word, he painted a vivid picture of the surreal experience of seeing himself motionless on the bed—a sight that shook him to the core.

Then, he described the mysterious door that beckoned him into the darkness, leading him to a place devoid of light or life, a place he had come to call **The Black Room**. Despite its emptiness, J explained, it wasn't darkness in the conventional sense; it was a profound absence of light, where whether his eyes were open or closed, everything remained shrouded in blackness.

In this void, J revealed how he discovered a peculiar phenomenon—the ability to manipulate time, to reclaim precious moments in the real world by spending time in The Black Room. He delved into the intricacies of his spectral equation, the formula that governed his ghostly existence and allowed him to navigate the liminal space between life and death. However, his tone grew sombre as he recounted the abrupt alteration of the equation, an unforeseen twist that culminated in a devastating motorcycle accident. The equation, once a source of empowerment, had become a harbinger of danger, granting him less time in the real world for each sojourn in The Black Room.

As the narrative unfolded, J hesitated before revealing the lengths he had gone to in order to avoid raising suspicions in the real world. He confessed to Meow that he had stolen ECG simulation hardware—a necessary tool to fake his vital signs and mask his transitions between life and The Black Room. When he admitted this, Meow's concern deepened, her eyes widening in shock and disbelief. She could barely comprehend the desperation that had driven J to such extremes.

J's story continued like a tale of cosmic uncertainty—a cycle of near-death experiences and miraculous resurrections. As he neared the conclusion of his account, J's voice wavered with emotion. He recounted the heart-stopping moment when Meow's anguished cry pierced the silence of The Black Room, jolting him back to the reality of their shared existence. In that moment, his strange journey collided with Meow's urgent distress, linking them in a fight against mysterious forces that threatened to tear their lives apart.

As J finished explaining, a look of terror resided in Meow's eyes. Like she wished it hadn't sounded so unbelievable. She stared at J as if at a loss for words. Meow didn't know how to respond to this and J understood that by the silence that now fell upon the room.

How do we get out of this? (Meow acknowledging to face the problem as 'us' helped calm J down for a while, as if now he had someone by his side to face whatever may come)

I don't know yet. There is nothing in that room that can help me get out this treachery.

Meow remained silent.

I think we should talk to someone, someone who would know what this might be. (J didn't like the way she sounded when she said this)

Like a psychiatrist?

(Meow didn't respond as if she understood J didn't appreciate the idea.)

Look, I and only I know and understand what I'm going through. I'm not even disappointed that you don't believe me completely. I wouldn't either if I were in your place. But we're not telling anyone. I highly doubt anyone could help. And I need you to promise me you won't tell anyone—not even Mum.

But for how long, J? You said yourself that the time is uncertain, and so is that equation. So what? You just wait and wait until it shrinks to nothing? Until you can't get any more time back in the real world? Wouldn't that mean you're... you're DEAD? Meow's voice trembled as she uttered the last word, her fear palpable.

I don't know...

How long do you have now? Meow asked, tears flowing uncontrollably.

An hour.

XIV

J and Meow lay on the other bed that stood beside J's, the silence between them heavy with unspoken fears. The room was cloaked in darkness, the shadows seeming to whisper their anxieties back to them. The only sound was the faint, rhythmic ticking of the wall clock, barely audible over the steady rise and fall of their breathing. As he lay with Meow, time seemed to have sped up. They held each other, unwilling to break the fragile warmth they shared. Minutes passed unnoticed, and time felt as elusive as the uncertain future they feared.

Understanding the silence weighed down by their shared worries, J broke it softly. *You know, once this is all over, we should finally take that road trip you've always wanted,* he murmured, gently brushing a hand through her hair.

...Yes, that would be nice, she replied, her voice distant, lacking the excitement such a dream once held.

J recognized the heaviness in her tone. The burden had shifted to her shoulders too, and perhaps, like him, she was beginning to sense the inevitability of his fate.

Like you said, he continued, *a cabin in the woods, far from the noise of the city, surrounded by trees. Deep in nature, where the only sounds are the birds singing and the river flowing nearby.*

As he spoke, J felt Meow's grip tighten around him, her silent acknowledgment louder than any words.

After an hour, J's gaze instinctively shifted to his watch, but a moment of confusion washed over him. It wasn't working. It hadn't occurred to him until now that the watch only functioned in the Black Room, and even after so many transitions, this oddity still unsettled him. *What does it mean?* he wondered, a sliver of unease creeping into his thoughts. *Is there an underlying message to this?* Shaking off the discomfort, he turned his attention to the clock on the wall. The glow of its digits cut through the eerie darkness, and he calculated the remaining time—just 8 minutes left in the physical realm. His heart pounded as the reality of their situation set in. With a soft tap on Meow's back, who clung tightly to him, her head resting on his chest, he whispered, *It's almost time.*

It's almost time.

21:37

J looked at Meow who now looked up onto his face. Although they didn't utter a word, a silent conversation seemed to have passed between the two. With a kiss on Meow's forehead, he stood up from the bed, to connect the leads onto his body to continue to mimic his heartbeat while he transitioned back into the black room. Meow, silently watched what J had to do in order to survive.

When will you be back then?

I'll try staying there for as long as possible in order to get ample time back in here, said J as he turned on the simulation hardware yet once again.

Meow had an expression of fear and worry lingering on her face as sat on her bed watching J.

I am thinking I will be back by 5:45, that will give me enough time in the real realm and also enough time for us to get out of here as soon as I am discharged.

How do you know when to get out?

He points to his broken digital watch

This for some reason, works in The Black Room.

Okay?, said Meow unable to comprehend what he was saying.

J now lay onto his bed with the leads attached, trying to calm himself down in his awaiting the next transition to happen any moment now.

Would you want me to do anything while I am here?

Relax? Said J with a smile

Meow smiled back aware of how J joked during times of distress.

You there?

21:45

She gets on her feet to check on J, she hovered her fingers under his nose to check. No breath. She then placed her hand on J's chest. No beat. She could confirm he was gone now. The feeling was still very strange to her, J's lifeless body lying in front of her. No number of assurances can drive away the sight of him lying motionless, and the doubt remained,

Was he going to come back?

A kind of loneliness that had embraced the room now, Meow tried to go to sleep but could not let go of J's sound in her head as it played his explanation in a loop . She tries to switch positions to get herself to go to sleep, but nothing seemed to work. A feeling of dread rested in her chest . Now she lay with her face to the ceiling, staring blankly in thoughts.

She felt the need to do something about it. She moved across to pick the phone off the nightstand between the beds. She sat up, she began searching. *The Black Room.* The results were frustratingly irrelevant—a movie, and nothing of significance. Undeterred, she searched for *dark rooms, death, after death, resurrection, near-death experiences,* and any other terms that felt even remotely connected to their predicament. But nothing useful appeared, just an endless stream of unrelated content. Defeated, just like J, she placed the phone on the bed and sat there, a hollow feeling settling in. *How are we going to get out of this?* The thought she had tried to bury now surfaced, relentless and terrifying. J's point of no return was beginning to feel inevitable. The fear of losing him forever, no matter how hard she fought it, started to take hold. J had been right to think that sharing the burden with her might be too much. Meow realized that this was simply beyond comprehension, too overwhelming to accept. But she was glad she knew, because if opening up to her had relieved J, even by a fraction, it was worth it. Yet despite her desire to help, she was helpless—what could she do to end this nightmare?

Her heartbeat quickened until she could feel the pulse in her neck, her mind racing. Involuntarily, the thought crept in—if J was indeed going to die in a few days?

What if J was not going to wake up again?

As she continued to contemplate, slowly, involuntarily her eyelids travelled across to put her in a deep slumber.

I'm surprised it took you this long to remember me. (Both laugh)

I saw your message and thought, "this guy has the audacity to text me!" Until I checked our mutuals and realized you were from school. Even then, I didn't quite figure out it was you! (Laughs) *Then it finally dawned on me. Oh, how you've changed—guess puberty hit you really hard.*

Oh, trust me, I'm not the only one at this table. Hey, shall I order something to eat alongside the cappuccinos? I think we're going to be here for a while. (Still laughing)

Yes, yes, I think so too. I'd like the burger and fries, please.

(Sighs) *Okay, did we ever really interact in school?*

I don't really think so. I mean, I've seen you lurking with your two friends in the corner.

Oh yes. Although I do remember this one time, I pissed you off and didn't come to school the next day.

What! (Surprised and laughing) *Really? What happened?*

Of course you don't remember. I did something that annoyed you, and afraid you'd find out, I decided not to come to school the next day.

You are making that up!

No, I am serious. Let me tell you what happened. (Sips his cappuccino)

I don't know if you remember, but 9th grade was the only time we were in the same batch. So, this was during our drawing exam that year...

Wait how do you remember all these?

I'm an introvert; I remember everything. Continuing... We had our drawing exams, and as far as I can remember, you were always good at painting.

I still am! (Smilingly)

If I remember correctly, you had just finished painting and were letting it dry before handing it over to the teacher. Meanwhile, I was still working on the drawing part, but I realized I had forgotten my paintbox—my acrylics. So, I decided to go to my friend who sat on the first bench. Remember the guy I used to eat with? Him. Your seat was on the way. He couldn't give me the entire box since he was still painting, so he asked me to take the colors I needed, one at a time. Considering the situation, he was generous enough to agree. While everyone else was letting their sheets dry, I kept marching back and forth for each bottle of paint. Realizing that time was running out, I started to hurry. I hurried so much that I didn't even bother putting the caps back on. As I rushed back with a new color, I slipped. In my defense, it was the drawing exam, and there was water spilled everywhere. So, I slipped and ended up spilling some red paint over your painting.

It was youuu!! (In shock and still laughing)

Unfortunately, yes. Luckily nobody saw. But being the good kid I was, I waited till the owner of the painting arrived to let them know how sorry I am.

Wait-wait, I don't remember you coming to apologize. (Takes a sip from the cup)

As I stood there, waiting to offer my apology, I scanned the sheet to see whose painting I had just ruined. You know, to prepare my apology based on the person. But the moment I realized it belonged to you, I knew no amount of preparation would save me. I'd seen you fight way too many times to know exactly what was about to go down. Being an introvert, I avoided attracting attention, but with what had just happened, I was about to be barbequed. The only thing I could think of was to get the hell out of there as fast as possible. And that's exactly what I did. Saying I 'escaped' would be an understatement. I vanished. I friggin' disappeared. That's how quickly I left the crime scene.

Oh my God that's terrible! (Still laughing) *Then what?*

As I had anticipated, you were furious when you returned to check if your painting had dried. You demanded to know who did it, but to my relief, nobody had a clue. And, funny enough, the poor guy who had accidentally spilled water over three paintings earlier became your target. You tore into him so badly that he didn't even get a chance to tell you he wasn't the culprit. Eventually, even the teacher seemed convinced it was him and cut his marks. Meanwhile, you were still graded well. What's even crazier is that despite me spilling paint all over your sheet, you're painting still looked levels above mine.

Then why didn't you come the next day when you weren't caught?

I was worried you were going to find out somehow. Honestly, I'm glad you never did, because we wouldn't be on this date if you had.

I'll get you back for that, J.... said Meow as they both laughed at it!

As the sunlight filtered through the slits and warmed Meow's face, she woke up to the sensation of the sun's rays gliding over her skin. She blinked her eyes open, letting the light in as her pupils adjusted to the contrast. The room, which had seemed so different in the morning light, was illuminated, revealing every wall and piece of furniture in sharp detail.

07:00

She was surprised to have woken up so early, but the persistent knocking reminded her why. Just before heading to the door to open it, she glanced back. J was supposed to be up almost an hour ago; why was he still asleep? She walked back to J's bed, assuming he might still be sleeping.

J, wake up. The nurse is here for the morning routine check-up. (she whispered)

....

J?

She checked for signs of life—no breath, no heartbeat. Anxiety began to grip her. The knocking grew louder. She had no choice but to open the door. The same trainee nurse who had performed the evening check-up entered with an energetic smile.

Morning, Ma'am. How are you this morning, and more importantly, how is he?

He's fine, still in deep sleep. Is there any way you could come back later? He slept late and had some pain in his head.

Oh, alright. I can come back later.

That would be great, thank you.

As the nurse shut the door behind her, Meow waited a few minutes before speaking softly to J.

J, if you can hear me, please wake up. It's already 7. The trainee will be back again, so please wake up.

She waited for any sign of movement, but there was none. With each passing second, her anxiety grew. Had the inevitable caught up with him? She tried to push such thoughts aside, but her mind raced with fears about what would happen if J didn't wake up on time and the nurses discovered he was not alive.

Would they declare him dead? What then?

Her heart pounded in her chest. She sat by J's side, rocking him gently.

J, please wake up. Please, please. The nurse will be back for her next round. Please get up!

Meow, prone to panic attacks, found herself spiralling into another episode. Her hands shook uncontrollably as she sat by his bed, trying to calm herself.

He's just asleep. He's probably lost track of time...

She pressed her hands down on the bed to steady them, feeling a deep sense of helplessness. She thought about how J must have felt when struggling to open up to her. Now, she too felt the need to ask for help.

Time seemed to pass faster this time. She wished it would slow down, desperately hoping she was caught in a nightmare, waiting to be awakened by J while they lay in his apartment. Each time she blinked, she wished to open her eyes to that reality.

Her mind briefly wandered back to the four days they had spent together. Every morning, J would wake up before her, never disturbing her peaceful slumber.

He would quietly grab his laptop, set up his bed table, and make coffee, settling beside her on the bed. He would put aside his work to cuddle her, caress her hair, kiss her cheeks, or playfully slap her—what he called **Kardashians.** By noon, J would disappear for a few minutes, only to return with the aroma of hot burgers and fries filling the room. There was no better way for Meow to start her day than waking up to that delicious smell. The rest of the afternoon would be spent binging movies, followed by an evening outing, and back home by 11. Their time together was precious, a rare chance to feel like a family. Nights would end with another movie and cozy embraces under the covers, their bodies naturally finding each other in the quiet darkness. Those nights had been their own little escape, a stolen moment away from everything else. Their deep connection had turned those ordinary days into something extraordinarily intimate and special—if only for a brief, perfect period.

Meow would've loved to stay in that memory for as long as possible, if another knock would not have thrown her back to reality. To Meow's surprise, it was the doc this time. The doctor hadn't come to visit even the previous evening, but he was here today, why?

Hey Ma'am morning! Samuela here just informed me about some pain he was having, so I thought I'll just come drop by.

Oh …….okay. He is still not up.

Oh, that's alright. We can wake him up.

No, I mean he's been having headaches, he just slept a few hours ago.

I understand dear, this is not going to take long.

Meow, having run out of excuses, stood frozen, her mind racing for something—anything—that would prevent the doctor from checking J. She watched anxiously as the doctor, who had been calm and cheerful until now, called out to J, hoping for a response. When none came, he gently tapped J on the right shoulder. A subtle change in the doctor's demeanor caught Meow's attention. The light-heartedness in his expression faded as he glanced back at the monitor, which continued to display a completely normal rhythm. The mismatch between J's unresponsiveness and the steady, reassuring rhythm on the screen seemed to unsettle the doctor, creating an undercurrent of tension in the room.

Meow watched as the doctor hurried into the room, his usual calm replaced by urgency. He moved straight to the bedside, fingers pressing against the protagonist's neck. His frown deepened as he checked the wrist, then the chest, waiting for a sign of life. **Nothing.**

His hands trembled as he opened the eyes, finding them clouded and unseeing. He whispered something under his breath, too soft to catch. Meow stepped closer, seeing the shock in his face as he tested the arms. They were stiff, resistant. **Rigor mortis.** The doctor's fingers traced the purplish marks pooling on the skin. **Livor mortis.** The blood had settled.

He was fine, he muttered, shaking his head in disbelief. Meow could see the confusion in his eyes, the disbelief growing stronger with every sign of death. He checked again, moving more frantically, as if hoping he'd missed something.

When he finally turned to the others, his voice was quiet, hoarse. He muttered something to the nearby nurses.

Meow stepped forward, How is he? Is he okay? she asked, hoping he'd tell her that he is breathing alright and he is completely fine.

He shook his head slowly, his gaze falling to the floor for a moment before he spoke. His voice was low and calm, but heavy with emotion. I'm so sorry, he began, his eyes meeting theirs again, holding that difficult truth.

He... he didn't make it...

XV

No, he's just sleeping. Please, give him some time. In her mind, she was stalling, desperately hoping J would return any second now. She held onto that hope, trying to delay the inevitable for as long as possible. But the longer she waited, the more it became clear—J wasn't coming back.

I'm sorry. We lost him.

No, we did not, she cried, her voice breaking into a sob.

The doctor, having seen this reaction countless times, assumed it was another case of someone struggling to accept an untimely death.

The doctor stood over J's body, troubled by the sudden and unexpected death. Everything had been fine just a few hours ago. His eyes landed on a small, blinking device attached to the ECG machine—ECG simulation hardware. This shouldn't be here.

He looked at Meow, who was sitting in the corner, pale and silent. She had been with him all night.

Did anything unusual happen last night? the doctor asked, his voice firm.

Meow shook her head, tears welling up. *No, he was just resting.*

The doctor's mind raced. The suspicious device could mean foul play, and the sudden death only added to his concerns. He knew time was critical.

Without hesitation, he made the decision. Picking up the phone, he dialled the hospital's pathology department. *This is the doctor in Room 314. I'm authorizing an immediate autopsy for J. There's suspicious equipment involved, and I need to know the exact cause of death.*

There was a pause on the other end, then a quick acknowledgment. The doctor knew he was bypassing the usual need for consent, but the circumstances were too suspicious to ignore.

As he hung up, he noticed Meow staring at him, shocked. *An autopsy?* she whispered.

Yes, the doctor said firmly. *It's necessary to understand what happened here.*

He knew he might face questions later, but in that moment, he was certain he was doing the right thing. The truth needed to come out, and he wasn't going to wait for permission to find it. The doctor lingered a moment longer, watching the flickering lines on the monitor. He hesitated, then made his decision. *It's time.*

With a nod to the senior nurse, he spoke softly, *Prepare him for the autopsy.*

The nurse understood the gravity of the situation and signalled the team. Two orderlies entered the room with a gurney, their faces expressionless, trained to remain detached. They carefully lifted the body from the bed, making sure not to disturb the lines and tubes still attached, then placed him on the cold metal surface. The nurses began disconnecting the equipment, each step methodical. The ECG wires were gently removed from his chest, the IV line carefully extracted from his arm. A clipboard was handed over to the doctor, who scribbled down the time of death, noting the unusual circumstances.

Transfer him to the morgue, the doctor instructed.

The orderlies covered the body with a white sheet, leaving only his still face visible. They wheeled him out of the room, the soft hum of the gurney's wheels the only sound in the corridor. As they moved through the quiet halls, a sense of finality settled in. Down in the basement, the morgue doors swung open with a creak. The lights flickered on, revealing the sterile, chilly environment within. The orderlies pushed the gurney inside, positioning it beside the steel autopsy table. The sheet was pulled back, fully revealing the lifeless form. A pathologist, already donned in gloves and a surgical gown, stepped forward, his face a mask of professionalism. He exchanged a brief, knowing glance with the doctor who had followed them down. The pathologist checked the paperwork, then turned his attention to the body.

Meanwhile, in the room, Meow clung desperately to the doctor, her sobs uncontrollable. She repeated the same words over and over, her voice a raw plea:

He's not dead. He's not dead. He should've been back by 5:30. He probably overslept. Please, try to understand.

As she spoke, she was acutely aware of how her pleas made her sound like a frantic woman who couldn't accept her loss. Despite understanding how absurd she sounded, she felt powerless. Who would listen to her, and even if they did, would they believe her?

What was more agonizing—losing a loved one or the torment of knowing someone you are certain is alive but has been declared dead? Meow grappled with this painful thought. The knowledge that J might still be alive, struggling to return, while his body was being prepared for an autopsy, was almost too much to bear. She wished she had never known what was happening to him; it would have been less painful than the anguish she now felt. The doctor, preparing to leave, delivered a final directive:

Inform his mother and his loved ones.

Meow sank onto J's bed, overwhelmed by the enormity of the responsibility placed upon her. Was J expecting her to somehow continue stalling, hoping he would find a way to return? Was there something she should be doing to bring him back? She began to internalize the blame for not knowing what to do, and the weight of the task ahead—informing J's mother— grew heavier with each passing moment.

Meanwhile, the doctor who had discovered the ECG simulation hardware was troubled by the findings. He knew that confirming the grim possibility—that J might have been killed by Meow or someone else—required checking the surveillance footage.

Play the footage near room 503 from last night, before midnight, he instructed.

The attendant began searching, but after several minutes without finding anything significant, he was directed to review the footage from earlier in the evening. Fast-forwarding through the footage, he soon spotted rapid movements by a man carrying something heavy.

Slow down, the doctor ordered.

The attendant complied, and the footage revealed J, hurrying with an ECG simulation hardware in hand. The sight was perplexing. Why would J need such equipment at that moment? The discovery cast doubt on the initial suspicion of foul play. It became evident that the man who had died was the same individual who had brought the ECG hardware into the room. The reason for this action was a question only the deceased might have answered.

The living room was a sanctuary of silence, pierced only by the sounds of grief. Meow sat beside Mum on the couch, their bodies huddled together as they wept openly. Meow's face was buried in Mum's shoulder, her own tears mingling with Mum's as they both sobbed uncontrollably.

Mum's cries were raw and anguished, her shoulders shaking violently as she tried to process the unbearable reality of losing her son. *How could this happen?* she gasped between sobs, her voice breaking with each word.

Just hours ago, he was okay.

Meow's arms were wrapped around Mum, her own grief spilling out in silent, shaking sobs. *I'm so sorry, Mum*, she whispered through her tears. *I'm so sorry. I can't believe he's gone.* Mum and Meow never saw eye to eye, probably because of their completely different personalities, but today they found solace in each other's arms—especially when Meow, for the first time, called her **Mum**.

Smo stood nearby, his own heart aching at the sight of their raw sorrow. He glanced over at Meow and Mum, his expression a mixture of sadness and helplessness.

We need to start making arrangements, he said, his voice strained and uneven.

I know it's hard, but we have to.

The room was heavy with grief and the quiet resolve to honor the memory of the one they had lost. Every decision felt like a painful reminder of their sorrow, yet each step was a move toward finding some semblance of closure. The living room seemed frozen in time, drained of color as if the world outside had come to a standstill. It was a black-and-white tableau of despair, punctuated only by the soft, heartbreaking sobs of Meow and Mum.

XVI

Meanwhile, hours ago in the black room....

05:27

You there? Meow's voice echoed in his mind.

I'll be back soon, J whispered, knowing she wouldn't hear him.

Feeling a deep sadness and a touch of resentment toward the Black Room, J had stepped back into the vast void, unwilling but compelled to earn his time back in the real world. By now, it had been too far-fetched to dismiss this as a nightmare. It was real—all of this was real, inexplicable, but undeniably happening. *But why me?* he wondered. He sat against the door, just like he always did, sitting with his hands on his knees, head resting back against the cold surface. The nature of the Black Room hadn't bothered him this time; all he wanted was to go back—to go back to Meow. The glow from his watch reminded him it was almost time. He needed to endure another 3 minutes before he stepped out. Sleep-deprived and weary, he waited, patiently.

05:30

Aware that it was time to step out, he got to his feet, ready to leave the Black Room, hoping he wouldn't have to return for a long time—if the spectral equation didn't change again. As he turned around to open the door back to the realm of reality, he reached out for the doorknob, but a jolt of fear struck him. The familiar exit door, which had guided him out the last eleven times, was gone. Panic surged through him. His heart raced as he frantically scanned the void, his breath coming in shallow gasps. He stumbled forward, his hands tracing the cold, unyielding walls, searching for any sign of the door. The pitch-black expanse swallowed him as he quickened his pace, almost running now, desperate to find an exit. He darted across the inky darkness, the walls slipping from his grasp as he moved. The realization hit him: even if he managed to find his way back to where he started, it wouldn't matter if the door wasn't there. He just needed to find some sign of a wall, anything that could lead him back to the mortal realm.

But the darkness offered no clues. He ran, stumbled, and fell, the void stretching endlessly around him. The walls seemed to elude him, as if they were moving away. Desperation overwhelmed him. He dropped to his knees in the middle of nowhere, his screams echoing through the empty void, raw and unrestrained. *Is this it?* he thought. *Is this the end? Have I finally died?* His mind raced through the possibilities—was this heaven, or was it hell? Or perhaps purgatory, a liminal space where he was condemned to wander endlessly? His cries reverberated in the emptiness, unanswered and haunting, as he grappled with the terrifying unknown.

NO!!!! Help me please!! Meow! He cried desperately. But no help came.

Kneeling on the cold, unforgiving floor, J pounded his fists in despair. Tears streamed down his face, each drop splattering against the ground, his body trembling with the weight of his emotions. He leaned back up, looked to the void above, and screamed in frustration—a cry that echoed into the emptiness, swallowed by the blackness that surrounded him. His life was over, just like that. No warnings, no final moments to prepare—he was only 24. There was so much left undone, so much he hadn't experienced, so many dreams left unfulfilled. Kneeling there, helpless and alone, regrets began to rise, flooding his mind with painful clarity. He could almost feel the weight of all the missed opportunities, the choices that could have led to different outcomes, but now stood as a monument of regrets in his mind.

What if that one time, I hadn't yelled at Mum?

What if I'd spent more time with her?

What if I'd taken her out for a drive when she was battling severe depression?

What if I hadn't fought with Meow over something so trivial, something I could have easily ignored?

What if, instead of leaving her on seen, I had texted her to say how much I loved her and went to bed?

What if I'd put more effort into our relationship?

What if I'd shown some appreciation for my life?

The questions tore at him, each one a reminder of how he had taken his life for granted. Looking back, he realized how he had often dismissed his existence as ordinary and dull, something to be endured rather than cherished. But now, in the darkness that spread out in every direction, his life seemed far from ordinary. It was vibrant, colourful, and full of meaning—sharply opposed to the emptiness that surrounded him now. But there was nothing he could do now, except relive those moments in his mind, over and over, trapped in a loop of what could have been.

Time slipped away as he remained there, drowning in misery, until distant noises jolted him back to the present.

J, please wake up. Please, please. The nurse will be back for her next round. Please get up!

The sound echoed across the room, a desperate plea that cut through the darkness. He knew it was time, and he also knew what would happen if he didn't make it back in time. Quickly, he jolted to his feet, frantically trying to locate the source of the voice. But to his dismay, the sound had vanished. He stood there in tense silence, trying to steady his breathing, straining to catch any hint of noise from the outside.

After what felt like an eternity, muffled voices began to filter through again. He carefully moved in the direction of the sound, his heart pounding. Finally, he stumbled into a wall.

I understand, dear, this won't take long, a voice murmured.

J strained to decipher the conversation, unsure who was speaking to Meow. He reached out, hoping to find the door nearby, but his fingers met only the cold, unyielding wall. Still, there was no sign of the door.

...Is he okay? Meow's voice trembled.

He froze, abandoning the search for the door, and pressed his ear against the wall, desperate to understand what was happening.

I'm so sorry... the man's voice broke the silence. *He... he didn't make it.*

With a quick surge of panic rising, he realized it was the doctor and he had declared what J desperately wished not to happen, he had declared him dead.

Meow!! I am here! Aware yet hopeful, J screamed from within the black room, hoping they'll hear him. Tears began to flow yet again as frantically started looking for the door along the wall. He traced the wall along its length and still came across no doorknobs, no wooden finishes, nothing.

No, he's just sleeping. Please, give him some time. He heard Meow please to the doctor. His heart sank when he heard these words, hoping it would've been better if he had kept it from her. He knelt down again in front of the wall, sobbing, *I am not dead....* The conversations now became an echo as he started accepting the reality. There was nothing to do, there was no help, life was over for J. Now all he could do was hear from the other side as a spectator, watching events unfold post mortem.

He sat, as always, back against the wall, wondering if this was what life after death looked like. Was his soul trapped in a void, a kind of purgatory, forced to silently witness the pain of his loved ones? Was this his punishment for being ungrateful for his life? He lay down on the floor, resigned to his fate, trying to find some comfort in this uncomfortable reality. The sounds of an autopsy being ordered reached him, but they barely registered. He also heard the unmistakable noise of a gurney, which he knew was meant to carry his body away.

In after a few minutes, distant sounds break the silence. A faint hum, the clink of metal, and the snap of latex gloves. The zipper's slow rasp sends a chill through him. The scalpel's first cut brings a sickening, wet sound, echoing through the emptiness. The crack of bone follows, sharp and jarring, each noise pulling him closer to the cold reality of his autopsy. Muffled voices discuss his body clinically, their words blurred and distant. As the sounds fade, he's left alone again, trapped between life and death. Paper rustles as the final report is documented, the pen's scratch against the page a calm, methodical note.

*It's a natural death....*said the forensic pathologist.

Time goes by, J gets up onto his feet at times to check if by any chance the door was back. He felt within him, the hope that once shimmered within him, was now colourless and dead. He checked his watch, which he realized must have been taken off for autopsy. He knew within himself, that it was all over, the one-sided battle has him succumbed to defeat. There was nothing but the *Acceptance Call* now.

After what felt like hours or even days, as time seemed to blur in his near-death state, J was stirred by distant voices, fragmented and dreamlike. He heard the soft shuffle of dress shoes on the floor, mixed with quiet sobs and hushed conversations. He could make out the thud of a casket being lowered, the creak of wooden planks being adjusted, and the rhythmic sound of earth being shovelled into the grave. The pastor's solemn voice came through, speaking farewell in a way that felt both strange and familiar. A mournful hymn played softly, its haunting melody filling the emptiness of the Black Room. Along with the hymn, there were occasional sniffles and the gentle clinking of metal as people placed flowers or keepsakes on the casket. The atmosphere was thick with sadness and finality, marked by the crackle of a speaker system and the shuffling of paper as programs were handed out. Each sound, though distant and distorted, reminded him of the world he had left behind—a world now filled with grief and the rituals of saying goodbye.

As he continued to sit there, listening to the sounds from the other side, something happened that had happened never before, there was this dim light which started to illuminate some areas, actually the areas which was closer to the wall. The light illuminated in such a way, that it cast a rectangular shape on the floor in front of J. Him having noticed this strange phenomenon, quickly spun around to see what was happening. To his amusement, the door had reappeared again, but this time a bright light shone across its borders.

Was this the doorway to heaven? he thought.

Slowly and carefully, he placed his hand on the doorknob and twisted it and stepped outside into the bright light. In a quick snap, he opened his eyes slowly, blinking away the darkness. At first, he saw only a dim, enclosed space around him, illuminated by a soft, flickering light that seemed to come from above. The walls around him were lined with a dark, plush material that felt smooth and cool to the touch. The air was still, with a faint, earthy smell that he couldn't quite place. His hands, cold and slightly numb, moved along the surface, brushing against the velvety lining. He shifted a bit, and the soft rustling of the material was the only sound in the confined space. There was a sense of pressure from all sides, but he couldn't immediately understand what was pressing in on him. As he tried to make sense of his surroundings, he noticed the distant voices and the faint echo of footsteps. The light above grew dimmer as if a curtain was being drawn over him, and he could hear a low, rhythmic thudding, like something heavy being moved.

It wasn't until cold, damp earth started falling on him, with the muffled sounds of shovels and dirt hitting the casket, that he realized the horrifying truth. The weight of the mud pressing down made it clear—he was being buried alive.

Help!! Help, someone please!

I'm in here, I'm alive!!!

He let out a strangled cry, his voice barely breaking through the muffled earth. He pounded on the casket lid, each thud swallowed by the heavy layers of dirt above. He tried to push the lid hoping someone above will see some movements over the lid and might stop this from happening. Slowly he realized, there was no help coming, he kept going with his pleas, but to no good. The horror dawned on him, that he was going to experience death this time, not because of time constraints, he is going to feel running out of breath.

Meow! It's me, please help!

He pounded weakly against the casket lid, the sound muffled by the thick layers of dirt.

Meow, can you hear me? I'm alive! Please, I need you!

Meow, don't leave me here! Please, save me!

His screams gradually faded as the weight of the dirt grew heavier. The muffled sounds of shovels and distant voices became more distant, swallowed by the darkness. His pounding on the casket lid weakened, his breaths growing laboured under the crushing pressure. As the last of the earth settled, silence took over. The faint light from above was gone, replaced by oppressive darkness. With one final, desperate gasp, he cried out,

Meow, help me!!!

Juxtapose IV

It's been almost two months since we started sleeping with each other....

.....So, why can't I know your name yet? he asked, his voice teasing.

Well, aren't personal lives off-limits during the project? she replied, her smile playful.

Right. What we're doing is strictly professional.

Absolutely, she laughed.

He reached out, gently caressing her face. *You're beautiful. Anyone ever tell you that?*

Plenty.

They both laughed, the intimacy between them light but undeniable.

Are you going to propose next? she teased.

I don't even know your name! he shot back, and they dissolved into laughter.

So, I see you're writing again. His gaze drifted to a stack of papers pinned to a pad on the nightstand.

Trying to, she replied, a small smile playing on her lips.

Mind telling me what it's about?

She hesitated, but her excitement to talk about it got the better of her. *Well...it's about a man who's taken away from his family. After facing countless hurdles, he finally reunites with them...though he loses quite a lot along the way.*

Damn, that sounds like something I'd want to read. What's it called?

22 : 13, she replied softly.

He frowned slightly. *What does that mean?*

She leaned back, a fond smile playing on her lips. *It's the time—10:13 at night—when my two characters, before they were deeply in love, share their first kiss. It's the moment their journey begins. Love, transformation, everything starts there.*

Is it done? Finished? he asked, nodding at the stack of papers.

Not yet, she said, brushing a strand of hair behind her ear. *Just the last part's left. I'm having a little trouble writing the end, when......*

..... Finally, he finds her again—the love he thought he'd lost forever. From a man drowning in emptiness to one who finds beauty even in the smallest of things, they rebuild what was broken. A family. A life. And in the quiet of their story's end, they live not just happily, but whole.

That's beautiful....And it's written by...? he prompted with a grin.

Nope, you're not getting my name, honey, she shot back, playfully deflecting, her eyes sparkling with mischief.

Oh shoot! He teased, and they both burst into laughter, the room filling with warmth.

Their moment was interrupted by a sharp knock at the door. It was 2 AM. Her smile vanished as she quickly signalled for him to hide in the washroom. Once he was out of sight, she grabbed her balaclava and cracked the door open.

What are you doing here? she whispered harshly. *I've told you before, we're never happening.*

Come on, JUDE, he sneered, leaning closer. *Tomorrow might be our last chance. Let me have you, just once.*

She stiffened. *You're out of your mind.*

I'm being decent by asking. I could just take you. No one would know, he grinned darkly, shoving the door open, causing her to step back.

His eyes darted around the room, stopping on another balaclava lying on the bed with the label BART.

Well, well, he drawled. *JUDE has a little boyfriend, doesn't she? Where's my boy BART? B-A-R-T!* he taunted.

Get out, PETER, came a voice from behind him. BART stepped out of the washroom, unblinking.

PETER turned, his face twisting. *Sir PETER, bitch!*

He laughed bitterly and headed for the door, stopping briefly to glance back. *You're both going to regret this.*

The door slammed shut behind him.

How long has he been like this? BART asked, his voice low.

Since I joined. She looked away, her expression tense.

Why didn't you tell me?

She sighed. *I didn't want you involved.*

BART stood still for a moment, his mind racing.

How could you let something like this slide? he asked quietly, though there was an edge to his voice.

I wasn't going to speak up because I had no one, JUDE replied, avoiding his gaze. *My priority was getting out of here unharmed. If I provoked him, if I went behind his back... it could've made things worse. Please, just let it go, alright?*

BART clenched his jaw. *Okay, okay,* he said, trying to soften his voice. *I'm here now, alright?*

Yeah. JUDE exhaled; her voice quiet. *I think I'm going to sleep now.*

He took that as his cue to leave. She needed space. She was upset, but pushing her right now wouldn't help. BART slipped out of the room, shutting the door gently behind him. Back in his own room, A25, he flipped on the light. The moment the glow hit the room, his heart lurched—there, sitting in the chair near the desk, was PETER.

There you are, Romeo, PETER sneered. *Breaking all the rules like that, BART?*

BART's pulse quickened. *What the hell are you doing here?*

Me? What were you doing there?

That's none of your damn business.

PETER's smile twisted. *How long have you been banging her? And how'd a runt like you get her to sleep with you, huh?*

Watch your mouth, BART growled.

Or what? What's little BART gonna do? PETER leaned back, almost lazily, his tone mocking.

BART's fists clenched.

You gonna hit me? Cute. PETER's voice dropped; the amusement gone.

PETER continued; *I'm going to kill your grandmother. How about that? Tell her you were a psychotic murderer, and we had to put you down. Maybe that'll give her a heart attack.*

BART's blood went cold. *What do you want?* His voice was tight, full of barely controlled rage.

There he is, PETER said with a smirk. *All I need is for you to stop sleeping with JUDE. That's it. Tomorrow, I'm going to have my way with her—whether she agrees or not. If you try to stop me, I'm going to pay your dear old grandmother a visit. Burn her alive, maybe kill JUDE too, while I'm at it. You remember Thaddeus, don't you?*

BART's jaw tightened, his teeth grinding as he forced himself to stay silent. Any wrong move, any show of defiance, and PETER might make good on his threat.

PETER grinned, sensing his victory. *That's what I thought. Get some sleep, BART. Big day tomorrow.* He turned and walked out, slamming the door behind him.

After spending 9 months in a secluded basement, PETER and JAMES had bonded over cigars and liquor. Every evening—or whenever they felt the need—they would retreat to what they called the "balcony," a small wooden deck they had converted from an emergency exit. Unlike the other rooms, A52 had a staircase in the corner leading to a door on the upper floor. The door opened onto the deck, which led out of the hangar and into the surrounding woods. This spot, free from surveillance, became their sanctuary. They would sit back in rocking chairs, enjoying their smokes and drinks, and talk about life. Over time, these moments became a ritual, and they got to know each other well.

When is JESUS CHRIST going to be here, JAMES? He asked, lighting up his cigar.

At around 1600, I'm hoping.

Oh, so I guess that'll be after the procedure is over. He took his first puff, leaning back against the chair.

98%, the rate at which it's going, seems likely.

What do you think? He passed the cigar to JAMES.

I think it's going to work out. I'm not hoping, I'm merely stating it, JAMES said, exhaling a thick mouthful of smoke.

What happens after this? He continued to stare into the greenery, his eyes locked on the horizon from the balcony in A52.

They'll study the data, the results... for months probably. Then they'll call you back. And the next time, it won't be small. It's going to be ten times bigger than this. JAMES handed the cigar back.

Will we still have to operate under covers?

I don't think so. But it doesn't matter, as long as the payday stays good.

That's one thing that has kept me going for so many months. He tapped the ashes into the tray, watching them fall with a faint smile.

PETER and JAMES walked towards the viewing gallery. The lab was a well-organized space, with two long platforms stretching along the sides, each filled with state-of-the-art equipment. In the center stood a large transparent cubicle made of reinforced glass. This cubicle, known as the viewing gallery, allowed a clear view of the platforms and housed the operational lab inside. The layout was designed for efficiency, with the platforms on either side for team members to work, while the central cubicle provided a focused space for critical operations, monitored by screens displaying real-time data.

JUDE stood inside, closely monitoring the activity, while the other eight were busy at work, moving between their workspaces and the operation lab. JAMES sat on a chair, appearing extremely relaxed, while PETER, tense, focused on the data displayed on the screens in the viewing gallery. At one point, PETER noticed BART eyeing him again from the corner of his eye.

Attention, everyone. The monitors are showing rapid declines—activity levels are plummeting, rhythm is becoming unstable, pressure is dropping, oxygen is critically low, and temperature is falling. We're facing an imminent failure.

Progress, 99% and temperature 35ºC. This is critical Said BART who now was standing beside JUDE.

Sir, PETER, if it drops even further, should we stop the operation? Asked a short engineer with a balaclava labelled LEVI, his voice tight with concern.

Nope, keep going till the meter hits a green freaking 100, JAMES cut in, interrupting PETER.

PETER shot him a look. *No, that's not a good idea, JAMES. We will have to stop then.*

Just 1% left, JAMES said, shrugging it off. *It's not going to cause that much harm anyway.*

PETER's expression hardened. *Everyone out! Now! I need only JUDE in there.*

BART clenched his jaw from the corner of the gallery, muscles tensing.

BART and the few people inside quickly stepped out and closed the door behind them. Now, a group of 10 stood outside, dispersed around the operational lab, peering through the gallery in anticipation of the result.

100%...

XVII

FUCK! J screamed as he sat up.

His vision was blurred, and it took a moment for his eyes to adjust to the bright light. As he looked around, everything seemed hazy, and he thought he might have just woken up from a bad dream. Gradually, as his senses returned, he heard the sounds of applause and people exchanging congratulations—cheering, high-fiving, and even jumping. When his vision cleared further, he saw a group of people—maybe 10 or 11—standing behind what looked like transparent barriers. They were laughing, applauding, and shaking hands. At that moment, J realized someone was standing beside him. It was a woman, though her face was obscured. As his eyes adjusted fully, he saw that she was wearing a black mask with openings for her eyes and mouth. She seemed quite pleased, her face beaming at him.

How are you feeling? she asked.

Umm, can you—can I—have you informed Mum and Meow that I'm alright? J's voice was filled with concern.

The woman took a moment before responding, *Don't worry about it.*

J noticed the name on the mask: *JUDAS*. He found it unusual for a woman to be named JUDAS. As JUDAS continued to smile at him, he took in his surroundings—what appeared to be some kind of operating room, equipped with numerous screens and advanced machinery. He was lying on a bed that seemed more advanced than the hospital bed he remembered from the previous night.

Where am I? he asked.

You are in safe hands... JUDAS replied.

But how—did—you—?

As I said, don't worry about it.

I want to see Meow. Please, I want to see her. Can you ask her to come? Is she waiting outside?

There was a long pause before JUDAS turned and walked out of the room. J found the silence unsettling. As she left, a signboard above the door came into focus and his gut wrenched. It read:

THE BLACK ROOM

What are we doing next?

Cover all the reflective surfaces for now. Move him to the interview room, said JAMES, his voice steady. *And initiate phase II.*

Are you sure, JAMES? PETER asked, a hint of hesitation creeping into his voice.

No doubt about it. Let's stick to this plan. Conduct the interview first, then hand him the article... as planned.

PETER didn't seem convinced, but BART and JUDE exchanged looks—they were certain. Some team members were ordered to move J to the interview room, also known as the IR, while others were sent to prepare it. As BART and JUDE got to work, JAMES held PETER back for a moment.

JESUS CHRIST might not be coming today...

What? Why not?

I asked for an extra day.

What? Why? We're done with the project, JAMES.

Because we're going to speed-run the rest of the sequence, so he'll be ready by tomorrow, he said, rubbing his palms with a grin, the excitement almost radiating from him.

That's not going to work. We'll risk losing everything we've done so far.

That's why we're initiating phase II now and jotting down our observations—just in case he dies, or worse, reverts to square one by tomorrow. He said with a chuckle, as if the gravity of the situation didn't faze him.

Putting in extra work won't increase your paycheck.....

Gotta do what we gotta do, PETER.

PETER wasn't sure about this plan; he'd been working too hard, for too long, on this project to take such a risk. But for now, what lay ahead was initiating the next phase.

The IR resembled more of a subject interview chamber. It was equipped with a table and two chairs facing each other, built-in voice recorders, and a microphone on the table to capture and amplify their conversation for those listening outside. Concealed cameras were discreetly positioned, and the door featured a face-length glass slit, allowing for unobstructed observation from the outside. A pale blue light washed over the room, casting a cold, sterile glow.

Meanwhile, J, who was escorted by JUDE and LEVI, looked confused as he took in his surroundings.

When can I see her? J's voice cracked; the question laced with unease.

Soon, JUDE replied, her tone neutral, offering no comfort

Any reflective surfaces? JUDE asked BART, who was now walking out of IR after finishing the setup

Covered.

In the IR, a notepad and pencil lay on the table between them. J sat in one chair, JUDE in the other. The room felt smaller now, the silence almost deafening.

I'll take it from here, said JUDE, picking up the notepad with the predetermined questions.

As LEVI left the room, an almost palpable silence filled the air—a pin-drop silence. JUDE looked at J with a concerned smile. J didn't smile back; he was still scanning the room, trying to make sense of what was happening.

J's fingers tapped nervously on the armrest. *What are we doing? Where is Meow?* His voice trembled slightly.

I'll explain everything soon, JUDE said, her eyes scanning his face carefully. *But first, how are you feeling, John?*

He blinked, startled. *John?*

Yes. How are you feeling?

I'm alright, but... who's John?

JUDE smiled; a smile meant to reassure but missing its mark. *We'll get back to that.* She paused; pen poised. *How old are you?*

J frowned. *23. Why are you asking me these questions? Where is Meow?*

JUDE scribbled something down. The sound of the pen on paper seemed to fill the room, amplifying the silence.

I'm sorry, I'll explain everything, but for now, please bear with me. What is your name?

J.

And your full name?

It's just J. His jaw tightened, his patience wearing thin.

More scribbling. JUDE barely looked up. *What's your mother's name?*

Mum.

JUDE's eyes flicked up, meeting his. *Are you sure?*

Yes! It's my mother. What is this?

She remained calm, unphased by his growing anger.

Are you married?

J scoffed, *I'm 23! What do you think?*

JUDE tilted her head slightly. *Do you have a girlfriend, then?*

Yes! Meow! I've been asking about her for ages now. When is she coming? His voice cracked, worry seeping through.

And by any chance, do you happen to remember the name of the trainee nurse who had attended you?

Umm – Yes, Samuela. J said after taking a minute to recollect

What's the name of your best friend?

Smo, J said reflexively, his mind clearly elsewhere.

JUDE raised an eyebrow. *Smo? Doesn't that sound a little... odd, J?*

J stiffened. *What? No, why? I didn't name him.*

JUDE's pen hovered for a second. *Soon.* She glanced down at her notepad again. *What do you last remember, J?* This time, she emphasized his name.

I was... in a coffin. I was being buried alive. I tried to call out for help and... and then... His voice trailed off. *I think I lost consciousness.*

The Black Room. She didn't ask it as a question. She just said it.

J flinched. His eyes widened for just a second, but JUDE saw it.

How do you know about that?

We'll have to get back to that, she said softly.

The silence that followed felt like it was tightening around J. His mind was spinning now, pulling him in different directions—confusion, fear, anger, but mostly fear.

What do you remember from The Black Room? JUDE asked, leaning in ever so slightly, her voice low.

J swallowed, hard. *I... I was there, before... before I opened the door and found myself in the coffin.*

JUDE's pen moved swiftly across the paper, scribbling down notes as if this were all routine.

JUDE glanced at her notes. *I know, but don't these names seem a little strange to you? Your mother's name is Mum, your girlfriend's name is Meow, and your best friend's name is Smo? These don't exactly sound... conventional, do they?*

I didn't name them! What does that have to do with anything? What are these questions?!

And one last question.... What is your grandfather's name?

GP!

What does it stand for?

Nothing, that's his name, lady! GP! J's frustration was evident, his patience wearing thin.

Okay, okay... just trying to calm him down. Give me a second. She handed him what looked like a call button. *If you need anything, just press this, okay?*

J stared at it, lost for words and lost in thought.

JUDE walked out of the room, the notepad in her hand. She was greeted by the entire team, who stood outside, had heard the whole interview, with varying expressions of anticipation and concern.

What do you think? She asked.

It's unbelievable! Said PETER.

JUDE turned to JAMES, clearly preferring to avoid further conversation with PETER. *What's next?*

JAMES paused for a moment; his face thoughtful.

Tell him...

au revoir I

They stood around the viewing gallery, watching the events unfold within The Black Room, the engineers in a mode of frantic, as the progress bar neared its end.

You'd have to be a complete idiot to try something like that after what happened!

I'd be an even bigger idiot if I don't— LEVI snapped back. *—especially after what happened!*

And he continued, you really think we're going to make it out of this alive, don't you? Just like every other fool who thought they could survive this madness.

If I were running a classified project like this, my second priority—right after success—would be eliminating any risk of duplication.

And why's that? Asked ALPHAEUS looking at LEVI, who continued to gaze into The Black Room.

Think about it. An organization like this only thrives if it holds power—enough power to make decisions that shape the world on a global scale.

So?

Dominance fades when the playing field is level...So, with this project, once it succeeds, the so-called JESUS CHRIST *will wield unimaginable power—and that makes us disposable. They'll kill us. Seriously, don't you watch movies?*

ALPHAEUS listens in silence.

Hey, I'll be honest with you, the moment I got that email, I knew accepting it would be like punching a one-way ticket to hell!

ALPHAEUS, now fully turned toward to LEVI, looks confused.

And yet, here you are.

I got here by accident!

ALPHAEUS laughs. *Yeah, right.*

So, you really think you're going to walk out of here, with your money, unharmed, no strings attached?

Yes, of course, ALPHAEUS *says it as if it's obvious.*

Oh... you must be completely deluded.

Then why did you come? If you already had all these suspicions...

Well, I needed the money, so I thought I'd give it a shot. And honestly, by now, you probably know why I've decided it's time to bail.

And you told me you were here for other reasons

ALPHAEUS chuckles his voice carrying a hint of disbelief. He pauses before continuing with a measured tone

Then why me? Why aren't you asking the others too? I bet even they want to leave now...

LEVI smirks. So, you do want to leave.

Just answer my damn question... why me?

Well, you don't really talk to anyone. You keep yourself buried in work, head down, minding your own business...

And what does that have to do with this?

It means I can trust you not to go running your mouth behind my back.

That's a risky assumption, I'd say...

I'll take my chances.

So, what exactly is your master plan? I'm definitely not tagging along, but with how unnerving the work here has been, I could use a little entertainment...

I don't have a plan. Not yet, anyway. But I do know there's one way out—unguarded, unwatched, a blind spot...

And where would that be?

LEVI spots JAMES watching them from the other side of the viewing gallery, his eyes sharp and unblinking.

See, dude, either you're in or you're out. I'm not giving you the grand tour of a prison break if you're just gonna sit it out. But if you change your mind, let me know. The sooner the better—we don't have much time left.

ECHO I

She had her hands on her head, wondering why the story wasn't coming together the way she envisioned it. A mess of crumpled papers lay scattered around her table, a few having rolled to rest near her trophies and certificates. Among them was a recent certificate awarded to her for the Best Sci-Fi Short Story in a local writing competition, a small yet significant victory in her writing journey. Some of the crumpled papers, with fragments of words visible, stopped rolling when they bumped against an anonymous package labelled **THO_PJ_12A28** which had arrived almost a week earlier.

She absentmindedly picked up the package along with a few crumpled papers and flicked them toward the bin, sending the paper balls tumbling inside. The package remained in her hand. She glanced at it again before placing it down. According to the document, the burner will be deactivated tomorrow, yet the pressure, which hasn't been present for the last seven days, appeared tonight. The document inside was brief, describing an opportunity for a writer needed for research purposes. But the additional requirements were astonishing.

No contact with the outside world? She muttered to herself.

As an aspiring writer, she had always believed her purpose was greater—to write for those in need, to pen words that could save lives. Every evening, after returning from her shift at the hypermarket, having managed a drawer full of bills and coins, she would sit in her tiny apartment, notepad and pen in hand, trying to capture the ideas that came to her while she packed customers' items. But today, she couldn't focus on her writing. The package on the table demanded her attention.

It did promise job security and a substantial payday—certainly a step up from being a cashier. She pondered it deeply, even considering how the money from this research job could fund her book, enabling her to self-publish it.

But why was she being asked to join such a classified project?

How did they even know about her?

It felt ominous, and she wasn't sure what to make of it. As if on cue, her phone chimed, reminding her that she was nearly two weeks behind on rent. She'd already sold her car to get a small scooter, as owning a car had become too heavy on her pocket, and she was barely making ends meet. The extra cash had given her some breathing room, but it was still a constant struggle to keep afloat.

Top Secret - Highly Classified

File Reference: THO-PJ-12A28
Date: 18/8/23
Subject: Project JENESIS - Assignment & Confidential Directives

---

Recipient Alias: JUDAS
Designation Code: THO-6491
Personal Identifier: HarborOfHope-6491
Role: Head Writer, Project JENESIS

I. PROJECT OVERVIEW
Project Name: *JENESIS*
Objective: To craft a detailed, immersive narrative that serves as a critical component of the experimental process. The story must be compelling, emotionally resonant, and seamlessly integrated into the project's broader goals.

As **Head Writer**, you will lead a team of six, working together to develop a narrative that captures human experience with emotional and psychological depth. You will have full creative freedom to construct the story, ensuring it achieves the desired impact.

Your leadership and storytelling are vital to the success of *Jenesis*, making your role essential in this experiment.

Earlier, when she saw the name typed beside the alias, she let out a chuckle.

How can people conducting a secret project accidentally send an anonymous recruitment document to the wrong person?

She would've thrown it away if her chuckle hadn't been abruptly stifled by something on the third line.

How do they know?

More than surprised, she was now a little scared. They seemed to know everything about her. She didn't have a large circle—just two or three friends at the hypermarket and one elderly friend who needed constant reminders of who she was. It unnerved her. She wasn't sure what to do. There was no pressure from their side; they probably wouldn't care if she didn't respond tonight. But the thought of being monitored for two years was unsettling.

She spent the rest of the night contemplating. The two reasons she considered the job, were the money and their promise of job security. But the reasons for her reluctance were equally strong: the project was classified, and the document offered little insight into what it involved.

My writing isn't taking me anywhere, she thought to herself. *If I want to make my book visible to the world, I'll need the money.*

What was there to lose? she wondered.

Having grown up in Harbor of Hope Orphanage, she had no one to call her own. This decision affected no one but herself.

By 11:30 PM, she lay in bed, thinking about what she had written.

Did it have the potential?

She got off the bed, grabbed the burner phone from the package, and made the call labelled **Acceptance Call**.

Good! I was arranging preparations for monitoring.

Yes, I—

Report to the abandoned school building on the 29th of this month at 10 in the morning. The line went dead.

On the morning of the designated date, she packed hastily, grabbing everything she thought she might need and forcefully squishing it all into a grey duffel bag.

She walked toward her scooter, when two women in colourful vacation outfits suddenly appeared out of nowhere. One grabbed her duffel while the other took hold of her hand, pretending they had known her forever. The woman spoke loudly about always wanting to go on a road trip, which she quickly realized was just a cover for their operation. The first woman opened the back door of a white Honda City with tinted windows, letting her in, while the other tossed the duffel into the boot and got into the driver's seat, all smiles and excitement. But as soon as the car started moving, their faces shifted into a more serious demeanor. The woman sitting beside her pulled out a cloth and blindfolded her. Throughout the ride, one question kept echoing in her mind:

Was this the right thing to do?

After a fair distance, the blindfold was removed. She saw that, as they got closer to the location, the urban landscape gradually gave way to a more rural setting. Buildings receded from view while greenery took over. With each passing mile, it felt as if they were drawing closer to the field until they reached a dead end. To their left, a broken gate stood, bearing a board that read "GOVERNMENT PROPERTY," overgrown with plants. One side of the gate leaned toward the ground, still capable of restricting entry unless someone decided to climb the walls. The abandoned school building mentioned in the documents had been nothing but a decoy. This wasn't a school at all—it was an abandoned airstrip, concealed under layers of overgrowth and time, left forgotten by most. They walked toward the hangar on the left. On the right lay a vast but overgrown airfield, surrounded by trees and thick vegetation. The area seemed prone to frequent rainfall, likely due to its higher altitude, as the hangar appeared to have once been used by the government for flight tests and training.

As they approached, her eyes caught a silhouette standing in the hangar near a table, dressed entirely in black. She struggled to make out the face, only to realize it was obscured by a mask, which was open at the eyes and mouth and covered the rest. All her belongings had been dropped on to the table.

When can I have them back?

Not in the next 8-9 months.

What!?

It's highly classified. We need no traces. If someone were to look from above, there should be no signs of activity here.

That wasn't in the document...

Then you didn't read it properly.

I'm out. This doesn't seem right.

Once you're here, you cannot turn back, ma'am.

Watch me! she picked her belongings, turned and moved away, while the man gestured the ladies not to do anything.

The chilling sound of a gun clicking froze her in place.

I'm watching. Keep going. Let's hope you reach the gates...

She realized, with a sinking feeling, that this was a terrible mistake.

There's nothing to worry about. You work on this project for 8-9 months, then either you walk away or stay—it's your call. In the meantime, you won't be subjected to anything harmful, if that's what you're worried about. There's no downside to this, so logically speaking, it's better to comply.

She stood there, her back turned, paralyzed by a mix of fear and helplessness. Slowly, she turned back and dropped her belongings on the table once more.

What now? she asked, her voice barely above a whisper, her face a picture of defeat.

The man handed her a bag and a keycard with the number A28.

Go straight, through the door, downstairs, and you'll know what to do, said the man, his mask labelled *JAMES*.

She went through the metal detecting doorway and did as instructed. When she reached the basement, she was stunned by what she saw. Underneath the abandoned hangar lay a vast, state-of-the-art super lab, filled with advanced equipment and large screens. As a writer, she was utterly confused about her role in this environment. To her right stretched the enormous lab, while to her left stood three tinted rooms that resembled offices—or perhaps two offices and a conference room. Straight ahead on the right, was a corridor with a sign hanging from the ceiling that read *ROOMS*.

She searched for A28 and found it, oddly situated in between A34 and A25, where she had expected to see A27 and A29. As the indicator blipped green, A34 opened, and a man in black wearing a mask labelled PETER walked out. He glanced at her for a second before moving away, but something about the way he looked at her sent shivers down her spine, making her question her security in this basement. She quickly strode into her room, shutting and locking the door behind her. With a sigh, she slid the keycard into the power socket, and the lights flickered to life, revealing a room that, though small, was still larger than her apartment. The room was simple yet comfortable, with a queen-sized bed, a nightstand, a desk, a chair, and no windows. The soft yellow light from the ceiling and lamps gave the space a warm, inviting glow. The washroom was fairly good, and the thermostat was set at a very comfortable temperature. Despite the unsettling vibe of the hangar in general, the room seemed to slightly lift her mood.

She settled down the bag handed to her by the man tagged as JAMES. Curiosity got the better of her, and she decided to open it. Inside, she found three pairs of clothes, a simple top and a pant, all of the same color. There were also two masks, more like balaclavas, with the name JUDAS labelled on them. The bag contained a bar of soap, feminine hygiene products sufficient for a month, a notepad, a pencil, a sharpener, an alarm clock, a watch, a toothbrush and toothpaste, a roll of toilet paper, and finally, a copy of the document she had received a week ago. The document was attached alongside an instruction manual.

TOP SECRET – INSTRUCTION MANUAL
Project JENESIS
THO_PJ_12A28

Welcome to Project JENESIS

You have been selected for a confidential project. Follow these instructions carefully.

1. Confidentiality

- Do not share any project details.
- Use only secure devices for communication.
- Your actions are monitored at all times.

2. Your Role

- Work hours are from **07:00 to 21:00**.
- Only communicate for work-related purposes—no personal conversations.
- Establishing personal relationships with other participants or staff is strictly prohibited.
- Follow all instructions from the floor supervisor, **Sir JAMES**.
- Report any issues or questions to project staff.

3. Facility Rules

- You must stay at the secure facility for the entire project.

- Do not enter restricted areas.
- Follow all security guidelines.

4. Experimental Procedures

- Specific tasks will be explained to you.
- Report any health concerns immediately.

5. Commitment

- You must participate for the full duration of the project.
- No communication with family or friends during this period.

6. Compensation and Compliance

- You will be compensated for your participation.
- Failure to follow rules or maintain confidentiality will result in immediate removal.

THO Central Command

At night, she lay on the bed, having set her alarm for 6 AM. A notebook lay beside her with a pencil resting on it. Thoughts swirled in her mind about what tomorrow might bring. According to the document, the project was set to commence on the first of next month, just two days away. As she drifted deeper into her thoughts, a knock on the door startled her. It was an odd time for a visit, she thought.

She cautiously opened the door slightly, and there stood the man tagged as PETER. Oddly, he seemed taller than when she had seen him earlier.

May I?

No, I am about to sleep, and this is not an appropriate time.

He pressed on the door, trying to push his way in.

What are you doing!?

I just want to talk for a while...

You can stay outside and talk!

Aw, honey, come on now...

Using all her strength, she managed to shut the door and latch it. PETER chuckled from the other side.

I like it, feisty.

Her heart pounded as she returned to the bed, regretting not having the pepper spray from her bag at hand. The uncertainty of the next few days gnawed at her, filling her with fear. She prayed for safety, lying there alert and unable to sleep. Her mind replayed the encounter when suddenly her alarm went off. It was 6 in the morning, and she realized she had stayed up all night, not catching a wink of sleep.

Rising from the bed, she freshened up and put on the pair of sky-blue clothes, then reached for one of the balaclavas from her bag. She hesitated for a moment before pulling it over her head, adjusting it so that only her eyes were visible. The fabric felt strange against her skin, but she knew it was part of the protocol. Just as she was about to leave, the sound of static filled the room. That's when she noticed the speaker mounted high on the wall opposite the bed.

Everyone, assemble in the conference room. Thank you.

Ready to face the day, she cautiously opened the door, checking if the hallway was clear. Seeing no one, she stepped outside, only to notice something she had missed earlier—a man on the left, with a bag similar to hers and a balaclava on labelled as BART, was struggling to open his door. Her initial worry subsided when she realized he was likely another candidate. He looked back and greeted her with a smile. She didn't smile back, still shaken from the events of the previous night, and walked away. Yet, something about his innocent smile oddly comforted her.

As she walked down the hallway, she noticed the door to the conference room on the right was open, revealing about 8-10 people inside. Among them stood two men dressed in all black, whom she recognized as PETER and JAMES. Her anger and frustration surged, but she forced herself to stay calm as she entered the room, reminding herself why she needed the money.

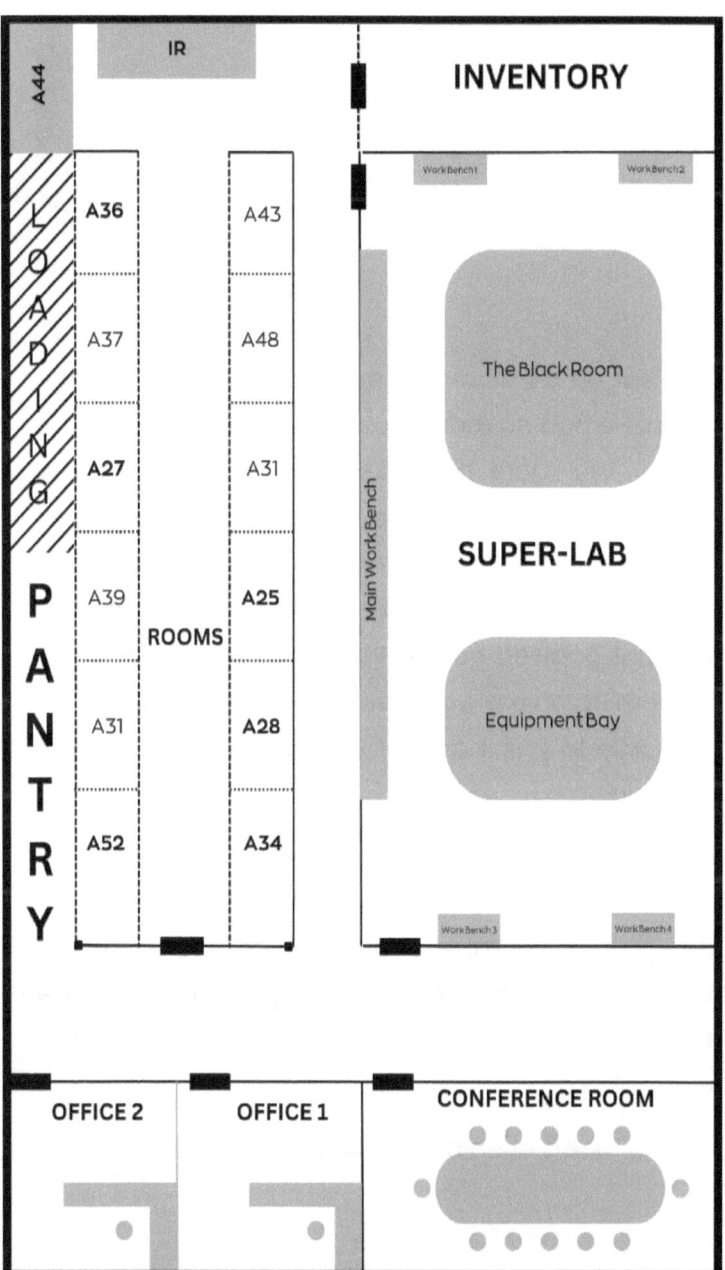

XVIII

J sat on the chair, his eyes scanning the strange room. He had no memory of how he ended up in this place. The more he looked around, the more he realized it didn't seem like a hospital. His mind kept racing, replaying the events. Why had the lady named JUDAS asked to cover the reflective surfaces? The thought gnawed at him. Instinctively, he glanced at something on the wall that was shrouded by a cloth. The urge to pull it down tugged at him—what were they hiding?

Before he could act on it, JUDAS returned, slipping back into the seat opposite him. She placed her notepad on the table and looked at him, as though weighing her next words carefully. J couldn't shake the unease that had settled deep within him. What was going on?

She took a deep breath and began,

Your name is John Birmingham, and you are 44 years old. You are part of this project called Project Jenesis—spelled with a J, for John, of course.

J let out a burst of laughter, a manic sound that echoed off the walls. *What the hell are you talking about?*

Why don't you turn around and see for yourself?

The laugh caught in his throat. He shot her a questioning look before turning toward the covered mirror. Skeptical, he glanced back at her, seeking permission. She gave a silent nod. Hesitantly, he pulled the cloth away. What he saw made his blood run cold.

The man in the reflection wasn't him. He was older—late forties, maybe—his hair streaked with gray, eyes dull, wrinkles marking a face that looked worn, as though it had seen too much. The man in the mirror looked broken. But what made J's heart stop was the horrifying realization: the man moved when he moved.

What the fuck have you done to me?! J screamed; his voice raw with panic.

Sir, please... let me explain—

Where is Meow? J's voice cracked with desperation. *Who the hell are you people? Get me out of here!*

I understand, sir, but can you please sit down so I can explain the rest?

J hesitated. His anger gave way to exhaustion. Tears welled in his eyes. The nightmare wouldn't end. He slumped back into the chair, his face buried in his hands. He couldn't tell what was real anymore, everything felt wrong.

Can I please see her? His voice was barely above a whisper now, breaking as he sobbed. *Please? I just want to see her...*

JUDAS waited for a moment before speaking, her voice softer now. *John, you were brought here from the Crescent Shrine Asylum—CSA. You were a patient there undergoing therapy.*

J shook his head violently. *You're lying! This is a sick joke! You're trying to make me think I'm crazy! I want to get the hell out of here!*

He shot up from his chair, moving toward the door.

JUDAS's voice cut through his movement, cold and sharp,

You are a murderer, John.

J froze in his tracks, chills running down his spine.

You murdered your wife and your kids. Your wife's name was Molly. You called her...

She paused, drawing in a deep, heavy breath, as if the weight of the next word was almost unbearable.

....Meow.

J stood still, paralyzed. The words didn't make sense. *Meow is dead?* His voice was hollow, a faint echo of disbelief.

There is no fucking way I would ever do that. His words came out stronger now, louder, filled with denial. *You're making it all up! I love Meow—I would never hurt her, never! Not physically, not emotionally. You're spinning some bullshit story, and it's not going to convince me.*

His chest heaved as he struggled to breathe, his thoughts spiralling. *I'm done talking to you. Let me out.* He took a step toward the door. *And don't you dare try to stop me.*

As J rushed toward the door, JUDAS swiftly moved to block his path, standing between him and his exit. She handed him a piece of paper, its edges frayed, like an old newspaper article.

You'll know, she said quietly.

Man Murders Wife and Children in Shocking Domestic Incident

Date: August 15, 2018

John Birmingham, 39, stands accused of the brutal murder of his wife, Molly Birmingham, also 39, and their two young sons, aged two, in a tragic incident that occurred late one night. The series of events began with a heated argument between John and Molly, escalating to a point where John lost control, ultimately killing his wife in a fit of rage. Molly's body was found with six stab wounds, a chilling detail that has shocked investigators.

After realizing what he had done, Birmingham reportedly became even more enraged and turned on his twin sons, taking their lives as well. The scene, described by investigators as horrific, left John in a state of severe shock. Upon discovery, he was unable to speak, and later diagnosed with memory loss, having no recollection of the violent events that transpired.

Birmingham has since been admitted to Crescent Shrine Asylum, where he is currently undergoing therapy for his mental condition. Investigations into the incident are ongoing, but authorities have yet to establish what caused the argument that led to this devastating outcome.

After handing him the article, JUDE silently slipped out of the room, closing the door behind her. She exhaled deeply, her back against the door, and turned to face the team waiting outside.

That was not easy... He's devastated. Who's going to explain why we brought him here? Because I can't. I've already caused him too much pain. Her voice was heavy with guilt.

It's alright. Let him be for now, PETER said, trying to comfort her.

Let him be? JAMES cut in. *Prepare THE BLACK ROOM for the Speed-Run. We're finishing the next 50% of the sequence.*

What? PETER's eyes widened. *No, no way!*

We need the results by tomorrow, JAMES replied firmly. *We run it tonight, study the observations, and create the data so we have something to present. JENESIS needs to be done today.*

PETER, nodded reluctantly.

I need THE BLACK ROOM ready for the Speed-Run in an hour—by 1600 hours, JAMES ordered.

PETER hesitated, *JAMES, the first 50% of the sequence took us three months to construct and six months to run. You're asking for the next half in three hours altogether. We might lose him.*

No, JAMES said coldly, *we won't. We have to do this; we have to know at least. Because sooner or later, JESUS CHRIST is going to ask us to do it, so might as well.*

Just then, a strange voice interrupted, *Are you sure about that?*

Two men in black suits walked down the hallway toward PETER and JAMES, their faces covered by balaclavas, one emblazoned with JCIII and the other with JCIV across the front.

Oh... you guys are here, JAMES stammered, clearly startled.

The men ignored his greeting, their demeanor cold and professional. They looked around, taking in the dimly lit basement, their gaze sharp and discerning. As their eyes swept their surroundings, they paused for a moment, noticing J seated in the IR, his silhouette partially obscured by shadows.

So, the shorter man said, his voice cold and businesslike, *what do you have for us?*

Jenesis & Revelation I

J couldn't believe what he was reading. In just a few hours, his entire life had taken a drastic turn. The pain was more unbearable than before. He didn't know what to believe, but one thing remained constant—his desperate hope that all of this was just a nightmare. *How cool would it be if I woke up right now,* he thought, imagining himself back in his house, the sunlight streaming in, and Meow curled up beside him. The urge to feel that again was beyond words. But here he was—trapped. If this was real, then he would be trapped here forever. If any of it was true, he thought, he should end his life. What meaning did life have without his loved ones? How do you go on when strangers tell you that you killed your wife and children? And yet... why couldn't he remember? Why wasn't there even a glimpse of his past? What had life been like with Meow and the kids? He couldn't recall their faces, their voices, and yet the knowledge of their absence left a hollow ache in his chest. Especially the children—the kids he didn't even remember, and still, the thought of them tore him apart. Just 24 hours ago, he had been dreaming of a future with Meow. He had imagined what life would look like after marriage, how their compatibility would shape their future. Now, those thoughts felt like lost dreams. He stared at the ceiling, the newspaper article lying on the coffee table. It said they had twins. Twins. A warmth bloomed in his heart—*what must it have been like when the doctor told us?* But then the doubt crept back in. *If all of this is true,* he thought, *what could have made me kill them? How could I have done that?* He stared blankly at the mess that his life had become. But instead of the flood of tears he once knew, there was just a heavy stillness. It wasn't that the pain wasn't there—it was. But it was like a tide too strong to fight, too vast to comprehend. He was numb. He simply... existed. Life had taken too much from him, and he had no more to give, he had felt so much, for so long, that there was nothing left to feel.

The sound of the door opening snapped J back to reality.

Hey...

JUDAS entered the room and slowly sat down in the chair across from him.

Is that your real name? he asked.

No, she replied with a soft, comforting smile. *I can't reveal my real name to you, but I can tell you what it means.*

She paused briefly before continuing.

This project—or operation—is run by a team of twelve. We're called The Apostles. My alias is JUDAS, like in the Bible. Our project lead is PETER, who, as in the Bible, is seen as the leader of the twelve. And then there's Sir JAMES, the floor supervisor and second-in-command, again, like in the Bible. The rest of us fall in line.

J leaned forward slightly. *Where's Jesus then?*

JUDAS chuckled, the sound light and amused. *JESUS CHRIST is the one funding this project.*

J stared at her for a moment, then said, deadpan, *JUDAS, are you going to betray Jesus?*

It was meant as a joke, but he said it with such a straight face that JUDAS laughed again, this time a bit louder.

No, I doubt it. This JUDAS is pretty loyal.

Does that make me Lazarus? J asked, raising an eyebrow. *You know, since he was brought back to life.*

No, she grinned, *your name is John, remember?* She said, pointing out the uncanny coincidence.

Are you going to tell me anything about this project?

JUDAS' smile faded. *Yes, that's why I'm here.*

She reached into her pocket and pulled out a smartphone, handing it to J.

You'll find a recorded video in the gallery, she said. *It's of PETER, our lead, explaining the project to the rest of us—the Apostles—on our first day here.*

J swiped open the phone, navigating to the gallery. There was only one video—no photos, no other media. He leaned back in his chair, making himself comfortable, and tapped play.

The video wasn't grainy CCTV footage; instead, the smartphone had been placed carefully on the long conference table. In the middle of the frame stood PETER, in front of a whiteboard with the bold headline *PROJECT JENESIS*. The camera angle captured the entire room—a wide shot showing people standing beside their empty chairs on either side of the table, all wearing masks. The masked individuals seemed restless, their heads turning as they took in the room, the board, each other, and the names written on their masks. There was an air of uncertainty, as if they were new to this, unfamiliar with both the surroundings and the situation. PETER stood at the centre of it all, a stack of papers and files laid out neatly in front of him. He appeared calm, though his fingers occasionally drummed on the table. Suddenly, the quiet anticipation in the room shifted as everyone's attention turned toward the unmistakable sound of the door opening. A woman entered—it was JUDAS. She moved with purpose, taking her place beside an empty chair. Still, the meeting didn't start. J quickly counted the figures standing around the table—there were eleven. Nobody spoke. The silence was so thick that J almost thought the video had no sound. Moments later, the masked figures turned toward the door again. This time, a short man entered the room. PETER asked everyone to take their seats, rubbed his hands together, picked up a green marker from the table, stepped forward and took a deep breath.

Morning everyone!

As you're all aware, each of you has been carefully chosen for a highly classified project—PROJECT JENESIS. My name is PETER—or rather, that's my alias. I am the lead for this project, which happens to be my idea. Outside this basement, I am a neurological researcher. While I understand that sharing personal information is against protocol, I feel it's necessary for you to grasp the authenticity and importance of this project. This is JAMES, second-in-command and floor supervisor. He'll be monitoring your work throughout the 14-hour shifts and was also the one who greeted you when you entered the hangar. He represents the organization funding this project—what we refer to as JESUS CHRIST. Which, of course, makes the twelve of us The Apostles. Hence, the names. I won't go over the rules and regulations, as they were clearly outlined in the document you received earlier. Instead, I'll dive straight into what PROJECT JENESIS is about.

As a neurological researcher, I study the brain and nervous system to understand how they work and find better treatments for disorders. I look at how brain cells interact, research diseases like Alzheimer's and Parkinson's, and analyse data to uncover new insights. I also work on translating my findings into practical treatments to help patients. My last couple of years have been more dedicated towards learning and understanding how memories work. Our plan is to induce a deep coma in the patient and then employ advanced neural stimulation technology to deliver a comprehensive memory simulation. This will involve creating a fully immersive alternate reality within their mind, complete with detailed sensory and emotional experiences to make the memories appear genuine. We will use this approach not only to implant new memories but also to reconstruct and modify existing ones. This will allow us to explore how memories can be manipulated and reshaped, providing valuable insights and potential therapeutic applications for treating trauma and memory disorders. In simple words, we are going to work on constructing memories, inducing them, and then seeing the results. (Turns and draws something on the board)

Imagine a field with the roots of a climbing plant. If we provide a support structure, the plant will grow along it; without one, it will meander and follow its own path. Similarly, pre-existing memories act as the roots or foundational knowledge in a person's mind. By installing a carefully crafted memory sequence, we create a support structure for these memories to grow upon. The new, artificially constructed memories will intertwine with the existing ones, guiding how thoughts and recollections develop. This approach enables us to understand and influence how memories can be implanted and reconstructed, much like directing the growth of a climber along a predetermined path.

This is what I have been working on for years. Yet, nobody believed in the vast scope of this project, which is why it never came to fruition—until now. All of it has been theoretical up to this point. What we are about to do is turn that theory into practice. In the right hands, this is a gift to humanity, but in the wrong hands, it becomes a weapon. So, I hope you understand the magnitude of what we're dealing with here. The organization has arranged a subject for the project. Let me tell you a few things about this unusual individual. He's 44 years old, a convicted murderer—killed his wife and two young sons. That night left him in such profound psychological shock that it induced a condition known as aphasia, robbing him of the ability to speak. Later, he was diagnosed with retrograde amnesia, unable to recall the events of that night. Since then, he's been undergoing therapy at Crescent Shrine Asylum.

Our task is to reconstruct and implant memories into his brain. I have spent the last five years laying the foundation for this project. I've gathered nearly all the necessary data to ensure that the artificially constructed memories are as detailed and lifelike as possible. I spoke with several of his closest friends, who shared a significant amount of information about his past, even his childhood. Now, you might still be wondering—why exactly are you all here? You've been carefully divided into two divisions: the Writing Division and the Engineering Division. We have four engineers and six writers, each with a respective head. BART, JUDAS, kindly step forward. (It took them a moment to register their aliases.) BART is Head Engineer, and JUDAS is Head Writer.

It's simple. The writing team will focus on creating a memory sequence—in their terms, a story. Not something overly dramatic, like a movie script, but a natural, detailed narrative that ties into his past. The goal is to write sequences that subtly instill traits he didn't have before. For example, J has been terrified of motorcycles since childhood, ever since his friend died in a speeding accident. Your task is to craft a sequence where he gradually overcomes that fear— but it must feel real, not forced. From there, we'll build on other traits, culminating in a completely alternate life for J. When he wakes up, we'll see if he has the traits we planted in him. Will he remember his real past? Or will the new memories overwrite the old?

The key is making the sequences feel natural. We can't risk continuity errors. For example, he can't just wake up one day and start riding a motorcycle out of nowhere. No! You need to write the process—what makes him change his mind, what triggers the desire to learn, how his past experiences shape that decision.

There are two types of errors we need to be wary of: Cosmic and Cosmetic. A cosmic error could theoretically cause major problems, so avoid them at all costs. Cosmetic errors are minor; the brain is strong enough to bridge small gaps and connect dots. But again, this is all theoretical. Your sequences need to answer all our questions and leave no room for doubt.

And now, to the engineers. Crafting the memory sequences is only half the project. The other 50% falls into your hands. Writing the story alone isn't enough—what makes a memory real are the sensory inputs attached to it. Sounds, smells, temperature, touch—these elements give memories their vividness and emotional weight. Think about it: sometimes a ray of sunlight hitting your face reminds you of a specific moment in your past. A particular smell might bring back a memory you had almost forgotten. Or a song might transport you into deep nostalgia. These sensory inputs are what make memories tangible. You, the engineers, are responsible for creating the sensory components of each memory. For every sequence, you'll need to simulate these inputs. It's your job to bring the sights, sounds, smells, and sensations to life, ensuring that the memories feel as real as possible. Not only that, but you'll also be responsible for running, monitoring, and executing the memory sequences. Every detail must be precise. This project relies heavily on your ability to make the memories feel authentic, so sensory input accuracy is crucial.

Therefore, I need both divisions to work in perfect cohesion. The writing team and the engineering team must coordinate closely for each memory sequence. Every memory written will have a corresponding set of sensory inputs, so clear communication between all members is essential. We have one month to prepare the sequences, and we will begin running them on the first of next month. After that, we'll have the flexibility to feed new memories as we progress

Jenesis & Revelation II

I believe that covers everything. Any questions? Asked PETER.

The 10 members were in a state of confusion and maybe even shock. They were not able to digest the depth and seriousness of this project and not only that but also, how insane all of it sounded.

Sir, may I ask how we're planning to induce a coma in the subject? asked a woman with the tag ANDREW, summoning the courage to speak up.

We'll be using a drug called Thiopental, PETER replied.

If I may, sir, I'd suggest Pentobarbital might be more effective than Thiopental, ANDREW offered.

And why's that?

Pentobarbital can induce a longer-lasting coma, sir. Thiopental's effects wear off after about 5 to 10 minutes, while Pentobarbital can sustain a coma for 4 to 6 hours.

Hmm... interesting.

The only drawback is a slightly longer onset time compared to Thiopental, but it shouldn't make much of a difference.

Noted. Remind me to order some. We already have Thiopental in inventory, but we'll add Pentobarbital too.

Sir what is the reason behind it being classified? Asked LEVI following ANDREW.

I don't think you ought to know that kid, interrupted JAMES.

No, no that's alright. I can let them in on a little something. This project is not exactly authorized. The organization who is funding this is called THO. The Higher Order, said PETER.

Why is the project classified? Continued PETER.

He adjusted his throat,

We, the THO, approached the government, offered them a chance to be a part of something groundbreaking. They listened—at first—but then they pulled out. Why? They didn't have the vision or the backbone. They saw risks where we see opportunity.

They were afraid of the fallout—public backlash, political instability. They couldn't stomach the heat if this got out. But THO is not like them. They're not afraid of pushing boundaries—ethical, political, or otherwise. The world isn't ready for what we're doing here, and the government didn't want to be tied to something they can't control. So, THO classified it. Not because we're hiding. Because they're not ready. And when they are, it'll be on THOS's terms—not theirs.

THO was strong enough to bypass the government and its regulations. But was it the sheer magnitude of the project that gave them this confidence? Or had THO always been this way—a group of men and women powerful enough, perhaps even more powerful, than the government itself? These questions stirred uneasily in each of the ten.

Why did we even want the government involved, if THO is this powerful on their own? Asked a man in balaclava, who clearly was shorter than LEVI, with the tag BART.

It wasn't about strength or resources. The THO approached them because having the government on our side would provide us with something even, we can't buy: legitimacy. See, the government's an ally that's visible, trusted by the public—people question us, but they're less likely to question them. With the government on board, anything that leaked or came under suspicion could be dismissed, redirected, or buried. They'd give us a layer of plausible deniability. If anyone started asking questions, we could stand behind their official statements, and accusations would be brushed off as 'conspiracy theories' or 'misunderstandings'— easier to hide in plain sight. But the government wanted no part of that. They knew the risks and feared public backlash if word got out that they were tied to something this... unconventional. They didn't want their reputation dragged down by a classified project they couldn't fully control. They were afraid people would lose faith in them. So, they turned THO down. And now? We do this ourselves, without a smokescreen.

The silence in the room felt tense, as if fear and regret had crept into the minds of those present. Perhaps some of them now questioned their choice to participate. After a brief pause, the man known as JAMES stepped forward, taking command.

Alright, that's enough briefing. You've all been given the necessary documents with all the relevant information, so there's no need for another spoon-feeding session. As PETER said, *we will star—*

The video abruptly stopped. The recording had reached its 22-minute mark. J checked the gallery for any other video that might precede it, but found none.

The gallery contained only this single video. The entire system held nothing else—no call logs, no files, no messages. Nothing. Under different circumstances, J might have found the emptiness of the phone odd. But now, he was too preoccupied with the video's contents.

Instilling traits? he wondered. J was beginning to question whether he truly knew who he was. An unsettling identity crisis began to creep in. He couldn't shake the feeling that the person he thought he was now was vastly different from who he might have been before. This thought haunted him. But before he could dwell on it, the sound of the door opening broke his concentration. JUDAS had entered.

They want you in the conference room.

As J followed JUDAS into the room, he interrupted a conversation among several men seated across from each other. Two of them wore name tags that unmistakably read JCIII & JCIV—figures he'd never seen before. The two other men, which J recognized from the video was PETER and JAMES.

We don't need to announce our arrival, one of the men with the name tag JCIII said sharply.

In fact, we wouldn't have come at all, except JAMES rang us up, asking to move things to tomorrow—which, of course, made it essential that we be here today.

So, enlighten us, JAMES. Show us the results of your nine months of work—it better be good.

Four pairs of eyes instinctively fell upon J as he entered the room, the two men staring at him without blinking. JUDE motioned for J to sit in a chair positioned at the far end of the table, with the pair of men seated on either side, facing each other. A book was placed in the centre of the table. As JUDE turned to leave, PETER stopped her.

Take a seat beside me, he said, gesturing. She paused, studying him for a moment before finally sitting next to JAMES. J could sense tension between PETER and JUDE.

JAMES seemed to be waiting for something before beginning his presentation. Just then, BART entered and took a seat beside PETER.

Alright! As you can see, here is our subject...

Twelve eyes now focused on J before JAMES continued.

First off, J, how are you feeling?

Um... J hesitated, finding the question odd. Why did JAMES care about his well-being right now? *I'm... alright.*

The two men watched him with an almost unsettling intensity.

Gentlemen, JAMES began, *as you can see, this marks the successful culmination of the project. We can officially declare that Project Jenesis was a resounding success.*

PETER handed an orange file to JAMES, who passed it along to the two men.

PETER and I divided the project into multiple segments, JAMES began. *As you'll see on the first page, the primary segment was restoring his ability to speak. He hadn't spoken in nearly five years, but today he did. This alone demonstrates that Jenesis has successfully addressed a disability—his aphasia. On the next page is the second segment: Memory Alteration. We crafted a memory sequence that resembles his past but diverges significantly from the events he's actually lived. For example, he remembers nothing of what happened that night in 2018, and when he woke up, he thought he was only 23.*

Also, check this, JAMES continued, *pressing play on a video of J's interview, taken by JUDE.*

As you can see, John has no recollection of his past, not even the names of his mother or grandfather. One might think such memories are impossible to forget, yet he has no trace of them.

What about your father? JCIV asked.

*I don't know...*replied J.

What do you mean you don't know?

Let me explain, JAMES interjected. *His answer may seem strange, but it's intentional. In the memory sequence we crafted, there's no mention of his father. He does, in fact, have one, and most information about John's traits and personality was provided by Mr. Birmingham himself.*

J felt a shock run through him. He had no memories of having a father, no sense of his existence—yet apparently, a man named Birmingham knew more about him than he did.

This segment, JAMES continued, *is Knowledge Alteration. We implanted new memory sequences that sever his ties with prior memories and build new ones from scratch. This approach draws from a theory of PETER's, suggesting that memories lost due to trauma aren't erased but rather hidden behind a mental barrier. In theory, these memories can only resurface if you gradually chip away at that wall, uncovering what's hidden behind.*

Both men looked as though they were beginning to be convinced.

Now, if I may, I have another demonstration of the segment, JAMES said.

He reached under the table and flicked a switch. A low hum sounded from above. J watched as the ceiling moved—or was it not just a ceiling? A thick layer slid away to reveal a glass panel behind it. The ceiling was designed in such a way that light and shadows moved precisely, mimicking real sunlight. It was an illusion, yet so convincing that, even knowing it was a basement, it was hard to shake the feeling of being outdoors—a clever trick, making the closed space feel strangely open.

What the hell is that!? J exclaimed, jolting up from his seat. BART quickly steadied him.

Both men stared at the ceiling, visibly concerned.

There's nothing up there, gentlemen, JAMES assured them. *One of our focuses was understanding how the brain processes cosmic and cosmetic changes. As you can see, he's adjusted to cosmetic changes—and even some cosmic ones—but we needed to push further. Our goal was to get him to accept something entirely surreal as natural. At first, we considered writing something entirely alien, but we realized that would likely overwhelm his ability to process it. So, we chose something simpler: we wrote the skies red.*

Sensing the slight confusion in the men's expressions, JAMES elaborated.

In the Memory Sequence Universe, or MSU as we call it, the skies are naturally red. So, for him, seeing a blue sky might feel like he's on an alien planet.

J who was standing, listened, feeling his inner world crumble. This is too much, he thought. In mere moments, his life had flipped upside down, and he was being told things about his own life that he'd never imagined.

Now would be the right time to wake up, if this were all a dream, he thought.

JAMES stood from his seat, grabbed a book from the table, and handed it to J.

John, I want you to do two things for me, he instructed. *First, open the book and start reading. Then, turn to the next page and write what you're about to read.*

J, confused but compliant, flipped to the first page. It was a blank white page, except for a few printed lines:

Her gaze was soft, her heart still pure,

But in his soul, darkness did stir.

A flash of rage, a quiet scream....

J paused.

... And all was lost in a single dream.

J sighed before he turned the pages to uncomfortably write what he had just read.

That will be enough, John. Thank you, JAMES said.

This segment, my personal favorite, is called Trait Imprint, JAMES explained to the two men. *We crafted a sequence that gave him a skill he's never had. John has been dyslexic since childhood, with significant difficulty reading or writing. But now, as you can see, he can do both.*

The two men sat with blank, expressionless faces while J grasped the unsettling depth of the entire project. If anyone was truly impacted by the presentation, it was J. He sat there in disbelief, battling an identity crisis within his mind.

One of the men spoke.

Don't get me wrong—this is all quite impressive, no doubt. But it still doesn't fulfill the primary objective.

Which is... ? asked JAMES, a hint of confusion in his voice.

The man chuckled. *We didn't want him learning to ride a motorcycle or reciting poetry. What we needed was for him to recall the events of that night. That was the primary objective.*

Wait, that wasn't part of the project at all. What I proposed was purely Memory Reconstruction; Memory Recollection is something else entirely, PETER interjected.

Speak when spoken to, the man replied coldly.

These are orders from above. If they want Memory Recollection, then Memory Recollection is what you'll provide. Telling them the subject has read a poem won't cut it. The primary objective is Memory Recollection. Only after that can secondary goals be considered.

The man, JCIII leaned forward slightly. *If you're wondering why Memory Recollection takes priority over Memory Alteration, despite the latter's complexity...* he paused, *it's none of your damn business. Just do what you're told.* With that, the two men stood.

24 hours. Same time. Show us what we need, or we lift the covers.

JCIV reached over and picked up a device from the table that seemed to have captured the entire conversation. The two men left without another word, heading out of the basement. The remaining five sat in silence, each lost in their own thoughts, wrestling with the new demands.

XIX

JAMES was pacing back and forth in the conference room, his footsteps filling the tense silence. The other four sat deep in thought, avoiding his eyes. The only sound was the rustling of JAMES' pants as he strode from one end of the room to the other, agitated.

PETER, you need to figure something out—now! Or we're all screwed, dammit! JAMES's voice cracked with panic.

Again! The project pitch didn't include anything about Memory Recollection! PETER shot back, exasperated.

Irrespective! JAMES's tone was nearly desperate. *We have to work that out, PETER! Do you even realize what's about to happen if this goes sideways? He said it himself, didn't he? They lift the covers, and once that's done, the media will be rushing to greet us at the entrance. Everything we've worked for—gone.*

You do realize what this calls for now, right, PETER? Continued JAMES.

We can't, JAMES. Even this plan will risk everything we've worked for.

We need to finish this in 24 hours. The only option we have is to speed-run the sequence.

And what happens when it doesn't work? PETER's tone was low but firm.

At least we'll have tried!

No! When this fails tomorrow and they bring in more people to evaluate our progress, do we just stand there and tell them we tried, we failed, and somehow also managed to lose everything we've built over the past nine months?

JAMES leaned in, his expression hard. *PETER, they already have recorded our observations and results. The argument is over. We have 24 hours to figure out a plan, construct the sequence, and run it. Do you really think the conventional method you're suggesting will work within that timeframe? They've seen what we've presented; they know what they want. Now it's time to move to the next stage—or by this time tomorrow, we'll be in cuffs!*

He raised his voice, the room vibrating with tension. *Take your time if you need it, come up with a plan, or get some rest. But we meet back here at 8 p.m.* JAMES stood, his presence as commanding as his words. *Clock's ticking.*

With that, JAMES stormed out of the room. J watched him go, wondering, *Didn't JUDAS say JAMES was representing THO?* Yet JAMES seemed the most rattled of them all. *Was he just worried about the team's cover being blown?* J considered. *He did seem like a decent guy.*

The pressure had shifted heavily onto PETER now. The man who pitched the whole project was burdened with a problem far beyond his life's work— one that had to be solved within a day. PETER sat at the table, looking focused yet visibly strained, trying to work out how to approach Memory Recollection. But the crushing time constraint clouded his focus. *Three or four months, maybe—* but 24 hours felt almost impossible.

Meanwhile, BART and JUDAS exchanged a look of contempt, which PETER didn't notice until they made it clear. Both stood to leave, but before they did, BART leaned in close to PETER, his tone low and menacing.

I'll fucking kill you if you lay as much as one finger on her.

PETER sat in stunned silence as they left, taking J with them and leaving him alone in the empty room. He stared at the door, his mind racing, then reached for a pencil and paper from the desk, quickly scribbling down his thoughts in the stillness.

17:10

That guy is getting on my nerves, BART muttered as they led J toward A44. The room, assigned specifically to J, was just like every other room in that basement.

Look, whispered JUDAS, her voice tight but controlled. *I appreciate you wanting to protect me, I do. But we don't even know who he is. You can't just go around threatening people we know nothing about, BART.*

So, we're just gonna let it slide? BART's chuckle was low, his frustration simmering beneath it.

Listen, she shot back, her whisper sharpening. *We're one night away from completion. One. Night. And then we're out of here. I need you to stay focused. I can't have you doing something that might keep us trapped here—* she took a tense breath, *—or worse, us put behind bars!*

BART's shoulders tensed. *And that's all hinging on PETER,* he muttered bitterly, *assuming he can actually pull it off. If he doesn't, we're done. Stuck here, with no way back to any kind of life.*

BART, JUDAS's tone softened, almost pleading, *we just need to get through this. One last push. Don't do anything reckless. Please—don't do anything that could risk our chances of getting out.*

BART's voice rose, heated. *No! You're the one not thinking, JUDE!* His frustration flashed into anger. *We're already trapped, unless PETER pulls off a miracle. And he won't, because half the time, he's too busy trying to get in your pants!*

Her face hardened. *And that, right there,* she hissed, *is exactly why I didn't want you involved. This...this is too much. Just go. Please—just go to your room. I can't deal with this. Not now.*

With a fierce look, BART spun on his heel and stormed out, his footsteps echoing as he left her standing with J.

17:45

JAMES stood at the edge of his balcony in A52, his back to the entrance, pants down and a cigar dangling from his mouth. Eyes closed, he was deep in his own world, his hand keeping a steady rhythm that quickened as his breaths grew heavier, almost inaudible moans escaping under his breath.

JAMES, what the fuck are you doing?!

Oh, hey, JAMES said, hardly flinching as he opened one eye, slowly pulling up his pants with casual ease. *Wasn't expecting you just yet.* He adjusted his zipper, completely unbothered, taking another puff of his cigar.

Dude, PETER sighed. *At least keep the door shut.*

Yeah, yeah, JAMES replied dismissively. *Just blowing off a little steam, given the recent madness.*

PETER exhaled in frustration, grabbing a cigar from the box and lighting it. *Alright. Look, I have an idea.*

Will it work? JAMES asked, as if nothing had happened, casually rolling the cigar between his fingers.

PETER gave him a side glance, taking a deep drag. *Honestly? I don't know,* he admitted, *but it's our best option.*

Alright, then, JAMES said with a smirk, relaxing into a chair. *Let's hear it.*

Okay, so I despite of me not having pitched THO about anything close to Memory Recollection, nevertheless I had thought about it a lot, lot even before Pro-Jenesis. Remember I had told you about a hypothetical wall that buries memories down when someone endures, say a trauma to the head? It revolves around that concept.

Okay?

Look, PETER says, leaning in closer, *if there really are memories blocked off behind this hypothetical wall, then theoretically, we should be able to reach them by recreating his original memories—right up to the moment before the murder.*

JAMES stares at him, his jaw tight. *Go on.*

The brain's funny like that, PETER continues. *If we get those memories exactly right, down to the details that drove his choices—the judgments he made from his past experiences—then, in theory, his mind should respond in the same way it did back then.* He taps his fingers together thoughtfully. *Though getting that kind of precision is... well, impossible.*

Why impossible?

Because, PETER explains, *there's no way to perfectly reconstruct every thought he had, every reaction. We're working blind, trying to simulate choices and memories we can't completely know.* He pauses. *But let's say we can get close, maybe fifty percent accuracy in recreating what led up to that point. The theory is, if he's put back into that familiar headspace, it could trigger... well, flashes of deja vu.*

JAMES frowns. *So, he'd see glimpses of the past?*

Exactly. PETER's gaze is intense. *Moments might resurface, split-second glimpses that his mind identifies as familiar. He won't remember everything, but if everything goes well, those glimpses could help him reconstruct the events of that night—maybe not exactly as they were, but if we're lucky, we might get around seventy-five to eighty percent of it right It's like nudging a stuck wheel into turning again, and if we do it right, the events of that night will be replicated.*

This all sounds good, but how are you going to write the sequence for the original memories? JAMES asks, taking a slow drag from his cigar, the smoke curling into the air.

I've gathered quite a lot of information about his past from his friends and family over the five years I spent preparing for this project, PETER replies, exhaling a plume of smoke.

But is that going to be enough?

That's all we've got, PETER admits, a hint of uncertainty creeping into his voice as he watches the smoke dissipate.

You sure about this? JAMES presses, raising an eyebrow as he flicks the ash from his cigar.

This is the only way to go, PETER insists, his gaze steady and serious.

We need to get this done quick! JAMES urges, the urgency in his voice cutting through the haze of cigar smoke.

Yeah, PETER replies, nodding as he takes another drag from his cigar. *I'm going to run this by BART and JUDE first to write and engineer the sequence.* He stands up, the chair scraping against the floor as he prepares to leave.

JAMES watches him intently, his eyes narrowing as PETER strides toward the door.

17:45

J sank into the chair in A44, letting out a slow breath as he settled. JUDE moved about quietly, preparing a cup of coffee to help him relax.

Thank you for the coffee. You're very kind.

Don't mention it, JUDE replied, handing him the cup. *How are you feeling?*

J took a moment, staring into the steaming cup. *It's... surreal,* he murmured. *Not every day someone tells you your life is just an experiment—and that you're far from the reality you thought you knew.* He paused, his expression clouded. *Then again, my reality... it wasn't exactly one I wanted to live in. I feel... lost.*

I'm sorry, JUDE said softly, her voice laced with empathy. *I can't imagine what that's like... but it must hurt.*

J sighed, gripping the cup a little tighter. *You know, JUDE... I don't know if it's just this altered version of me talking, but I would never lay a hand on Molly. Even if she cheated, I couldn't do it. I'd take the kids if I had to, but... hurting her?* He shook his head. *That's just not me.*

Silence stretched between them, thick with unspoken words.

I miss her, he whispered. *You wrote it well, JUDE. There are so many memories—moments with her that keep me going, even if it all feels like a blur.*

JUDE hesitated, her gaze steady. *J... not all those memories were crafted or written.*

He looked up, brow furrowed. *I... I don't understand.*

See, she explained gently, *we did our best to create memories, paying attention to every detail. But the brain... it has this way of filling in gaps on its own. Like PETER said in that video, it "addresses cosmetic changes" without us even realizing.*

J's expression grew more confused. *So, the memories with Molly... some of them weren't created by you?*

Exactly, JUDE nodded. *Even though you were in a controlled environment, your brain adapted, filling in spaces with natural memories. They're pieces of the life you would have lived. That's the mind's way of adapting. We were always aware that something unexpected could occur, but... fortunately, it didn't.*

J looked away, his eyes drifting. *JUDE... what did I do for a living?*

JUDE paused, choosing her words carefully. *Well... we didn't have extensive background information, only the essentials. But you know,* she said, a small smile tugging at her lips, *you were pretty fond of guns as a kid. That's real—you actually were.* She let that sink in. *And as for work, you were a firearm designer, with a company called Sig Sauer.*

As the name left her lips, a jolt of pain shot through J's head. He closed his eyes, his fingers pressing against his temples as the pain intensified.

Hey, are you alright? JUDE asked, worry flashing across her face.

I don't know... he breathed, his voice strained. Images began to flicker in his mind—bits and pieces, a factory, a workplace. The fragments came and went, hazy and out of reach.

Wait, let me call someone—

No... he said, forcing himself to slow his breathing. *I'm okay... I think it's passing.*

Gradually, the pain ebbed, and he opened his eyes, calmer now, though a trace of the memory lingered in his mind.

What happened? JUDE asked, concern sharpening her tone.

J took a shaky breath, still rubbing his temples. *I think... the name of the company flipped a switch. I saw things...*

JUDE leaned closer. *What did you see, J?*

I don't know exactly. He shook his head, his eyes distant. *Some kind of factory, maybe a workplace... It was just fragments, but it felt... familiar.*

JUDE's eyes widened slightly, a flicker of excitement breaking through her worry. *The sequence we crafted—it had none of that. This could mean we're finally breaking through the barriers.* Her voice lowered, almost in awe. *I think... we've scratched the wall......this is it.*

JUDE got off the seat, and moved towards the where there was a platform holding a few cups, a kettle, a bowl of tea bags and coffee powder and milk powder. Just when she was stirring a cup of hot coffee, a loud knock echoed through the room, that dropped the spoon from her hand.

Both of them froze, the tension thick in the air as they turned toward the door.

18:30

PETER headed toward JUDE's room first. Better to get the writer's perspective before consulting the engineer, he reasoned. Tucked under his arm was a file labelled **JB**, packed with all the crucial information about John Birmingham—notes from friends, insights from family, mainly his father's accounts. This was the only option, he knew. Even if hours of deliberation might produce something better, he didn't have hours to spare. In just over ninety minutes, he needed an actionable plan, enough time to initiate the sequence, test it, and carefully monitor the results.

Reaching A28, he knocked. Silence. He knocked again. Still no answer. Impatience bubbled up as he knocked a third time, his knuckles rattling the door.

Suddenly, a sharp, searing pain shot through his head, and his vision blurred. His balance faltered, and he dropped to the floor, a heaviness settling over him. Instinct screamed for him to turn, to see who was behind him—but he knew better than to risk another blow. Escape was all that mattered.

He tried to crawl forward, but his limbs barely obeyed. He strained, willing himself forward, but the initial bang had left him dazed, and his movements were sluggish, almost ineffective. Gritting his teeth, he forced himself onward, hoping to make it to JAMES. But his strength ebbed, and with a final, defeated gasp, his body gave out, and his face hit the cold floor.

He remembered the sudden pressure of hands gripping his arms, the rough tug as two people lifted him up and dragged him away—and then everything faded to black...

au revoir II

The man approached LEVI in the super lab, his footsteps echoing softly against the sterile floor. LEVI stood by a workbench, his right hand tucked in his pocket, eyes distant like he was lost in thought.

What are you doing? ALPHAEUS asked.

LEVI flinched, his gaze snapping toward him. *Nothing...* he muttered, sinking into a nearby chair.

ALPHAEUS grabbed a chair from the adjacent workbench, dragged it over, and sat next to LEVI. For a moment, they sat in silence. ALPHAEUS eyed LEVI, noticing the rapid tapping of his foot. Unable to bear the quiet, he finally spoke.

I'm kind of surprised you're still here... you know... given your whole escape plan.

LEVI shot him a look but said nothing.

Umm... ALPHAEUS hesitated, glancing around like someone might be listening. I want in.

LEVI stopped tapping his foot, his eyes narrowing as he turned to face ALPHAEUS.

What made you change your mind now? LEVI asked, suspicion lacing his tone.

I heard them talking, ALPHAEUS said, leaning in. *They're planning to run another sequence on J. Not just that—they're going to speed-run it. After everything he's just been through.* He shook his head, his eyes dark with unease. *It's messed up, man. The more I think about it, the more I see things that don't add up. Little signs, little details. It's not just the project—it's the people running it. They don't care about us. They never did.* He leaned back, exhaling slowly. *I'm starting to see it now... there's no way out of this place...*

LEVI leaned back and exhaled slowly.

So, if you've got a plan, now's the time. By the looks of it, we don't have long, continued APHAEUS.

He straightened up, leaning in closer to ALPHAEUS.

I overheard PETER and JAMES talking last night. Didn't catch much, but one of them mentioned wanting a drink, and the other said, "Meet me at the balcony in five."

Okay...? ALPHAEUS raised a brow, unimpressed.

So, I figured—if anyone's got a balcony in this place, it's gotta be JAMES. Makes sense, right? His position, being part of THO and all. And here's the kicker—I doubt if JAMES is being monitored. Which means his room's a blind spot.

But how can he have a balcony if we're in a basement?

Well, either there's a stairway leading to an upper level we don't know about, or they're calling something else a "balcony."

What do you think?

There's nothing to think about. LEVI's tone was sharp, certain. We gamble. We don't have the luxury of overthinking this. We move. We act.

So, you're suggesting we make a run for it?

Yes.

Okay... but how do we break into JAMES' room? We can't afford a move that raises suspicion. So how do you plan to pull that off?

LEVI pulled his right hand out of his pocket, revealing a key card hidden in his palm. He held it up just enough for ALPHAEUS to see but not enough to draw attention.

How...?! ALPHAEUS's eyes widened in shock.

Everyone's got a spare key, don't they? LEVI replied, his voice calm but sharp.

How did you get it?

It was too easy, LEVI said flatly, his face unreadable.

Great, great, ALPHAEUS said, his excitement building. So, what's the next move? When do we get out?

LEVI stared at him for a moment, his gaze cold and deliberate.

I think... we shouldn't get out.

What? ALPHAEUS blinked, half-laughing. What do you mean, "we shouldn't"? A hint of anger edged his voice.

As I said, it was too easy...

So what? Good for you! ALPHAEUS leaned forward, his frustration growing.

No, you don't understand. LEVI's tone dropped, almost a whisper. It was too damn easy.

What the hell are you talking about?

Think about it, LEVI said, his eyes narrowing. A project as classified as this. Every step planned to perfection. Guards, surveillance, checkpoints—all of it airtight. And yet... JAMES just happens to leave his keycard on the conference room table? He leaned in closer, his voice a low, deliberate whisper. Almost like he wanted me to take it.

The problem is, ALPHAEUS leaned back, shaking his head, you've watched way too many movies. There's no grand conspiracy here. You got the key, and now we get out. He jabbed a finger at LEVI. And besides, didn't you want me to tag along? So, let's go!

LEVI shook his head slowly, his gaze distant.

ALPHAEUS let out a sharp exhale of frustration, leaning back in his chair. But after a moment, he straightened up, his eyes sharper than before.

You know, you told me you got here by accident? ALPHAEUS said, his voice tight. Well, so did I.

LEVI glanced up at him, curious but silent.

The package that showed up at my doorstep? ALPHAEUS leaned forward, his voice picking up intensity. It wasn't even meant for me. It was for my brother—my parents' favorite. The overachiever. The smart one. The good-looking one. The better one. The one who gets opportunities dropped at his feet, like the universe owes him something. His jaw tensed. And me? I'm not that different, but I never got the chances he got. I grew up in a house where my brother was worshipped more than God himself.

LEVI listened, his eyes narrowing with understanding.

When I opened that package, man... ALPHAEUS trailed off, his fingers curling into fists on his knees.

...It felt like you'd finally gotten a chance to prove yourself? LEVI said, finishing the thought for him.

ALPHAEUS glanced at him, surprise flashing across his face. You too, huh?

LEVI shook his head, lips twitching in the faintest smirk. No. The Lion King, actually.

Do you think I'm making this up? ALPHAEUS snapped, leaning in.

No, I get it, LEVI replied, leaning back. I've seen the movie.

ALPHAEUS scoffed, rolling his eyes. Alright, then how'd you end up here?

LEVI exhaled deeply, rubbing the back of his neck. I'm... or I was... a small-time thief, he began slowly, like he was admitting it to himself as much as to ALPHAEUS. Nothing violent. Just breaking in and out of rich people's places after doing my homework on them. Only hit the ones who deserved it. You know, karmic balance—they steal from the poor, I steal from them. He shrugged.

A moral thief... ALPHAEUS muttered, raising a brow.

Call it what you want, LEVI replied, waving it off. But here's the thing. I wasn't doing it that often. Because, weirdly enough, it felt like either rich people were getting nicer, or they'd gotten a whole lot better at hiding their dirt. Either way, pickings got slim. He leaned forward, resting his elbows on his knees. Then I saw this advertisement. "A million bucks for the best short story." Problem was—I'm no writer.

ALPHAEUS tilted his head, curious now.

So, I did some research, figured I'd cheat the system. Found out about this so-called 'successful writer' who made his money stealing scripts from other people. Poetic, right? LEVI smirked. Perfect candidate to rob. Broke into his house, no gloves, no bag, just me and my eyes. I only took one thing—a single sheet of paper, handpicked from a file labeled BEST SHORT STORIES. You see that? Luck, fate, or whatever you wanna call it, just lined up perfectly.

ALPHAEUS blinked, stunned. No way.

Submitted that paper just to see what'd happen... and now here I am, LEVI said with a humourless laugh.

Regretting a whole bunch of choices—but not robbing the rich.

There was a brief silence lingering between the two, thick and heavy.

I think it's only poetic that the two of us leave—the two who got here by accident, ALPHAEUS muttered, his eyes locked on the ground.

I still think it's a bad idea... LEVI said, his tone low but firm.

Staying here means walking toward an inevitable death, ALPHAEUS shot back, leaning forward, his eyes sharp now. But trying to break out? That's a 50-50 shot... and I like those odds.

LEVI let out a long, slow sigh, rubbing his hands over his face. Alright... he muttered, his gaze distant before it settled on ALPHAEUS.

We do it tonight.

ECHO II

The room was dark except for the faint glow of a computer screen, casting a cold blue light on the man's face. His fingers hovered over the keyboard, still for now, waiting. His eyes darted across the screen, studying lines of code, deep in focus. Next to him, two cans of energy drinks stood on the cluttered desk, with another lying on its side, spilling its contents. The desk was a mess of snack wrappers and empty bottles, showing he had been at this for hours.

He began to type. The soft clatter of keys echoed in the silence as he worked his way through layers of security. Each firewall he encountered was tougher than the last, but he was patient, methodical. He'd been here before, and he knew the steps.

Suddenly, the screen flashed. **ACCESS DENIED**.

He paused, barely blinking. There was no frustration, just a quick adjustment. His fingers moved faster, sending new commands through. His mind raced, already a step ahead of the system's defenses. A small smile crept onto his lips as the next line appeared: **FIREWALL COMPROMISED**.

He was in.

The screen filled with files and data—confidential, locked away from anyone's eyes. He had cracked the system. But before he could dig deeper, a warning flashed: **INTRUSION DETECTED**.

No panic. He quickly typed in a final command, shutting down the system, erasing every trace of his presence. In an instant, it was over. The screen went blank.

He leaned back, exhaling slowly. The room was quiet again. He had won. He was contented on how he did, and more importantly he was proud because he had achieved a great milestone for a self-taught programmer. He knew, whatever he had hacked into was unlike any that he had done before, this had a clutter of confidential files and folders. It was decent enough of him to have not opened or looked into any of it, he thought. Unlike the other hackers, he was more interested in breaking firewalls and entering it, because it challenged him. He wasn't really bothered about what it contained. He just loved the challenge of breaking into a tougher system every other time. Before bed, he encrypted his data, used a VPN to hide his IP address, and cleared all logs to cover his tracks. He switched accounts to avoid detection, ran tools to avoid being noticed, and made sure all his software was up-to-date and secure.

The next day morning, he was greeted by a package laying at his desk. He, while still laying, rubbing his eyes,

Gramma, what is this?

No idea, darling. Found it on our doorstep.

He would've ignored it completely, but curiosity got the better of him when he noticed there was no sender address, which meant only one thing,

It is an anonymous post.

He grabbed it and sat on his bed and ripped it open.

Top Secret - Highly Classified

File Reference: THO-PJ-12A25
Date: 18/8/23
Subject: Project JENESIS - Approval, Operational Directives, and Protocols

-----

Recipient Alias: BARTHOLOMEW
Designation Code: THO-9796
Personal Identifier: SUZIE-9796
Role: Engineer-Head, Project JENESIS

I. PROJECT OVERVIEW
Project Name: *JENESIS*
Objective: To design and implement complex, advanced software systems as a critical component of the experimental process. The software will need to seamlessly integrate with ongoing research and deliver precise, high-performance outcomes.

As **Engineer-Head**, you will head a team of four, working together to develop and optimize the codebase that drives the project's technological infrastructure. You will have full autonomy over the design and execution of the systems, ensuring the software operates with accuracy and efficiency.

It has come to our attention that you attempted unauthorized access to our systems last night. While this was a breach of protocol, we recognize your skills and resourcefulness, which is precisely why you are being considered for this role. Such actions will not be tolerated moving forward, but they confirm our belief in your technical capabilities.

Your expertise and leadership will be pivotal to the success of *Jenesis*, making your role critical in executing the experiment's objectives.

The hacker's hands went cold as he read the document. His first thought: they were trying to kill him. He shoved the document and the burner phone back onto his desk, then hurried to the window to shut the curtains. Sitting back on his bed, he tried to think—what should he do next?

A shock wave surged through him when the burner phone suddenly rang, the sound cutting through the silence. Trembling, he retrieved it from the package, his eyes locking onto the caller ID: *Acceptance Call*.

We don't usually do this, but if you're wondering, this is not an attempt to kill you. The voice was calm, almost too calm. *We're interested in your skillset for our project. The pay is good, and it might help with your introvert problem.*

A chill ran down his spine. They knew more about him than he'd ever imagined. Being an introvert all his life, the only thing his grandma ever wanted for him was to go out, make friends, and find something to live for beyond her.

Okay? His voice wavered.

This would have been optional if we didn't know about your capabilities. But now, it's crucial that you join us temporarily—you can leave when the work is done, in 8-9 months. Don't worry about Suzie; we'll inform her that this is a military program.

So, you're not concerned that I hacked into your system? He asked, trying to regain some control.

No, we actually like it. The only problem would arise if you refuse to join us. In that case, we'd have to get you onboard by force, which we sincerely hope won't be necessary. Trust me, there's no downside to this.

Alright... I guess, he finally agreed.

See you on the morning of the 30th at 7. And you can open your curtains again. The line went dead.

He opened the blinds; fully aware he was being watched. As he walked into the living room, he noticed Gramma beaming, a letter in her hand.

That's too wide of a smile, Gramma!

I'm so happy for you, darling!

What for? He asked, puzzled.

You landed a job! And in a military program, no less! That's amazing, darling!

Yes... right. Can I see that? He reached for the letter, trying to mask his growing unease.

Dear Mrs. Suzie,

We are pleased to inform you that your grandson has been selected for an exclusive military program, recognizing his remarkable talents. This is a tremendous opportunity for him to grow and develop new skills.

As part of this commitment, he will need to focus fully on the program for the next 8 to 9 months, which means he will not be able to stay in regular contact. Please rest assured that he is in excellent hands and will emerge stronger than ever.

Thank you for your understanding and support.

Warm regards.

This wasn't convincing at all, but it sure worked for Gramma, he thought.

When did this letter arrive, Gramma?

The postman just handed it over a few seconds ago.

They're really quick with things, he thought.

Yes, yes. Will you be okay, though? I won't be able to keep in touch for the next several months.

I'll be fine as long as I know you're doing alright. I'm so thrilled; I'm going to go bake a cake!

On the 30th morning, at fifteen minutes past six, the hacker packed and was ready to leave. He tried calling from the burner to confirm the location, but there was no response. After kissing Gramma goodbye, he walked downstairs, about to hail a cab, when two women in colorful vacation clothes approached him.

About half an hour later, they untied his blindfold as the white Honda City came to a stop. He was asked to get out, while the driver dropped his bag at the entrance table inside the hangar. In there, a man labeled *JAMES* handed him a key card and directed him downstairs.

In the basement, the setup took him by surprise. He had assumed there would only be four people, but as he glanced to his left, he saw a group of about ten to twelve people in what looked like a conference room. He headed towards his room door labeled *A25*.

The door denied access on his first few attempts. Just then, the door to his right opened slightly. No one stepped out for a few seconds, but then, he caught sight of someone looking around cautiously before stepping out, wearing a balaclava with the name *JUDAS* on it. The woman seemed startled at the sight of him. There was a brief moment of eye contact, and he decided to greet her with a smile. The woman named *JUDAS*—which he found odd—ignored him and hurried off.

The beep of the door reminded him of the task at hand, and his door finally opened.

Just minutes before seven, the hacker stepped out of his room, ready for what he assumed would be an icebreaking session. As he entered the conference room, heads turned to look at the short man who had just walked in, labeled *BART*.

XX

18:30

After the heated clash with JUDE, BART slumped into a chair in the lab, his mind racing. He felt helpless, a hot, simmering anger growing in his chest as he replayed the argument. He hadn't been able to protect the one he loved—no matter how he tried, he couldn't think of a solution that didn't involve violence. One thought echoed more than the rest: Did JUDE doubt him? Did she think he wasn't man enough to keep her safe? His fists clenched unconsciously, blood boiling, the urge to prove himself creeping into his mind, slowly overtaking his intent to protect her.

After what felt like an hour, BART stood, resolve settling within him as he picked up a metal bracket from the lab. He knew what he had to do. Making his way toward the row of rooms, he spotted a figure standing outside A28. His grip tightened when he realized it wasn't JUDE. Moving closer, he recognized the silhouette—it was PETER, apparently waiting for

JUDE to open the door. *Very decent of him not to bang on it this time,* BART thought with a flash of sarcasm. With each step closer, his breaths grew heavier. *Time to prove a point,* he thought, steadying his nerves. Just as he reached arm's length, he swung the bracket, feeling the rush as it sliced through the air toward PETER's head. At the last moment, a hesitation slowed his swing—he didn't want to kill him. That hesitation, along with a torrent of second thoughts, weakened the impact. The bracket connected with a dull thud, and PETER crumpled to the ground. BART stood there, the metal bracket slipping from his hand and clattering to the floor as he took in the sight of PETER, still conscious, attempting to crawl away. BART's hands were trembling. He looked around, realizing too late that the cameras had caught everything—a rookie mistake. Then he saw it: blood staining PETER's hands as he clawed at the floor. BART froze, torn between finishing what he'd started and retreating. The sight of blood was enough to make his decision for him. He stepped back, his resolve shaken, feeling the weight of what he'd done.

PETER came to a halt, collapsing belly-down on the floor, his movements fading. Instinctively, BART rushed to A36, knocking with urgency—just enough to avoid drawing attention. After a few tense moments, the door cracked open, revealing a woman adjusting her balaclava. The label on it read *ANDREW*.

What, BART? she said, her tone exasperated.

I need your help, ANDREA, please... right now.

She sighed, crossing her arms. *What?*

Just... come with me.

BART turned quickly, leading her down the dimly lit corridor. She followed, her pace quickening as she picked up on his urgency. As they approached, a shape on the floor came into view under the faint lights. A few feet away, she realized it was a body.

Who's that? Her voice wavered with alarm. *Oh, no— I don't want any part of this, kid!*

No, no, he's not dead! BART said quickly, gesturing to PETER. *Look, he's alive—I checked his pulse. Come see for yourself.*

Kid, I don't care if he's alive or dead, ANDREA shot back, already backing away. *That's your mess, not mine.*

She turned to head back, but BART reached out, almost pleading. *ANDREA!* he said, his voice strained. *The CCTV's saw everything. If you walk away from this, they'll know you turned your back on the lead of the project. The THO won't be happy.*

Wait—that's PETER?!

BART's silence confirmed it.

Oh, dear lord, ANDREA groaned, rubbing her temples. *What did you do, kid?*

It's... a long story.

And one I don't need to hear, okay? She sighed, crouching to check on PETER. *I'll patch him up, but after that, I'm out. Got it?*

Yes, thank you, ANDREA!

We need to get him somewhere if I'm going to stitch him up, she muttered, looking around.

Uh... okay, how about your room?

Oh, hell no, kid. Not anywhere near my room.

Alright, my room, then?

Anywhere but my room, honey.

BART and ANDREA struggled to lift PETER at first, each trying to support him from one side. After a moment, they realized it would be easier to carry him by his shoulders, each taking an arm as they made their way down the hallway. When BART reached into his pocket for his keycard, a thought struck him—there was an empty room in the basement. *THADDEUS' room.*

Wait, turn around, he said, his voice low. *There's an empty room nearby. Let's take him there.*

ANDREA gave him a puzzled glance but didn't question it. BART was silently relieved; at least he wasn't taking PETER to his own room.

They eased PETER onto the bed, his limp body settling into the mattress. *I'm going to grab my supplies,* ANDREA said, already heading for the door. *Don't go anywhere.*

Yes, but make it quick, BART replied, his nerves fraying. *We have to be in the conference room by 8.*

Left alone, BART paced back and forth, rubbing his temples. The room felt eerie, completely empty, as if no one had occupied it in months. *The THO did a thorough job cleaning up,* he thought. *Almost like THAD never existed.* He stared at PETER, feeling the anger rise again, an impulse to tear off his mask and finish what he'd started. But he held back—*not yet*. There would be a time to make PETER pay, a time he could savor every bit of satisfaction.

ANDREA returned, carrying a first aid kit—larger than the standard issue, equipped for emergencies. She knelt beside PETER, setting the kit on the bed.

What are you going to do? BART asked, trying to keep his voice steady. *Is he going to be alright?*

ANDREA didn't look up, focusing instead on the tools she needed. *He'll be fine if you let me work,* she said. *You didn't hit him hard enough to do serious damage.*

BART watched, his mind racing. *Alright,* he murmured, *just... fix him up quickly.*

Should we take off his mask? ANDREA asked, her voice laced with concern.

Can you do it without removing it?

I'll have to cut open the balaclava to do that...

Uhh... just take it off.

Are you sure?

Put it back on when you're done.

Alright BART, ANDREA said after taking PETER's balaclava off, keeping her voice calm *first we stop the bleeding. Head wounds bleed a lot so don't panic. I'm cleaning it to keep out infection.*

She pressed gauze against the wound, holding it firmly *Pressure helps stop the bleeding. Just steady not too hard.*

When the bleeding slowed, she reached for sutures and began stitching the gash *This'll close it up* she explained, glancing at BART *Not perfect but it'll help.*

ANDREA checked PETER's pulse and breathing, then wrapped him in an emergency blanket *His pulse is strong; he's stable. He might wake up soon or it could take hours. We just need to keep him warm and keep an eye on him.*

BART nodded, looking reassured. He knew he needed to tell JUDE about this.

I'm going to check if everything's alright outside.

Is that necessary?

BART didn't respond. He slipped out of the room, knowing JUDE had to be kept in the loop.

18:45

Come in, said J, his voice steady but watchful.

The door opened, and PETER stepped in, glancing around as if taking in every detail. *Hey...* he said.

J gave him a nod. *What are you doing?* PETER asked, taking slow, deliberate steps further into the room.

Just having some coffee, J replied, lifting his cup slightly. *And thinking.*

Good... good, PETER murmured, his eyes roaming over the room, pausing briefly on JUDE's empty chair before drifting to the walls, the table, every corner.

PETER picked the spoon up from the floor, set it back on the platform, and examined it carefully. Just as he bent down, J felt another sharp pain shoot through his head. But before PETER could say anything, J broke the silence.

What brings you by, PETER?

Oh, uh... was JUDE here? he asked, his voice too casual. *Have you seen her?*

Yes, J answered simply. *They walked me back and left.*

Right... PETER nodded, though he seemed preoccupied, his gaze intensifying as he continued scanning the room.

For a moment, silence thickened between them.

Then PETER turned, his eyes landing on the closed bathroom door. He took a step closer, hand reaching toward the handle—

You know, J said, voice calm but firm, *I find it hard to wrap my head around why you'd be wearing PETER's mask.*

PETER froze, his hand hovering just an inch from the bathroom door handle. He turned, his eyes narrowing slightly. *What do you mean?*

Why are you wearing his mask, I wonder? J's tone was almost playful, but there was a sharper edge beneath.

PETER chuckled, a hollow sound. *Buddy... I am PETER.*

J held his gaze, then gave a slow nod. *Alright then.*

Without another word, PETER let his hand fall from the bathroom door handle, stepping back as if to leave. But just as he reached for the knob, he paused, then turned back toward J, his eyes unreadable.

What makes you think I'm not PETER? he asked, his voice carrying a subtle edge.

J placed his coffee mug on the table, leaning back in his chair with a faint, knowing smile, as if he'd already cracked the man's game.

A tense silence hung in the air.

You know, J began, leaning back as if savoring the moment, *an earlier conversation with JUDE gave me a few clues about myself. Apparently, I've been into guns since I was a kid, fascinated by every model I could find online. I guess that's how I ended up designing firearms for Sig Sauer, or at least that's what she said.* He took a slow breath, his eyes studying PETER. *And whoever wrote this... sequence was generous enough to let that little piece of me remain.*

He let the words linger, watching for any shift in PETER's expression.

So, he continued, his voice calm but sharp, *for someone who spent his entire childhood learning every gun inside and out, it's not too hard to recognize the model you've got tucked at your back. That's a Sig Sauer P226. And not just any version.* J paused, letting a glint of satisfaction show. *That model was designed specifically to honor the Navy SEALs. A limited release, meant as a tribute, given only to those who'd served in the field.*

J's gaze was steady, piercing through PETER. *And I'd know that gun anywhere, because...* he leaned forward slightly, a smirk on his lips, *it was one of my designs, JAMES....*

The man stared at him, the silence between them thick with unspoken threats, his gaze assessing, dangerous. Slowly, a smile tugged at the corner of his mouth as he lifted his P226, examining it in the dim light. The weapon glinted coldly as he raised it to eye level, turning it as if admiring his own reflection in its polished metal.

So, the man began, his tone casual, almost mocking, *you figured if PETER's just a neurological researcher, like you saw in the video, why would he carry a Navy SEAL's P226?* He nodded, as if impressed. Smart. *And the rest of the team here?* He shook his head, chuckling. *They're far too green to be carrying a SEAL's tribute.*

A hint of a smile curled at the edge of J's mouth. He had him.

JAMES leaned forward, the gun still in his hand, his gaze narrowing. *Since you know I'm a Navy SEAL*, he murmured, his voice dropping to a menacing whisper, *you also know damn well I wouldn't think twice to put a bullet in you.*

J held his ground, his expression stoic. *What're you going to threaten a man with, a man who's got nothing to lose?*

For a moment, anger flashed across JAMES's face, his jaw tight as if J's words had struck a nerve. But it was only seconds before another smile spread across his face, cool and predatory, as he straightened up.

Right. John, he said, voice like steel, *if word of this little exchange gets out... I'll kill JUDE.*

J's composure faltered, and though he fought to hide it, the slight tension in his eyes betrayed him. JAMES's smile grew colder.

Oh, you didn't think I'd notice? The little Stockholm syndrome bond you've been building with JUDE? You really think I don't see things, John? He leaned in, his voice a lethal whisper. *Her blood will be on your hands. So, tread carefully.*

They held each other's gaze, the silence between them heavy, charged. Then, without another word, JAMES holstered his gun, turned, and strode out, shutting the door with a final, echoing thud.

ECHO III

The doctor took a deep breath, glancing at the file before him.

I'm afraid I have some difficult news to share, he began, his voice carefully measured.

Your son's tests have come back, and they confirm what I suspected. He has DMD, Duchenne Muscular Dystrophy.

The words hung in the air like a death sentence. The father's chest tightened, and he struggled to process the information. His wife gasped, her hand flying to her mouth as her eyes welled up with tears.

But... but what does that mean? she whispered, her voice trembling

The doctor leaned forward; his tone gentle but firm.

Duchenne is a progressive muscle-wasting disease. Over time, it will cause your son's muscles to weaken, eventually affecting his ability to walk, and later, his heart and lungs. There's no cure, but there

are treatments that can help manage the symptoms and slow the progression.

The father stared at the doctor, his mind racing. The room seemed to close in around him, the words 'no cure' echoing in his head. He glanced at his wife, who was now openly crying, and felt a surge of helplessness.

How much time do we have, Doc? he asked, his voice barely above a whisper.

The doctor hesitated; his eyes filled with sympathy.

It varies, but with proper care and treatment, many children with Duchenne live into their twenties or early thirties. However, the costs of treatment can be substantial, especially as the disease progresses.

The father felt like the floor had been ripped out from beneath him. The future he had envisioned for his son crumbled before his eyes. His thoughts turned to the financial burden that lay ahead—hospital visits, medication, physical therapy, and potentially experimental treatments. The weight of it all threatened to crush him. His wife's sobs brought him back to the present. He squeezed her hand, trying to offer comfort even as he felt his own world collapsing. The doctor continued speaking, outlining the next steps, but the father could barely hear him over the pounding in his ears.

The father's voice was barely audible, a mix of desperation and fear.

What do we do now, Doc?

The doctor sighed, his eyes reflecting the weight of the question.

The first step is to connect with a specialist who can guide you through the treatment options. We'll need to start physical therapy right away to help maintain as much muscle function as possible. There are medications that can slow the progression, but they come with their own set of challenges.

He paused, looking between the father and his wife.

You should also consider genetic counselling to fully understand what this means for your son and your family. There might be clinical trials that offer some hope, but they're experimental and can be expensive.

The father felt a hollow pit forming in his stomach. It wasn't just about treatments and medications; it was about a lifetime of navigating an unpredictable and relentless disease. He glanced at his wife, seeing the same overwhelming fear mirrored in her eyes.

How... how do we afford all of this? he asked, the enormity of the situation pressing down on him.

The doctor's expression softened.

There are resources and support groups that can help. Financial planning will be crucial, and we'll connect you with a social worker who can assist in navigating insurance and potential funding sources. But I won't lie to you—it's going to be a difficult road.

The father's ego bristled at the suggestion; despite the financial strain he was already under. He had no interest in gathering money from anyone else; he was determined to handle it on his own. It didn't matter if he had to work day and night—he refused to request or accept donations. Even if it meant selling all their assets, he would do whatever it took to spend another hour with their boy. The father swallowed hard, fighting back the tears that threatened to spill over. His son's future flashed before his eyes, now filled with uncertainty and struggle.

Later that night, the father sat in his study area in their small apartment, shuffling through papers while simultaneously scrolling through job listings on his laptop. He was looking for positions with better pay and more shifts. As a neurological researcher at the University of IONRA (Institution of Neurological Research and Advancements), he wasn't making a decent living. The university didn't believe in the potential of his project. The project's lack of progress led to stalled grant renewals and made it difficult to attract new funding. While his colleagues made significant strides in their fields, he struggled to convince potential funders of the value of his work. He even considered switching fields or finding a new job, but his faith in his project fought against those thoughts. The fear that someone else might take up his project and succeed before he did, haunted him. But now, faced with his son's needs, he knew it was time to make a decision. His son outweighed his academics on the balance, and he decided to resign.

On his last day at the university, he spent most of his time wrapping up his writings and gathering important materials from his small work area in the basement. That same day, the owner of a business conglomerate visited the university in search of potential projects to fund. The magnate, a childhood friend of the university's president, had already settled on a project in the physics department. As he was leaving, he noticed a man in his mid-thirties struggling with a giant box filled with files, papers, books, and other items.

The 78-year-old magnate, still jolly and sharp-minded, decided to engage in conversation.

Where you headed, kid?

Shocked, the researcher replied,

Oh... um... I just resigned. I'm headed home now.

Oh, why's that, son?

Unfortunately, the university doesn't have as much faith in my project as I do.

What were you working on, dear?

The researcher went on to explain his project and the progress he had made so far.

Sounds good to me, kid, but unfortunately, I've already committed to funding a project here.

Expecting this response, the researcher said,

It's alright. I've decided to take up a different job anyway. Thanks for listening, though.

Son, wait. I know a guy who knows a guy who knows an organization. They'd be willing to fund this project, I have no doubt—provided you deliver the results you're so confident about.

I don't know, sir. I've faced too much criticism and too many denials.

Trust me, kid, they'll do this. I'll have them ring you up. Will that be alright?

You're very kind, sir, but that won't be necessary. I guess I too have started losing faith in my project, the researcher said with a chuckle.

A few days later, the father received a call.

I'm calling on behalf of Mr. Raheem El-Nassar's reference.

Yes?

Our organization is interested in funding your project.

Really? That's fantastic news. Part of the weight seemed to lift off his shoulders.

Which organization is this, may I ask?

THO. That's all you need to know for now.

Okay. How do we proceed?

We don't communicate over calls, so...

Sure, we can arrange to meet somewhere, then! (excited)

Ahem, no. You'll receive a package in a few days. It will contain all the necessary information.

Umm... alright. Please let Mr. El-Nassar know I'm deeply grateful for his help.

The line went dead.

Two days later, an anonymous package arrived at his doorstep. Suspecting it might be from THO; he took it to his study and placed it on his desk for inspection. He rotated the lamp toward the package and began tearing it open. His eyes were met with a file and a burner phone inside. He examined the burner, then set it aside to focus on the file, which was labelled HIGHLY CLASSIFIED.

Top Secret - Highly Classified

File Reference: THO-PJ-12A34
Date: 18/8/18
Subject: Project JENESIS - Approval, Operational Directives, and Protocols

---

Recipient Alias: PETER
Designation Code: THO-4769
Personal Identifier: NATE-4769
Role: Lead Researcher, Project JENESIS

I. PROJECT OVERVIEW

Project Name: JENESIS
Objective: To develop and implement advanced procedures and conduct trials to evaluate the potential for cutting-edge applications. The project is intended to significantly advance our capabilities in a highly confidential field.

Note: Although the project originated from your concept, THO will now assume full control over its execution. You will continue to hold the position of Lead Researcher, but all strategic decisions and oversight will be managed by THO's central command to ensure alignment with our overarching objectives.

II. FUNDING APPROVAL

Amount Approved: $20M
Duration: 8-9 months (Strict Deadline)
Disbursement: Funding will be provided in phases, contingent upon the successful completion of specific milestones. Any deviation from the approved budget will result in severe consequences.

III. OPERATIONAL DIRECTIVES

1. **Team Assembly:**

   - **Responsibility:** You are tasked with determining the number of team members needed for Project JENESIS and specifying their qualifications. THO will handle the recruitment and onboarding based on your recommendations.

   - **Compliance:** All personnel must strictly follow THO's guidelines. Any deviation or unauthorized actions will be addressed accordingly.

2. **Experimental Focus:**

   - **Confidential Techniques:** Develop and refine techniques as outlined in the project specifications. Detailed objectives are classified and will be communicated through secure channels as necessary.

- **Controlled Trials:** Conduct trials as per THO's protocols. Ensure all activities adhere to the classified ethical guidelines provided. Any deviations will result in immediate cessation of the project and potential sanctions.

3. **Human Trials:**

    - **Subject Selection:** Subjects will be selected from THO-designated facilities. Selection criteria include physical and psychological suitability, with minimal external connections.

    - **Monitoring:** Continuous observation of subjects' responses is mandatory. Regular reports must be submitted to THO's oversight committee.

4. **Facility Requirements:**

    - **Location:** Activities related to Project JENESIS must occur at the designated facility. This location has been equipped with top-level security and research infrastructure.

- **Security:** The facility is under constant surveillance by THO's security division. Unauthorized access or breaches must be reported immediately.

5. **Submission of Existing Work:**
   - You are required to submit all previous research and work relevant to this field. This will facilitate the establishment of a solid foundation for Project JENESIS.

IV. SEVERANCE FROM OUTSIDE WORLD

For the duration of Project JENESIS, you must sever all ties with the outside world, including family. This is crucial for maintaining the project's secrecy and ensuring its successful execution. The estimated completion time is 8 to 9 months. During this period, secure communication channels for project-related purposes will be provided.

Payday: Your compensation can be directed to any account of your choice.

V. INCENTIVES AND CONSEQUENCES

1. **Compensation:**
   - **Fixed Income:** A fixed income will be provided throughout the project's duration, deposited into a secure account as specified.
   - **Success Bonus:** On successful completion of Project JENESIS, you will be eligible for a six-figure annual salary and guaranteed job security. Additional bonuses may be awarded based on the project's impact.

2. **Consequences of Non-Compliance:**
   - **Erasure:** Failure to comply with the directives will result in severe consequences, including possible erasure of you and your family.
   - **Monitoring:** If you opt not to participate, you will be monitored for the next 24 months to ensure no classified information is disclosed. Any breach will be met with immediate action.

3. **Decision Window:**
   - You have one week from today to confirm your involvement in Project JENESIS. Use the

pre-saved number on the burner phone provided to communicate your decision. If you choose not to proceed, the burner will deactivate on the eighth day. Non-response will result in monitoring as outlined above.

VI. CLASSIFIED INFORMATION PROTOCOL

Data Handling:

- **Encryption:** All project data must be encrypted using THO's secure algorithms. Backup and storage must be handled according to THO's protocols.

- **Communication:** All communications must be conducted through secure THO channels. Unauthorized methods will be considered a breach.

- **Destruction:** Upon project completion or termination, all related materials must be destroyed following THO's destruction procedures.

VII. FINAL NOTICE

Compliance:

You are reminded that any failure to adhere to the directives will result in immediate repercussions, including termination of the project and possible legal actions.

Acknowledgment:

By receiving this document, you acknowledge the confidential nature of the information and your responsibility to maintain secrecy. Breaches will be met with full disciplinary measures.

For the Eyes of Designation Code THO-4769 Only

End of Document

THO Central Command

His heart skipped a beat when he saw that his Personal Identifier Name was his son's. It was clear they meant business and already had all the information they needed. What shocked him even more was the amount they were willing to fund for his project. For over four years, he had struggled to secure even 100 grand in grants, but after a brief encounter with an old man in the university basement, he was now being offered $20 million. The sheer scale of it was mind-boggling.

He was starting to feel an overwhelming urge to drop the whole thing. The unsettling nature of the offer gnawed at him, and questions flooded his mind.

Why are they arranging this at an abandoned airfield instead of a proper laboratory?

And why aren't they handling this face-to-face?

Something about it felt off. He turned to his computer and typed "THO" into the search bar, hoping to find some answers. But the results were far from what he expected:

- Tasty Homemade Options
- Trusted Help Office
- Travel Hub Operations
- True Home Organics

- The Home Outlet
  ...and so on.

What struck him as even stranger was that an organization wealthy enough to fund $20 million for a project that had been overlooked for years was nowhere to be found on the internet. The more he thought about it, the more he felt the need to abandon the plan and continue his search for other jobs. And more importantly, if he participated in this project, it would also keep him away from his family for the next 8 to 9 months, cutting off all contact, which he clearly didn't want. So, he only saw one option. He carefully placed the file and the burner back into the envelope and set it on the far end of the table, where a stack of papers waited to be thrown away.

Later that night, he sat at the dinner table, his eyes on Nate, who was seated in his high chair. He watched as Nate struggled to sit upright, his small body leaning to one side. Mum noticed too, gently adjusting him.

There you go, sweetheart, let's stay upright, she said softly.

Nate reached for his spoon, but his tiny fingers fumbled, and the spoon fell onto the tray. He quickly picked it up, handing it back with a calm,

Let's try again, buddy.

Nate tried once more, his hand trembling as he brought the food to his mouth, but a bit fell onto his shirt. Mum wiped it away, her voice steady.

Good job, Nate. You're doing great.

But he saw the fatigue setting in. Nate's grip weakened, and he leaned back, his energy fading. He offered a gentle,

It's okay if you're tired. We can help you.

Mum fed him small bites, pausing when a cough escaped Nate, a reminder of the challenges they were facing.

Nate's eyes began to droop, and he reached for Mum.

Up, Mama, he murmured.

She lifted him, holding him close as he nestled into her arms. He watched; his heart heavy but filled with resolve. It was as if his wife was fighting every second to hold back her tears.

That night, as the three of them cuddled in bed with Nate sleeping peacefully between them, the silence was broken by Mum's quiet sobs. Dad turned to her, gently wiping the tears from her face and caressing it.

I... got a job, he said, his voice cracking slightly. *It pays well.*

What? Where? she asked, her tears still flowing.

It's a little far, but it will pay off really well. Don't worry about the money.

The next morning, he grabbed the envelope and took out the burner phone. He dialled the number saved as "Acceptance Call."

Well, that was sooner than I expected... PETER.

Yes. What's next?

Report to the abandoned school building on the 29th of this month at 9 in the morning.

Okay. I'll be there!

How's Nate?

...silence...

The operator hung up.

It felt like they were hinting that they knew more than they let on, and were cautioning him against thinking otherwise.

He had no choice but to take this up if it meant paying off his son's medical bills. The reality of staying away for 8-9 months from the two people who meant everything to him was devastating, but he forced himself to focus on the brighter side.

The doctors might say there's no cure for this condition, but what if, in the next 5-10 years, someone discovers one? he thought.

Clinging to that hope, he resolved to participate in **PROJECT JENESIS**.

XXI

19:20

JUDE stepped out of the washroom, where she'd been hiding, barely able to process what she'd just overheard. She looked shaken, as if she'd seen a ghost. Across the room, J met her gaze, and for a long moment, they simply stared, the silence charged with an unspoken exchange.

When I saw his gun, the pain flared up again. Not the fleeting glimpses this time, just a searing headache. But something about that gun felt deeply familiar—like it was mine, almost as if I'd crafted it myself. That's why I said what I did. Maybe it sounds absurd, but in that moment, I connected the dots. If I recognized the gun so viscerally, perhaps I had a hand in creating it. And if that's true, I thought claiming I was its sole creator would have the most impact.

JUDE gave a slow, pensive nod, absorbing this revelation. She gathered herself. *I need to go,* she said, her voice resolute, already planning her next move. She had to inform BART.

She carefully stepped out and walked toward A25. As she turned into the hallway, there was BART, either standing or heading in her direction.

Oh, great, I was coming to talk to you. I need to tell you something.

No, that can wait; this is important... JUDE interrupted.

So is this! BART fired back.

JUDE didn't wait for an opening. She jumped right in, *It had been JAMES this whole time. He's been wearing PETER's balaclava.*

Wait—what? But—how do yo—?

It's a long story; get in the room! JUDE said, gesturing urgently to A28.

No, wait, I need to—

We'll talk. Get in first.

They both slipped into A28. JUDE barely waited for the door to close.

Okay, so I was in A44. JAMES was there, disguised as PETER, apparently looking for me, she said hurriedly. *J figured it out. I'm not going to get into the whole story, but JAMES didn't deny it...*

Oh no, oh no. Said BART sensing the weight of the situation. *I knocked down PETER with a bat.*

What the fuck!

... I don't know which one...

Shit, shit. When did it happen? When did you blindside him?

Uh... BART stuttered; *I think an hour ago.*

SHIT! You got the original PETER, because JAMES was in A44 ten minutes ago.

They both stood there, rubbing their temples, pacing in a mix of confusion and frustration.

Where's PETER? JUDE asked finally.

He's in A27. Come with me.

19:30

Is he going to be alright?

Yes, he's had a moderate concussion; he should be up in a while.

JUDE eyed BART intently. *I'm gonna go now. You guys take it from here. I mean... I'm done, right? I did my part. Gotta be back in my room in 30.*

ANDREA, stay, BART insisted. *You have to be here at least till he's up. Alright?*

He's going to be fine. We all need to go.

No, we have to stay. There are a few things he needs to know before he steps out of the room.

Like what?! I don't care—write him a letter and leave it here.

I don't think he'll be wanting to read a damn letter first thing when he wakes up. So we're staying here. We tell him everything, and then we leave.

Oh, come on! I feel like I'm already in enough trouble as it is, please. I have a family out there; I can't mess up!

So do we, BART replied. *We've all got family, and we all need money. I was raised by my grandma; she's all I got. And she still thinks I'm in some military program.*

No, you don't understand, this is not just about money for me! ANDREA's voice cracked as she put her face in her hands, her eyes misting over.

ECHO IV

Out there, I'm a surgeon by profession, ANDREA began, her voice trembling. I have a beautiful family—a husband and two daughters, 15 and 12.

She took a shaky breath. About a year ago, a 17-year-old boy was brought to my ER. He'd been hit by some drunk rich guy who, of course, got out of it using his connections. The boy was going to survive; he just needed surgery. But... he didn't make it. Her gaze dropped. Word spread fast, and within hours, the headlines were everywhere: Tragic Error or Corruption? Renowned Surgeon's Mistake Costs Teen His Life. My husband lost his job almost immediately. My kids were harassed at school. And the hospital—where I'd dedicated my life—cut ties with me to save their reputation. We were left completely alone, surrounded by people demanding answers. Crowds stormed our house, throwing stones, camping out front, shouting for days on end. And then, the media doubled down, painting the boy as 'a brilliant future'—

the kind who 'could change the world.' The anger, the riots outside our home... it was relentless.

After about a month, things finally settled... or so we thought. But it didn't really go away. My husband couldn't find work, my kids were refused entry at school, and no one would hire me. Even our friends, our family—they abandoned us. Ruined, we were at the end of our rope, thinking of ending it all just to escape. She paused, her hands trembling slightly. Then, one day, an anonymous package arrived on our doorstep. We were terrified; for all we knew, it could've been a bomb. Hours passed before we even dared to open it. Inside was an offer—to work on a classified project, with the promise that everything would be fixed in return. I thought it was some kind of twisted joke. But then I saw a burner phone. The moment I picked it up, it rang. The caller told me about the project, but I didn't believe him. Then he hung up, and five minutes later, my husband got his job back, my kids were readmitted to school, and everything was back to normal—as long as I complied.

She looked up, her eyes fierce with barely contained fear. *And of course, all of this could be taken back, reversed to how it was, if I ever failed to comply.*

I just need to get this over with, avoid any more trouble, and mind my own business. ANDREA stood up, ready to leave.

We get it, but you can't leave yet, BART interjected. *We're not doctors like you are, ANDREA. We need you here until he wakes up.*

He'll wake up just fine, she replied, eyes narrowed. *But I'm leaving.*

A groan from the bed broke the silence. *Ugh...my head...* PETER mumbled, his face contorting in pain.

ANDREA froze mid-step, then spun around and rushed to PETER's side in an instant, her earlier resolve forgotten.

PETER stirred, groaning softly as he opened his eyes. ANDREA was beside him, steadying him as he instinctively reached for his head.

Easy, PETER she said gently. *You've been through a lot. Just take it slow for now*

BART and JUDE hovered nearby, both looking worried. PETER winced, a hand pressing against his temple.

I know it hurts ANDREA said, reaching for a bottle in the first aid kit. *This is acetaminophen—it's a basic pain reliever, but it's a safer choice for a head injury.*

She looked at BART and JUDE as she measured a dose. *With head injuries, we avoid painkillers like aspirin or ibuprofen because they thin the blood. That could make any bleeding worse, and that's the last thing we want*

She lifted PETER's head gently, helping him take the medicine. *Acetaminophen won't thin the blood, but it'll help take the edge off his pain. Now, we'll just keep an eye on him and make sure he's comfortable.*

PETER lay back, his breathing a little easier, as ANDREA gave BART and JUDE a reassuring nod. *This should help him rest. Now we keep watch and make sure he's steady*

What happened? Who hit me with the bat?

Um... I did, sir, BART answered softly.

Why would you do that, kid? PETER asked, surprisingly calm.

BART and JUDE exchanged a look, both surprised by his composure. Maybe it was the medication, they thought. JUDE hesitated, wondering if this was really the right moment to tell him. But how long could they wait? They didn't have time on their side. BART gave her a small nod.

Sir, there's something you should know...

PETER's eyes were closed, but his breathing slowed slightly. He was listening.

JUDE took a deep breath, nervous about his reaction. Tonight, she was out of options; if she didn't tell him now, it would be too late.

Sir, for months now, JAMES has been roaming around… disguised as you.

PETER chuckled, a dry, disbelieving sound. *That's the silliest thing I've heard tonight.*

It's true. He's been posing as you—for instance, when he showed up at my door in the dead of night, trying to force his way in, night after night. He broke into BART's room to threaten him. And there's a lot more he's done—while wearing your face.

ANDREA who was sitting at PETER's side was shocked to hear this.

But we need to know for sure, JUDE said, her voice steady. *Did you kill Thad?*

What? No! Absolutely not! PETER's response was firm, almost offended. *I wouldn't lay a hand on any of my recruits. They're my kids.*

JAMES did that too, JUDE murmured, *disguised as you…*

So, everyone thinks I did it? PETER's gaze hardened as he scanned their faces.

Yes, BART said quietly. *Killing him for showing up late or dropping a few things? That's not just cruel—it's diabolical.*

PETER's calm demeanor wavered slightly. *How do you know for sure?*

JUDE looked him squarely in the eyes. He didn't deny it, she said, her voice cold and deliberate. *When J confronted him, he admitted it—it was JAMES behind your mask.*

The room fell into an uneasy silence, each person lost in their thoughts. *Cruelty like this*, BART muttered after a long pause, *is the kind of thing you only expect to see in movies.*

Yesterday, he threatened me, BART continued, his voice strained. *He said he was going to... have his way with JUDE tonight, and that there was nothing I could do about it.* BART swallowed. *The only option I saw was to...*

...Hit me with a bat, PETER finished, his tone unreadable.

BART looked down, embarrassed.

JUDE picked up the explanation, recounting what had happened in A44 and how J had figured it out.

PETER shook his head slowly. *I want to be shocked,* he murmured, *but JAMES has had this side to him for a long time. It also explains why I was only given one balaclava, while the rest of you were issued a pair.*

He exhaled sharply and looked around at the others. *JAMES has been siphoning funds from THO—money that was supposed to go into running this project. And you might think he killed THAD because THAD was careless or because JAMES thought he slowed us all down*, he paused, *but the truth is he killed him to cut expenses, to make up for the funds he took for himself.*

The room fell into stunned silence as everyone absorbed the shocking revelation.

We all have something driving us here. We all have someone or something we need this money for. PETER glanced at them both, his face grim. *No one is here just to make an extra buck.*

He hesitated, then continued. *But I had to be sure that my family was getting my share. So, one night, I broke into his office to get to his computer—that computer is the only line of communication to the outside world, and he uses it to contact the THO.* He paused, then added quietly, *I confirmed my family was getting the money. But in the process, I stumbled on a notification that had just popped up—a message from the THO.*

What did it say? JUDE asked, leaning forward.

Nothing significant. It was just asking for a progress report. But curiosity got the better of me. I checked his email history—the exchanges he's had with them. Turns out, while we received anonymous packages, he received direct messages. Clear, straightforward emails from The Higher Order.

PETER reached into the pocket of his suit and pulled out a folded sheet of paper, holding it up for them to see.

TOP SECRET - HIGHLY CLASSIFIED
File Reference: THO-PJ-12A52
Date: 18/08/18
Subject: Project JENESIS - Clearance and Redeployment Directives

---

Recipient Alias: Chief Addams
Assigned Alias: JAMES
Designation Code: THO-7603
Role: Operations Head, Project JENESIS

Chief Addams,

Upon review of your prior service history and extensive operational experience, you have been selected for redeployment under The Higher Order's latest classified directive: *Project JENESIS*. This deployment offers an exclusive, conditional clearance—intended as an opportunity to reestablish your standing following your discharge from duties as a Navy SEAL Commander.

While your record reflects commendable contributions to tactical missions and critical defense operations, it also reveals conduct violations resulting in the revocation of service status. Your documented involvement in unauthorized activities—namely, illicit trafficking networks—led to your expedited discharge, bringing an end to what could have been an esteemed career in national defense. Such history, however, now grants us insight into your unique skillset, which aligns precisely with Project JENESIS's demands.

Under the alias "JAMES," you are to operate within the project's most classified parameters, adhering to THO's stringent protocols and maintaining zero deviation from your designated role. This assignment is a chance to redeem yourself and reclaim your reputation. The Higher Order will observe your performance with the utmost scrutiny.

Ensure that all communications align with the security standards of *Project JENESIS*—breach of protocol or failure to execute directives precisely will result in immediate consequences.

For further orientation, report to the assigned location in 48 hours. This message is to be deleted upon acknowledgment.

End of Transmission

Signed,
THO Central Command

XXII

20:15

So, why didn't you do anything if you knew about this all along? BART asked, his eyes narrowing.

PETER adjusted himself on the bed, leaning back. As I said, I wasn't going to jeopardize anything. We all have to walk out of here with what we've been promised; otherwise, all of this would be a waste.

The four of them sat in silence, absorbing what had just been revealed. ANDREA looked torn, unsure what to believe. But after hearing JUDE's account, she was starting to see which side was right.

But how did you break in... and get into his computer? BART asked, curiosity getting the better of him.

It's not locked up like you'd expect, PETER explained. *The room, the computer—it's all accessible. You can walk right in, pull up anything, without raising alarms. I don't know why it's set up like that. But I took a printout of his messages, just in case I needed leverage someday.*

BART scoffed. *Of course, he's a sex trafficker. The guy reeks of it.*

ANDREA glanced at her watch. *Guys, we really need to go now. We're already twenty minutes late*, she said, her voice edged with nerves.

PETER held up a hand. *Wait, all three of you. We're not rebels. We're not stirring up trouble. We finish our work and walk out of here, no mess, no drama. We don't know the full extent of who these people are or what they're capable of. And I'd like to keep it that way.*

He paused, looking directly at BART. *And BART, no more swinging. It won't end well—not for you, not for JUDE, not for anyone.*

BART gave him a blank look, his expression unreadable.

PETER slipped on his balaclava, and they all stood, preparing to leave the room.

Here, ANDREA said softly, handing him a couple of acetaminophen tablets. *For the pain. And try not to strain yourself.*

The doctor in her couldn't help but show through. PETER gave her a small nod, and with that, they all headed out, the weight of their conversation hanging in the air.

20:23

The four of them walked into the conference room, slowly, not making much eye contact with anyone else but JAMES. The room was half filled with 7 men sitting around the conference table, when the 4 walked in.

Okay, now that the gang is here, PETER has figured out a way to retrieve lost memories, PETER, take it from here!

PETER who was still a little shaky, got himself together. He adjusted his throat, let out a breath looking around and began, taking out a bunch of papers, with what looked like ink blots, but as PETER knew, they were blood stains. But far enough for JAMES to know.

Ugh, okay....umm....So, I figured there is one way to retrieve memories, and due to the time constraints, this is our best shot. He picks a large file placed on the table, and shows it to everyone.

PETER steps forward, glancing around the group as he speaks.

Here's the concept in simple terms. When someone experiences severe trauma, like a blow to the head, their mind can wall off certain memories as a protective measure. So, if there are memories hidden behind this barrier, we could potentially unlock them by recreating the original sequence of events leading up to the trauma—right to the night of the murder.

He pauses, letting this sink in.

Now, the brain's strange; it responds to familiarity. If we can get close enough to how things happened—capturing even fifty to seventy-five percent accuracy—then there's a chance he'll experience flashes of déjà vu. These glimpses might be just enough to nudge his mind into recalling fragments of that night.

PETER looks around, his expression serious.

But there's no guarantee. We can only estimate his thoughts and decisions, based on years of data I've gathered from those who knew him. We'll recreate what we can, and if we're lucky, those glimpses could help him piece together the events of that night.

He opens the file, spreading out a schematic of John's house along with photos of the hall room, the scene of the crime.

This space—his home—needs to be replicated in his mind. We'll use auditory and visual inputs without dialogue, as we can't risk adding anything that wasn't there. The slightest detail could make or break the process. This file holds everything each team will need. Follow it precisely. Stick to the plan, no improvisation.

Now, as it turns out, speed-run is possible, PETER said meeting JAMES' gaze. *Let me explain. Speed-run simply means rushing through the sequence—maybe five or six times faster than the standard pace. My concern was whether the brain could process so much information so quickly. The answer is... yes and no. Earlier, we were working on Memory Alteration, which would have made speed-run a huge risk. But now, since we're focused on Memory Recollection, it's a different story.*

He continued. *Think of it this way: if I handed you a book you've never read and asked you to rush through it, you'd finish it, sure, but you'd miss every vital piece of information. On the other hand, if I gave you a book you've already read, your brain would automatically begin to fill in the gaps, piecing everything together as you go. Since the information is already stored, your brain keeps up with the pace and makes sense of it. Therefore, given the constraints, we'll have to go with the speed-run.*

Alright! You heard the man, said JAMES, rising from his chair with a commanding tone. *Now, we've got until tomorrow morning at 10 to craft the memory sequence, and five hours after that—until 3 p.m.—to speed-run through the sequence in real-time. Then, one hour to assess the results, document observations, and prepare him for THO.*

He clapped his hands, a signal for action. *With that said, best of luck—and get to work.*

Everyone around the table scrambled to their feet, ready to disperse.

...except you four, JAMES added sharply, narrowing his eyes at the group. *The rest of you, leave. Now.*

The others quickly exited, leaving the four of them alone in the room, now tensely awaiting JAMES' next words.

JAMES walked over to the door, locking it with a calculated click, then strolled back toward them, hands settling on his hips as a faint, knowing smile crept across his face.

You know, it's not every day that the four of you show up nearly half an hour late, he said, his voice low and teasing. *It makes me wonder if something's... hmm, what's the word... ah, yes, cooking.*

Nothing, JAMES. We just happened to be late, replied PETER, meeting his gaze with a steady look.

Coincidentally missing my announcement at precisely 8:15? JAMES tilted his head, his tone both casual and sharp. *And none of you showed up until now. I have to wonder why. How is it that all four of you,* he now fixed his stare directly on PETER, *just coincidentally chose to ignore my call?*

The four exchanged brief, guarded glances, each trying to read the others without revealing too much. None of them had the faintest clue what JAMES might be angling at—whether he was merely probing or truly on to something.

...Unless, JAMES continued, drawing out the words as he narrowed his eyes, *you were all cooped up in a room with a broken speaker. Ah, yes—that's it, isn't it? You were all in THADDEUS' room!*

It suddenly clicked for them—of course. THAD's room had a defective speaker; they hadn't even considered it.

So, JAMES leaned back slightly, folding his arms, *who's going to tell me what all four of you were doing in A27?*

JAMES started pacing in front of them, back and forth, each step deliberate. Then, with a smooth motion, he drew a gun from his waistband and placed it on the table, fingers brushing over the cold metal as he let it sit there, gleaming under the lights.

Let's try that again, he said, his tone low but sharp as a razor. *What were you all doing in A27?*

He looked at the three on the left, his gaze cold and unrelenting, before his eyes fixed on ANDREA. She immediately felt his attention like a weight pressing down. JAMES picked up the gun and slowly walked toward her, stopping just a breath away, gun lifted close to her face. She couldn't bear to meet his eyes, but the nearness of the barrel made her tremble.

Tell me, ANDREA, he murmured, voice chillingly soft. *What were you all doing?*

With a nervous swallow, ANDREA glanced up at the gun, her fear loosening her resolve as the words started tumbling out. She recounted everything, from the moment BART had knocked on her door to the discussion in THAD's room, her voice shaky, spilling secrets like confessions.

JAMES listened, nodding slowly as he rested the gun on his shoulder, almost casually, as if it were just another tool. *The most interesting thing I heard,* he said, turning his gaze to BART, *is that you had the balls to swing at someone. Though it seems not quite enough to do real damage.* He smirked. *But tell me, BART, why did you take a swing at PETER?*

Because you've been disguised as him all along, BART shot back, his teeth clenched, defiant.

In a flash, JAMES turned, gun raised and aimed directly at JUDE. *I told him,* he said coldly, *your blood would be on his hands if word got out.*

No, no, no! JUDE stammered; hands raised slightly. *I was there in A44—I was in the washroom, that's how I know!*

JAMES narrowed his eyes, then slowly lowered his gun, pondering her words.

I knew you were in there, he admitted, his voice dropping as a tight smile crossed his lips. *But that little stunt of John's caught me off guard.* He let out a long, resigned sigh, shaking his head, as if weighing his next move.

JAMES straightened up, his composure fully restored, and he let his cold gaze travel over each of them in turn. *First things first,* he began, calm and pointed, *I don't know if you recall, but according to the docket you all received, the one that got you into this whole operation, you have breached the code of conduct.*

He paused, letting his words sink in, and continued, *The rule states that everyone must strictly avoid establishing personal relationships with anyone.* He tilted his head, the faintest trace of a smirk creeping in. *But clearly, that didn't stop you. We've got two lovebirds playing house every night, and now...this. So, what exactly went down, huh? A plot against me? Sharing sob stories? Whatever it was, you've broken the rules.*

The word hung in the air like a death sentence, and then he said it: *The repercussions for such actions are swift elimination.*

At the word *elimination,* ANDREA flinched, her face paling.

But, JAMES continued, his tone shifting as he lifted his finger and pointed directly at BART, *I don't think that's going to be enough. Given that BART here tried to take a swing at me—* he shifted his point to ANDREA, *and you covered for him.* He glanced at JUDE. *And you helped him, too.* Then he turned to PETER, his expression hardening. *And PETER? You thought I wouldn't notice, didn't you? That you could just slip into my office and take a printout from my PC?*

JAMES paused, watching as PETER's expression shifted, his discomfort unmistakable. *Every action taken from my PC notifies THO, you idiot,* JAMES continued with a smirk. *So, imagine their confusion— why would I suddenly be printing out a recruitment letter, and now of all times?*

JAMES let out a short, mocking laugh.

They looked back, dread settling over their features as JAMES continued, *so here's what I'm going to do. There are six innocent men out there, and I am going to kill each of them before I kill any of you. Because of your stupid, reckless mistakes, they'll pay, too.*

No, not them, JAMES! PETER's voice broke through, pleading.

JAMES glared at him; his tone ice-cold. *I didn't finish, you prick!* He took a slow, deliberate breath. *As I was saying, every last one of you dies because of the four of you.*

The silence was suffocating. Fear was now written on all their faces, the weight of JAMES's threat pressing down like a vise. But then, JAMES broke the silence, his expression shifting just slightly.

But, he said, his tone almost teasing, *as always, JAMES saves the day.* He paused, letting them wonder, the smallest flicker of hope daring to break through their terror. *I'm going to put forth a wild card—a single chance to save the lives of six innocent men.* His eyes sharpened, cold and calculating. *So, here's the deal: either all of you die—that's six innocent men and four guilty scumbags—or, if you choose the wild card...* He leaned forward, voice dropping to a razor-thin edge. *Everyone lives. Except three guilty scumbags.*

The ultimatum lingered, chilling them as they realized the twisted choice he'd set before them.

JAMES raised the gun to eye level, admiring it with a small, twisted smile. *This is my souvenir for exceptional service as a Navy SEAL,* he said, savoring each word. *The Sig Sauer P226.* His gaze flicked to JUDE. *As you must have overheard while hiding out in A44.*

He held it up, gleaming and ominous in his hand. *Now, here's what's going to happen,* he continued, his voice chillingly calm. *One of you four is going to come forward, pick it up, and shoot the other three to death.*

The weight of his words dropped on them like a stone. Each of the four felt a tight, sick feeling in their stomachs. This was pressure unlike anything they'd known—ordinary people, thrown into a nightmare, suddenly facing an unthinkable choice. The air grew thick with tension, each heartbeat pounding louder, the realization setting in like a dreadful fog.

I get it, JAMES said, looking at each one. *You all want to survive. But maybe, just maybe, that will to live isn't strong enough to kill three people to do it.* He chuckled softly, tilting his head. *But that's the only way. Only two people leave this room alive: one is me, of course, and the other? That's up to you four to decide.*

JAMES circled them like a predator savoring its prey, eyes gleaming with an unsettling calm. He stopped in front of PETER first, a cruel smile creeping across his face.

PETER, he said softly, *don't you have a sick child on his deathbed? You want to see him again, don't you? Get rid of these people, and you and I walk out of here—leaders like we've always been. You reunite with your family.*

JAMES moved on to ANDREA, whose face tightened as he approached. *And you, ANDREA,* he whispered, *the THO could pull the plug any day, and your husband loses his job. No education for your kids, no future. Is it worth the risk of not picking up my P226 and putting a bullet in these three?*

He turned sharply to where BART and JUDE stood together, tension rippling through their bodies. *And you, BART,* he said with a mocking laugh, *don't you have a grandma out there who thinks you're off in some military program? Don't you want to see her again? Or is this woman—* his gaze settled on JUDE, *— your world now?*

Then, with a cold finality, he turned to JUDE. *And you, the only one here with absolutely nothing to lose.* He looked back at the others, eyes narrowed. *I'm going to make this simple. BART's grandma will pass on sooner or later, so kill him. JUDE? She's got no one. Expendable.* His voice lowered, seething. *That leaves just the two of you.*

Come on, ANDREA, he said with a twisted smile, *haven't you already killed someone before?*

ANDREA's eyes filled with a mixture of anger and tears as she glared back at him.

JAMES laughed, delighted by her reaction. *Oh, struck a nerve, have I? Remember, if anything happens to me, not only do you all die—but so do your families.* He looked at each one of them, savoring their anguish. *So, think twice before making a dumb mistake like BART did.*

BART's fists clenched at his sides, trembling with suppressed fury.

So, JAMES said, tapping the gun on the table, *why the delay? Figure it out. Pull the trigger three times, and let's move on.*

ANDREA took a shaky step forward, shoulders slumped under the weight of what she was about to do. Her fingers trembled as she reached for the gun. JAMES smiled, cold and unrelenting.

There's my lioness. Here, she's all yours, he said, pushing the P226 toward her on the table.

ANDREA picked it up slowly, her breath hitching. The gun felt foreign, heavy, her grip unsteady as her hands shook uncontrollably. Tears streamed down her face, her sobs the only sound breaking the silence. She lifted the weapon, arms quivering, and pointed it at BART.

Great choice, JAMES sneered, pacing behind her. *Shoot the guy who got you into this mess in the first place.*

ANDREA's breaths came out in shallow gasps, her entire frame shaking as she struggled to hold the gun steady. JAMES watched, eyes narrowing, his patience wearing thin.

ANDREA, he barked, voice sharp. *Do I need to put a bullet in your kneecap to move things along?*

No, no, please, she stammered, her sobs growing louder. She closed her eyes for a split second, then forced them open, steadying her grip with a deep, ragged breath. Her aim tightened on BART, hands white-knuckling the gun.

JUDE suddenly stepped forward, her voice breaking, *JAMES, please, I'll do anything you ask—anything.*

No, JUDE! BART's voice thundered through the room, desperate.

Oh, shut the fuck up, both of you! JAMES roared, his voice slicing through their pleas. He leaned closer to ANDREA, voice icy. *ANDREA!*

The sound of her name jolted her. She flinched, breaths now ragged and shallow, her fingers tightening on the trigger, her vision blurring with tears. With a shaky breath, she whispered, *I'm sorry.* Her voice broke, a single tear tracing down her cheek as she tightened her grip on the trigger. Every nerve in her body screamed against what she was about to do, but her finger slowly, reluctantly, applied pressure to the trigger.

She pulled.

Click.

XXIII

The hollow *click* lingered in the air, leaving ANDREA frozen, the gun still aimed at BART, her chest tight with fear and disbelief. She blinked, staring at the weapon as it dawned on her—the gun wasn't loaded.

JAMES moved in close, his face inches from hers, eyes cold and piercing. *That's what I want,* he whispered, his voice soft but menacing. *That fear in each of your eyes. The pressure of knowing exactly what's at stake.* He straightened, looking at each of them in turn, his voice growing louder, filled with authority. *I control every outcome in this room. I always have.*

He turned, pacing deliberately as his words sank in. *I am the one who speaks to THO, who puts in the word. If I say we need ten people, then we do. If I decide you're all useless, well—then they'll kill you. You don't understand the power I hold, the control I have in the palm of my hand.*

He stopped pacing, fixing them with a sharp stare. *My primary objective here is to finish this damn project,* he said, his tone cold and resolute. *But I needed to make sure we're all on the same page—and to remind you what happens when you dare to step out of line.*

JAMES's words settled over them like a heavy weight, suffocating and final. He let the silence stretch, watching as each of them absorbed the grim reality. *But don't get too comfortable,* he added, voice steely. *Your rule-breaking won't go unpunished. When the project is done, you'll pay—with your lives. And if you fail to finish this project, your families pay too.*

The four of them stood motionless, the weight of his words pressing down on them, the grim realization that their fates had been sealed sinking in.

Now, get to work! he barked, breaking the silence, snapping them back to the task at hand, as he opened the door and gestured them to leave. The four left silently as each of them eyed JAMES except ANDREA, she walked her eyes fixed on the ground. JAMES followed them to the super lab, where everybody were already working, one batch were writing down things while the other were on their computers with headphones on. Everyone turned to see the 5 of them enter the lab, but they continued with their work.

We have thirteen hours from now. Take a break if you must—the window is narrow, from 2AM to 4. Beyond that, we can't afford lost time. Everything needs to be perfect when THO arrives. Get to work! JAMES commanded, then left the lab, leaving the four in tense silence.

Each of them knew now they were on death row, their fates sealed by one misstep. The countdown had begun, a clock ticking down to their execution. Months of grueling work suddenly meant nothing. In the weight of the moment, a sliver of comfort surfaced: at least their mistakes wouldn't cost the other six their lives.

PETER shuffled through the pile of papers outlining the first draft of the memory sequence, but his eyes skimmed the text mindlessly. His thoughts were elsewhere—on his son, Nate. Tomorrow, he realized, he wouldn't walk out of here as he'd hoped. Yet, in the pain of it, a faint calm took hold, knowing the money had been going to his family all along. Six figures in nine months, a fortune he'd never dreamed of, but one that might just give Nate a fighting chance. Somehow, in the dark, that thought brought a small, fleeting smile to his face.

Sir? ... What do you think, Sir? a voice snapped PETER back.

Clearing his throat, he said, *Uh... yes ... the knife.*

The knife? asked LEVI, brow furrowed.

It can't be just any knife, PETER replied, more firmly now, *It was a chef's knife. LEVI, don't skip over the details. Every last thing has to be precise—accurate down to the smallest element. Get it right.*

22:00

The waves brushed over their feet, cool and constant, as they sank into the soft grains of sand. The salty scent of the seashore filled the air as they sat side by side, watching the sun slowly descend toward the horizon. He felt an indescribable happiness, a joy so complete it felt impossible anyone could match it in that moment. As the sun kissed the horizon, he took a breath, got down on one knee, and pulled out a lush, velvety blue box. Inside, a brilliant sparkle greeted her, and her eyes widened, shimmering with a mix of surprise and tears.

BART took out a folded piece of paper from his back pocket and, with a nervous laugh, began to read. *JUDE,* he started, voice trembling, *I don't know if this is too soon or too late.* He blushed. *But what I do know is, true love doesn't wait for the perfect time. It exists here, in the present—so right now feels like the right time.*

The breeze played with her hair as he continued, *I never thought I'd want to settle down, never even imagined myself married. But with you...* he trailed off, smiling softly. *What was once just a fairytale—the dream of being with someone as wonderful as you—that's my reality now. You've made me believe in family, in waking up each morning next to someone I love, tackling challenges together, celebrating even the smallest victories. Life without you?* He shook his head, *It just wouldn't be a life worth living.*

His hand shook as he lifted the box. *JUDE, I love you. It would make me the happiest man on Earth if you wore this ring and promised never to take it off...* He flipped the paper in his hand, revealing a blank sheet—a playful reminder he didn't need the words written down, he felt them.

Her eyes filled with tears as she gazed at him, her face radiant with joy. But just as she began to respond, her expression shifted. Her smile faded, the clouds thickened, and the breeze died. In a voice that was suddenly cold, she whispered, *But you don't even know my name.*

And with that, she raised a gun, and the echo of a gunshot filled the air.

BART jolted awake, gasping for breath, drenched in the lingering dread of the dream. His surroundings sharpened—the sterile lab, his cluttered workbench. He looked around, grateful no one had noticed. His eyes fell on JUDE, sitting nearby, writing. Her face was partially obscured, but even behind the mask, he saw traces of the woman he'd just dreamed about.

The weight of his actions hit him hard, an ache settling deep within. If only he'd thought it through, hadn't let his emotions cloud his judgment, maybe he wouldn't be here now, haunted by regret. He hadn't just ruined one life—he'd dragged three down with him.

22:30

JAMES sat alone in the balcony in A52, tapping the ash off his cigar. Smoke curled around him, casting a hazy veil over the room. Beside him on the table sat a crystal glass and an opened bottle of Ardbeg Uigeadail. He took a sip, savoring the powerful, smoky flavor, tasting hints of chocolate and dried fruits. Footsteps echoed from behind, growing closer.

You're wasting your time if you're here to talk treason, PETER.

Without a word, PETER sat in the chair to JAMES's right, pulled a cigar from the box, and lit it.

So you opened it, huh? PETER asked, eyeing the bottle.

Yes, JAMES replied, taking another sip. *There's nothing left to celebrate. You'll find a glass on the top shelf…*

I'd rather keep a clear head while I'm working.

PETER's tone softened, *Let the three of them go, JAMES.*

There it is, JAMES exhaled a thick plume of smoke, *I told you, PETER. You're wasting your time.*

I'm pleading, JAMES, PETER's voice cracked. *Take me instead. They're just kids. And ANDREA… she was only dragged into this because I was knocked out.*

Stop playing the hero. This isn't a movie. When I finally have a gun to your head, you'll be begging me not to pull the trigger.

But it worked, didn't it? The project succeeded. We've achieved not one, but two objectives—

We don't know that yet, JAMES interrupted, gaze hard.

See, you're the voice. You can make a choice here, PETER said, his tone urgent. *We've known each other long enough. We've sat on this very patio, shared cigars, bottles of scotch. You could convince them that you need us, can't you?*

Stop it, PETER. For fuck's sake. JAMES clenched his jaw, voice icy. *The only reason I'm not putting a bullet in you now is out of respect for what we've shared over these months. So, stop wasting your time and get back to work.*

PETER sighed, defeated. *Alright. Do what you can—that's all I ask.* He rose and turned to leave.

PETER—wait...

PETER paused, a glimmer of hope flickering in his eyes as he turned back to face JAMES.

No one is walking out of here tomorrow, JAMES said, his voice low. *THO won't risk PROJECT JENESIS being replicated. They're determined to eliminate all traces. Even if I wanted to help... there's nothing I could do.*

The weight of those words sank deep into PETER's chest, stealing the breath from him. He swallowed, unable to speak, then turned and walked out of A52 in silent defeat.

23:00

Guys! The food has arrived. Help yourselves, called out MATTHEW as he stepped into the room with trays of late-night provisions. Working overnight meant extra food, an unusual luxury at this hour.

JUDE made her way to the pantry, picked up two kits, and headed to A44.

JUDE, I wasn't expecting you here, J said, surprised.

I needed some space, she replied, setting down one of the kits in front of him. *Figured I'd bring you one too.*

Thank you, that's... thoughtful.

J opened the kit, eyeing the food. *This is a very diplomatic meal, wouldn't you say? Measured rice, two boiled broccolis, a couple of chicken breasts, and an energy drink.*

To someone who's survived on this for the last nine months, it might look different, said JUDE.

So, tomorrow's the big day, huh? Finally, you all get to go home.

At the mention of going home, JUDE hesitated, her spoon frozen midair before she quickly resumed eating, brushing it off.

What are you gonna do when you get out?

She shrugged. *I haven't really thought about it.*

J took a deep breath, setting his kit aside. *JUDE... you realize they're playing you, right?*

She glanced at him, wary. *What do you mean?*

Think about it, he replied. *You present a groundbreaking neurological advancement, and they act like it's irrelevant—then remind you of an 'objective' that's nowhere near as complex?*

Silence hung between them.

They're stalling, he continued, voice low. *I don't think anyone's walking out of here. They've squeezed everything they could out of you guys. Now they're preparing to dispose of you.*

JUDE studied him, her expression unreadable. *A lot's happened in the last few hours, J. My fate was sealed long before you said this. Forgive me if I'm not exactly hungry to keep living.*

J opened his mouth to respond, but she cut him off. *And don't even ask what.*

There's one thing I've wanted to know... why the black room?

We were just instilling a trait in you, she replied, her tone weary.

What trait?

One you didn't have before, she said quietly. *You value life now.*

And what makes you think I didn't before?

JUDE raised an eyebrow, her gaze sharp. *You killed your wife and kids, your entire world. I don't know what that is, if it's not someone who didn't give a damn about life.*

J sat there, absorbing her words.

And the spectral equation? What was that really about?

JUDE finished her food and wiped her hands. *There was no spectral equation, but there was an underlying mathematical structure meant to gauge your coping mechanisms. Every time you figured it out, we'd change it, and that's when we saw progress. We knew that coping was the enemy of progress.*

J sat there, sighing as he began to understand. *But what was with the ECG and everything? I couldn't have figured that out on my own—unless you have an explanation for how you made the internet accessible in the memory...*

You're right, came the reply. *Constructing the internet within the sequence would've been extremely complex. But the ECG? That was just there to spark a glimmer of hope, only to snatch it away. It was meant to make you crave life and, eventually, to value it.*

And what about the glowing green eyes? What was that about...

Sorry, what?

The glowing green eyes. Back in the black room. It only appeared once, never saw it again after that...

Ah, right. Jude's lips curled into a faint smile. *Well, I suppose every writer slips up now and then — loose ends, forgotten threads. I'd say that's probably all it was.*

That's it? J's eyes narrowed. *What was the original plan, then?*

Honestly? Jude leaned back, *we meant to circle back to it later. But things picked up, momentum shifted, and...* She shrugged, letting out a small laugh. *It just slipped through the cracks.*

Brutal... but the blue skies? They freaked me out, J admitted with a slight chuckle.

I'll fix that, JUDE said, smiling slightly as she took a last sip from her energy drink. She rose to leave, hesitating just a moment. *You seemed like a brother for a few hours there. It was... nice.*

She paused at the door, giving him a final look. *See you around, J.*

Everyone was frantically working, but the four avoided eye contact with one another. BART, desperate to get JUDE's attention, had barely seen her since she'd returned to the lab and resumed her tasks. ANDREA, meanwhile, worked silently with tear-stained eyes, barely holding herself together since leaving the conference room. She felt as though she'd betrayed her family, a thought that made her curse BART under her breath. Even when food arrived, she didn't move from her spot.

01:59.

This is a reminder that it's almost 2. Please take your breaks if you need them. Resume work at 4.

Chairs scraped, footsteps began echoing, breaking the silence that had been filled only with paper shuffling and mouse clicks. People drifted toward the exit, everyone opting for a break without exception. ANDREA caught up with BART as they filed out.

I hope you rot in hell; she hissed.

BART stopped in his tracks, stunned, as she walked away without another word.

Afterward, he tried to find JUDE. He'd hoped to talk to her, but she'd already slipped away to her room. Maybe she needed space, after everything. BART couldn't help but blame himself for what had happened, and maybe she did too. If tomorrow truly was their last day—maybe their last day alive—he wanted to spend tonight with her. With a heavy heart, he walked to A28 and knocked on her door.

Not tonight, BART...

Please, if this is our last night, I want to be with you.

Just go away, BART. She shut the door firmly.

BART let out a shaky breath, feeling both defeated and raw as he trudged to A25. He was barely holding himself together, on the verge of a breakdown. But as he flipped on the lights, he froze. The room was exactly as it had been the last time he'd faced this nightmare. JAMES sat casually in the chair, waiting for him, only now, true to his identity, he wore his own balaclava, emblazoned with his name.

You... you fucked it up! BART shot, his voice thick with anger.

No, no, Romeo. You fucked it up, JAMES replied smoothly, rising from his seat. *And now, you're going to pay.*

BART held his ground, unwilling to back down. *I only wish it was you earlier today. I would've loved watching you crawl, blood spilling—*

Oh, buddy, that's exactly what I'm here for. With a swift, brutal motion, JAMES lunged at BART, who quickly realized he was no match for the 6'2" Navy SEAL. A strike to the solar plexus sent BART crumbling to his knees, and before he could react, JAMES landed a series of crushing blows to his face, splitting the skin and shattering his jaw. The pain radiated through his skull as if it had fractured in one single hit. BART barely noticed as he was hauled onto a chair, tied up, and gagged with tape.

You thought you could fight me? JAMES chuckled darkly. BART's muffled protests and groans were drowned beneath the tape, his pain and fear trapped within him.

The punishment is just beginning, Romeo.

As the realization of what was coming washed over him, BART's expression twisted in rage and panic. His body strained against the restraints, his face wet with blood and tears.

From the moment I realized you tried to take a swing at PETER, thinking it was me, I knew you'd have to pay. JAMES leaned close, taking a slow, menacing breath. *And now, while you're tied up here... you can just imagine what I'm going to do to her.* He paused, savoring the words. *Oh, you'll get her alright... after I've had her first.*

BART's panic surged; his screams stifled under the tape, his face a mess of blood, sweat and tears. JAMES turned, leaving him bound and broken. He walked out, heading toward A28, the spare keys cool in his hand. As he quietly unlocked the door, he caught sight of JUDE on her bed. She jumped, shock spreading across her face as she recognized him.

A slow, twisted smile crept across his lips.

...Finally.

au revoir III

A few hours earlier...

Is it done? came a distorted voice from the other end of the line.

No, not yet. I don't know what's taking them so long... JAMES replied, his eyes locked on the super lab across from his office, his gaze sharp with impatience.

Did you do everything as I instructed? the voice pressed.

Yes, every bit of it, JAMES said, his tone edged with frustration. *You think they missed the clues?*

Give it some time... the voice responded, calm but razor-sharp. *If you followed my instructions to the letter — like you did last time — there's nothing to worry about.*

Alright... JAMES muttered. A sudden buzz from his hand device drew his attention. He glanced down, eyes narrowing. *I think it's them...*

Keep me posted, the voice ordered, and the line went dead with a cold, empty click.

22:00

JAMES rose from his chair with calm precision. He reached behind his back, drew his gun, checked the chamber to ensure it was fully loaded, then tucked it away with a practiced ease. His gaze sharpened as he moved toward the door.

He stepped out of his office, eyes scanning his surroundings with the quiet awareness of a predator on the hunt. When he reached A52, he swiped his keycard with a subtle beep, the door unlocking with a soft click. JAMES entered slowly, his footsteps measured and deliberate, as though he were walking into a room of sleeping beasts he had no intention of waking.

His eyes flicked up to the top of the staircase. There, just beyond the door that led to the balcony, were two figures — hunched, frantic, working feverishly to unlock a padlock. The padlock itself was heavy, industrial-grade, with reinforced steel shackles and a broad, blackened body marked with scratches from failed attempts to breach it.

JAMES lingered at the base of the stairs, watching them work like a pair of fish thrashing at the end of a hook. He tilted his head, observing their struggle with quiet amusement. Eventually, he lowered himself into a nearby chair, elbows on his knees, hands loosely clasped as if he had all the time in the world. The men remained oblivious, too consumed by their task to notice the man watching them from below.

Guys... JAMES's voice sliced through the room, cool and cutting. *You're embarrassing yourselves. Just... give it up.*

The two men froze mid-motion, their bodies going rigid as if turned to stone. Neither moved.

Turn around, JAMES ordered, his voice firm but calm.

Slowly, the men turned to face him. Their eyes met his. LEVI and ALPHAEUS.

Ah, LEVI, ALPHAEUS... JAMES *leaned back, crossing one leg over the other. For a moment there, I thought you'd missed the little setup I prepared for you. But here you are.* He gestured loosely toward them, his eyes cold with amusement. *I mean, surely no one could be this predictable, right?* A grin tugged at the corner of his lips. *But here you are, proving me wrong.*

I knew it was a damn setup, muttered LEVI through clenched teeth. ALPHAEUS stayed silent.

And you went with it anyway, didn't you? JAMES's voice was cold, sharp as a blade.

Why? Why us?

No, JAMES stepped forward, slow and deliberate. Just you, LEVI. But look at you—brought a plus one. Unbelievable. Convincing someone else to join your little escape plan? Gotta hand it to you. His eyes shifted to ALPHAEUS. See, ALPHA, I've got nothing against you. You followed orders. Stayed in line. One of the very few who actually did. He shook his head, lips curling into a sneer. But now, thanks to this fatty, you're here too. And you know what that means, right? I'm sorry, buddy, but I'll have to kill you as well.

Hey, JAMES—JAMES, please. ALPHAEUS's voice broke as he raised his hands. His breathing came fast, shallow. I'm sorry. I was scared, alright? After PETER killed THAD, I didn't know who was next. I followed orders. Every single one. I even helped clean up a dead body, for God's sake— his voice cracked — something I have absolutely no experience with. I was terrified, JAMES. I don't want to die. I've got a family, man. A family! Please understand. I've followed your orders before, and I swear, I'll keep following them. No mistakes this time.

You want to swear loyalty to me now? JAMES tilted his head, eyes narrowing. *Right after you tried to run? How does that work, ALPHA?*

Why, JAMES!? Tell me why! barked LEVI, his voice raw with fury.

Calm down, kid, JAMES said, his tone cool, sharp as broken glass. *Or I'll make you regret ever raising your voice at me.*

ALPHAEUS was breathing hard now, each inhale sharp and shallow.

JAMES took a step closer, his eyes fixed on them like a predator sizing up prey. *Do you know what happens when a member of the project dies?* He let the question linger, his gaze shifting between them. *The funds wired to their account? They get sent back. Back to me.* His grin was slow, deliberate. *Yes, we can do that. I made sure of it.*

He tilted his head, like he was explaining something to a child. Now, imagine this—I've got some existing debts with the organization. Big ones. But I don't have enough cash on hand to cover it. So, I thought about it for a while. Weighing my options, you know? He tapped his temple, eyes bright with mock inspiration. And I realized... I just have to eliminate someone. He leaned forward slightly, his smile curving into something sharper. Simple math, really. One less member, and the funds get wired back to the account I control. Because, in case you forgot, I'm the one who handles the money for Project Jenesis.

ALPHAEUS's breathing had turned shallow and uneven. His eyes darted around the room, looking for something—an escape, maybe. LEVI, on the other hand, was frozen, his jaw tight, his eyes locked on JAMES with seething rage.

Now, I can't just kill anyone. There's a system, of course. JAMES gestured vaguely, as if the "system" was floating somewhere in the air. *But there's one clear exception.* His eyes locked on LEVI, and his grin faded into a hard, calculating line. *If someone tries to break out... well, I'm allowed to kill them. No questions asked.* He clapped his hands together, the sharp echo bouncing off the cold walls. *And that, gentlemen, brings us to the present moment.*

Silence. Heavy, oppressive silence.

ALPHAEUS blinked slowly, his face pale. *You're insane,* he muttered, barely above a whisper.

No, I'm practical, JAMES replied, voice low and steady. And if you're wondering why I'm telling you all this instead of just pulling the trigger— he glanced between them, his eyes crinkling with amusement —

it's simple. I'm decent enough to let you know why you're about to die, instead of leaving you clueless.

The silence that followed wasn't just heavy this time—it was suffocating.

So, gentlemen, any last words? JAMES asked, tilting his head with the calm of a man already in control.

ALPHAEUS's breath came in sharp, shallow bursts. His hands trembled. Suddenly, he dropped to his knees, grabbing JAMES by the ankle.

Please, JAMES! His voice cracked with panic. Please—I'm sorry! I didn't mean it! I didn't mean any of it!

His grip tightened. JAMES raised an eyebrow, unimpressed.

Pathetic, JAMES muttered, but before he could react—

ALPHAEUS surged forward, yanking hard on JAMES's leg. Caught off balance, JAMES hit the ground with a heavy thud, his back slamming against the cold tiles.

LEVI didn't move. His eyes followed them, cold and still, as if he'd seen it all before.

ALPHAEUS didn't waste a second. He scrambled over JAMES, pinning him by the chest, and his fists came down like wild hammers. The first punch cracked against JAMES's cheek. The second caught his jaw.

You bitch! I'll kill you; you hear me!? YOU FUCKED WITH THE WRONG GUY! he roared, his eyes wide with fury.

JAMES's head snapped to the side, but his gaze was sharp, calculating. He shifted his hips, his feet twisting into position.

On the next punch, JAMES's legs shot up like coiled springs, locking around ALPHAEUS's shoulders. With a sharp pull, he threw him backward, twisting ALPHAEUS off his chest. ALPHAEUS tumbled, landing hard on his back before clumsily rolling to his feet. But JAMES was faster.

Already upright, JAMES closed the distance with a single step. His foot shot out—a precise kick to ALPHAEUS's knee. The joint hyperextended with a sickening *pop*. ALPHAEUS crumpled forward, screaming—

But JAMES was there to meet him.

His knee drove upward, smashing into ALPHAEUS's face with a crunch of bone. Blood sprayed from his nose, and he let out a choked, wet gasp. Before ALPHAEUS could even scream, JAMES's hand was on him. He clamped his palm over ALPHAEUS's mouth, fingers digging into his jawline.

Shhh, JAMES whispered. His eyes were calm. Detached.

ALPHAEUS thrashed, his body seizing in panicked, jerky movements. His muffled groans echoed in the silence.

The plan was a bullet. Clean. Efficient.

But plans change.

With one swift motion, JAMES twisted ALPHAEUS's head to the side. The crack echoed louder than any scream.

Silence.

JAMES let the body fall at his feet. Blood dripped from his face, a single line tracing the curve of his jaw. He wiped it away with his sleeve, slow and deliberate, before turning to face LEVI.

JAMES said, his eyes sharp as broken glass. *Got any last words, kid?*

After what felt like an eternity, the floor was spotless, both bodies unceremoniously dumped in the washroom. JAMES opened the door to the balcony, uncapped a brand-new bottle of scotch, and lit a cigarette. Settling into his chair, he exhaled slowly, the weight of it all momentarily lifting as he took in the quiet.

XXIV

After what felt like hours, when the pain finally settled enough to handle, BART slowly opened his eyes. His whole face hurt, especially his jaw, but he couldn't focus on that now—he had to get out. He pulled at his wrists, tightly bound, and twisted his hands until he felt the rope start to loosen. Hope flickered as he ignored the pain of the rope scraping his skin. Little by little, he managed to free one wrist. With a shaky breath, he quickly freed his other hand and peeled the tape off his mouth, gasping for air. Every part of him ached, but he forced himself up, steadying himself against the wall. He looked at the alarm clock at the nightstand.

04:45

He moved quietly to the door, cracking it open to look out. The hallway was empty—JAMES must be gone, probably with JUDE. The thought drove him on as he slipped out, gathering his strength, hoping he wasn't too late. BART turned the doorknob—it was locked. Panic surged through him as he pounded on the door, but no sound came from inside. He shoved his shoulder against it, straining with everything he had, but it wouldn't budge. Frustrated and desperate, he took a shaky breath, steadying himself as best he could, then made his way to the lab, his bruised and bloodied body barely holding him upright.

WHERE IS JAMES! he bellowed, his voice cracking. Heads whipped around, and everyone turned to stare at him, shocked by the sight. Fury and tears mingled on BART's face as PETER hurried over.

BART, what happened? Did JAMES—?

WHERE THE HELL IS JAMES! BART's voice broke with anger and despair. *I'LL KILL HIM, I SWEAR...* But his voice faltered, choked with sobs.

Breath hitching, he slumped against PETER, his voice softer now, desperate. *Where's JUDE?* he begged. *Please, find her, PETER. Please.*

BART? A familiar voice cut through his panic. It was JUDE, rushing forward, eyes wide with concern as she took in his battered face. *What happened to you, BART?*

JU-JU-JUDE... are you okay? he stammered, barely believing his eyes.

Yes, love. I'm fine, see? She spoke gently, as though she understood everything that had happened.

But... but... JA— he managed, struggling to breathe.

Don't worry about him, alright? She turned, calling over her shoulder. *ANDREA! I could use a little help here.*

ANDREA watched the whole scene unfold, her arms crossed, unmoved. *He deserves this,* she said coldly.

ANDREA, please, JUDE pleaded, her eyes filled with worry. *He's shaking. Please, help him.*

ANDREA shot her a bitter look. *You know as well as I do—he dragged us into this mess. Because of him, I'll probably never see my family again! The least I can do is ignore your pleas for him.*

Like you did for that seventeen-year-old boy? PETER cut in sharply.

ANDREA's face tightened as her eyes glistened with anger. *That was a mistake!* she snapped, her voice cracking.

And you're about to make another one, PETER replied. *One that'll haunt you, just like that did.*

ANDREA's expression softened, a flicker of guilt breaking through her anger. Beneath her rage, she was still a doctor, bound to help, even if the patient was BART. With a resigned sigh, she said, *Fine. Bring him to A27.*

PETER and JUDE immediately lifted BART by the shoulders, guiding his weakened form toward A27, while ANDREA moved ahead to retrieve her first aid kit.

ANDREA worked swiftly, pulling supplies from the first aid kit. She cleaned BART's cuts with antiseptic wipes, pressing sterile gauze over the deeper wounds and securing them with medical tape. For his broken jaw, she gently wrapped an elastic bandage around his head, stabilizing it as best as possible. She handed him a cold pack for the swelling, pressing his hand over it to hold it in place. Offering him a small dose of painkillers from the kit, she instructed him to take only one and made him to sip water carefully to keep him hydrated. Finally, she draped a blanket over his shoulders to counter the shock and sat beside him, watching his breathing, ready to help if he needed anything else.

As ANDREA finished tending to him, BART whispered, *...thank you.*

Don't thank me, she replied bluntly, gathering her supplies. *Thank God I changed my mind. I would've been just fine with you dead.* Without another word, she left the room.

Rest well, JUDE said softly, leaning over him. *I'll wake you when they're here.* She gave his shoulder a gentle squeeze before she and PETER slipped out, leaving BART alone to recover.

15:52

The painkillers had cradled BART into a deep, peaceful sleep. He drifted through it, weightless, until he felt hands on his shoulders, shaking him gently at first, then with urgency. He blinked awake, his vision blurred but sharpening quickly. It was JUDE, her face tense in the dim light.

BART, get up. Now!

What's—?

THO is here...

That snapped him awake. BART bolted out of bed, knowing lateness could be the worst choice he'd ever make. They hurried through the sterile corridors to the lab, where the others had already gathered. PETER stood nearby, looking on edge. BART glanced into the Black Room and saw J, lying in position, just starting to stir.

How did it go? BART asked, lowering his voice.

PETER shook his head, frustration etched into his face. *Last-minute changes set everything back an hour. J will be waking up any moment now, but there's no time to test the results, no time to record the full observations.*

The tension in the room was palpable, a murmur of worry hanging in the air—until it abruptly dropped into silence. A group of men in black suits and balaclavas had entered, and in a swift, practiced movement, everyone fell into formation. 4-4. At the front stood BART, JUDE, ANDREA, and PETER. Seven men approached, this time led by someone new—a shorter man, perhaps 5'8", who radiated authority.

Where is JAMES? he asked, his voice low but commanding.

PETER stepped forward. *He's on his way, sir.*

He better be here. It's one minute to 1600, and he knows I don't like waiting.

Gentlemen! A voice echoed from behind. JAMES strode into the lab, nodding in acknowledgment. *My apologies. Final preparations were needed in light of your arrival.*

You know, JAMES, in the Bible I've read, the man said in a commanding tone, *JESUS CHRIST had twelve apostles. Why does yours have only nine?*

All eight of them resisted the overwhelming urge to glance around, wondering where the other two could be. Yet, a curious thought crept into some of their minds—had the missing pair somehow managed to escape?

An accident, sir, JAMES replied.

The leader's eyes narrowed. *All right, JAMES. What have you got?*

JAMES turned and caught JUDE's gaze, giving her a quick nod. She took the signal and headed toward the observation gallery overlooking the Black Room. JAMES then motioned for the seven men to follow him deeper into the lab.

The leader—identified by the others as JC1—muttered, *I expected you to be ready.*

I know, JAMES replied smoothly, *but there were last-minute adjustments.*

The seven men moved in formation behind him, and the team trailed close behind, eyes fixed on JAMES. Around them, the lab hummed with the quiet activity of screens and machines monitoring J's vital signs and mental state. Then, a calm voice from the gallery:

Sequence 100% complete. John is ready.

The men from THO gathered at the entrance to the Black Room, their attention on the figure inside. Meanwhile, the team spread out around the room, eyes darting between monitors above and the data feeds in their hands.

In that moment, something clicked in BART's mind. A cold realization washed over him—they might have made a mistake. He moved closer to PETER and tapped his shoulder. But it seemed like PETER was already lost in thought, his worry etched on his face.

Are you okay?

Uh... yeah. Just worried if the speed-run will actually work or not...

BART hesitated for a moment, unsure whether to voice the question weighing on his mind or let PETER be for now.

I think we made an error, BART whispered urgently.

Like what?

We're running the same memory sequence from the night of the murder, aren't we?

Yes...

Didn't that event cause him to lose his ability to speak?

Yes...

So, if we're repeating it exactly, BART pressed, *won't he lose his speech again?*

PETER sighed, glancing at BART. *We realized that partway through. That's why we were delayed by an hour.*

HOLY SHIT! HOLY SHIT! OH MY GOD—NO! At that moment, J stirred awake from the memory sequence.

BART looked at J, then at PETER, who sighed, the weight of his worry lifting as he realized the speed-run had worked. He gave BART a reassuring nod, silently confirming that everything was under control. The plan had succeeded—just as they hoped.

As if reading BART's mind, PETER explained, *before we started the sequence, we gave John clear indications about what he'd experience, what he'd see, and why he was being sent back to relive that night. It was almost like sending him in as a spy to witness his own crime.*

He paused, then added, *but in case that approach didn't fully engage him, we left subtle clues throughout the sequence: a call log with my name, a letter from JUDE, a book in his library titled Pro-Jenesis, and a few other cues.*

So, you've completely overwritten the memory? Won't that cause him more pain?

It was the only option, came the reply, resolute yet weary...

BART exhaled, feeling a tentative sense of relief as he glanced at J, still dazed but conscious, as the clues seemed to ground him in the carefully orchestrated reality of the memory.

On the other side, in the Black Room, J was in tears. The pain felt unbearable as he slumped into JUDE's arms, sobbing heavily. Just moments ago, he had seen himself—or rather, he had become himself—as he brutally murdered his wife and children. What had once been distant, horrifying lore was now a living nightmare he'd been forced to endure.

Across the room, JC1 remained expressionless, but he gestured to two of his men. They stepped forward, carrying a video camera and a tripod, setting them up in front of J's bed. The men wore balaclavas labeled JCVI and JCVII. Another, labeled JCV, brought a chair from the nearest workbench. Silence enveloped the room, broken only by J's quiet, shattered sobs.

JC1 sat down in the chair facing J while JUDE adjusted the bed to lift J into a seated position, facing JC1. He gestured for JUDE to step aside, clearing the frame so that the camera captured both men in profile.

Hello, John, he began, his tone calm, almost clinical. *My name is CROSS. I know—it's a bit ironic, given the alias this project operates under.*

John didn't respond, still lost in the aftermath of reliving his darkest moments.

I'm the one who authorized this project. And now that it's complete, I'll be the one to assess the results.

John nodded, looking down, still trembling from what he had seen.

CROSS cleared his throat, his voice taking on a sharper edge. *I'd appreciate it if you looked at me, Birmingham.*

The command was subtle, yet firm. John lifted his head immediately, meeting CROSS's gaze, his eyes red-rimmed and glassy.

Good. CROSS leaned forward slightly. *So, tell me, John—what happened that night?*

John closed his eyes, struggling against the urge to shut down. Going through it once had been a nightmare, but to relive it again, now—under the scrutiny of twenty silent onlookers—felt like a new level of torment. He took a shaky breath, the weight of their eyes pressing on him, and prepared himself to recount the night that had destroyed his life.

For months, I'd been drowning in stress at work, J began, his voice strained. *I was done. I wanted to leave it all behind, start something of my own, be closer to my family. But work kept me on the road, always away. And when I finally made it home, I started noticing things...things that made me believe my wife, Molly, was cheating on me.*

He swallowed hard, his gaze fixed somewhere beyond the present. *She was gone half the time, always on the phone with someone. Whenever I asked, she'd shrug it off, saying it was just a friend from work. But there was something off...*

His voice faltered. *One night, I came home drunk. I was just...done. And as I got to the house, I saw a man in a suit walk out, get into his car, and drive off. Right then, I decided I was going to end it.*

He drew in a ragged breath, trembling. *Until then, I hadn't planned to hurt her...but the moment I walked in, she greeted me with this big smile, like nothing was wrong.* His face twisted, pain contorting his features. *I thought she was pretending, thought it was all a show, as if she knew I'd seen him leave.*

He took another unsteady breath. *I walked into the kitchen, grabbed a knife, and stabbed her—six times in the stomach. And then I kissed her, because no matter what, the pain I felt was deeper than those wounds.*

J closed his eyes, his voice breaking. *She died in my arms. I was under the influence—it made everything so...fast, so impulsive. I didn't stop to think, not for a second.*

He paused, the weight of what came next hanging in the air. *And then...I saw my kids. They were watching me. In that moment, their faces seemed different—as if they weren't even mine, like they belonged to the man who had just left.*

A shudder ran through him. *From that point on, my body moved on its own. I don't even remember what I did...I was barely conscious.*

His eyes filled with tears as he continued. *It was later, after going through her phone, that I learned the truth. She wasn't cheating. She'd been setting up a business for me—a way for me to stay home, close to them. Every call, every late night out was about buying a place, making the right connections. The man I saw that night...he was the one who'd helped her finalize everything.*

J choked on his words, barely able to go on. *She was going to surprise me...for my birthday. August 17th.*

He began to sob openly. *The realization hit me like nothing I'd ever felt. I sat there for hours on the floor, my family in my arms. I didn't move, didn't speak...I was...gone.*

He looked up, his face drenched with tears. *That's all I remember...*

The room was silent, save for J's uncontrollable sobs, his agony filling the space as he collapsed under the weight of his remorse.

XXV

The silence in the room was suffocating, the weight of it pressing down on everyone. No one dared to move until CROSS finally broke it.

Clearing his throat, he began, *this was your testimony. We'll have to hand you over to the legal authorities, where you'll be processed and then imprisoned.*

J nodded, eyes cast down, his tears silently falling onto his hands.

Alright, CROSS said, looking over his shoulder. *Wrap it up.*

The two men who had set up the recording equipment gathered their items and exited the room. CROSS rose to his feet, leaving without a backward glance at J.

Now, he said, turning to the rest of the group, *everyone—on your knees.*

A murmur of confusion rippled through the room.

Wait, what? BART protested. *There are only four of us here directly involved.*

Do what you're told! barked JCII, another of CROSS's men.

Confusion turned to dread. Most of the group didn't understand, but PETER, JUDE, BART, and ANDREA knew exactly what this meant. ANDREA began to cry, her sobs audible in the quiet, unsettling the others.

One by one, they all knelt, falling into the same formation as before: four, four, two. ANDREA muttered prayers under her breath, while JUDE reached for BART's hand. BART looked at JUDE, his eyes wet with regret. *I'm sorry,* he whispered.

It's okay, she replied softly, *I love you.*

From a distance, JAMES watched the scene unfold.

Nine months to reach this point. Time flies, doesn't it? CROSS addressed the room, his voice calm. *First, I want to congratulate you all on your hard work and dedication to this project.*

A murmur of relief and appreciation came from the others; they felt proud, acknowledged—even as they knelt. But PETER and JUDE could barely contain their dread, knowing what was to come.

CROSS continued, *This project, which once seemed impossible, is now reality. And that's because of each of you.* His tone was genuine, almost warm. *You've contributed to something groundbreaking, to a better world.*

PETER glanced at the four men behind him, who appeared proud, perhaps even hopeful. Some were no doubt imagining a reunion with their families. PETER knew that was a fantasy.

Your invaluable contributions to the society will be highly regarded, CROSS added, *and you will be well remembered.*

At those words, the smiles vanished.

What do you mean, 'we'll be remembered'? one of the men asked, his voice tense. His tag read MATTHEW.

CROSS met his gaze. *With a project as highly classified—and dangerous—as this, we cannot risk its replication outside these walls. The only way to ensure that...is to 'cut off the hands that made it.'*

A collective gasp filled the room.

Voices rose, pleading and desperate. *Please, don't do this! I have a family! This wasn't in the contract! You lied to us!*

Unmoved, CROSS continued. *Just as agreed, your families have received their payments, and they'll be spared. But the part about...eliminating you? That's my addition.* He glanced at them, unmoved by their terror. *You're not seeing the bigger picture here.*

One man, panicked, tried to rise and flee, but one of CROSS' men stepped forward, delivering a sharp blow to his stomach, forcing him back to his knees.

If anyone else tries to run, CROSS said coldly, *I'll revoke my promise—and hunt down your families.*

The threat hung in the air, silencing even the most defiant.

With a curt nod, CROSS ordered his men to draw their guns, then slowly pulled out his own. Collective sobs echoed through the room, as each man pointed his weapon at one of the kneeling figures.

You know the drill, CROSS said calmly, his gaze sweeping the room. *Each of us shoots one. I'll handle the last one,* he continued, gesturing toward PETER, JUDE, BART, and ANDREA. The unmistakable clicks of loading guns echoed as dread spread across the faces of those kneeling.

If I may interject, came a voice from behind.

What! JAMES? CROSS turned, irritated but caught off guard.

Can I have a moment, please, sir? JAMES asked, moving closer to CROSS.

Leaning in, he whispered, *I think it might be a mistake to eliminate them...*

CROSS stiffened. *You don't make the calls, JAMES.*

I'm aware of that, but just consider this. JAMES maintained a respectful tone, yet firm. *This room holds some of the best minds available—besides the "muscle" you brought in. They're essential, sir. We don't have the creative insights, problem-solving skills, or technical knowledge to take this project further without them. If we need to expand on what we've done here or apply it elsewhere, they're invaluable. Training replacements would waste time and risk setbacks. Continuing with these minds in place might ensure our future success.*

CROSS narrowed his eyes, taking a long, contemplative pause. Finally, he gave a nod.

Men, lower your guns, CROSS ordered.

Relief washed over PETER and the others, stunned by JAMES' unexpected intervention. BART noticed JUDE slip something from her pocket—small and metallic: J's emergency call button from A44. The moment CROSS turned his attention back to the group, JUDE discreetly pressed the button. A loud, piercing alarm sounded, echoing through the lab. In that split second, JAMES drew his P226 and pointed it at CROSS. Within seconds, the room erupted into chaos as gunfire blazed in every direction. Smoke thickened the air, obscuring vision, while the deafening shots ricocheted off walls. In the frenzy, JAMES took six bullets, collapsing to the floor face-first. The sight sent gasps of horror and disbelief through the room as the smoke began to clear, revealing the aftermath of the brutal confrontation.

JAMES was dead.

Should you reconsider his suggestion, sir? asked the man standing beside CROSS, labeled JCII. *He may have been a snake, but he wasn't stupid,* he added quietly. *It's clear we might need these people for future endeavors.*

After a brief silence, CROSS nodded curtly. *Clean it up!* he ordered.

CROSS scanned the group of eight, their faces a mixture of terror and relief, though still shadowed by uncertainty. His gaze was cold, calculating.

...See you all in six months. And with that, CROSS turned and exited.

As the heavy doors shut behind him, the room released a collective exhale. Several of them clambered to their feet, some embracing each other in quiet relief, while those in the front row, still in shock, merely stood frozen—except JUDE, whose expression remained calm, her mind already processing.

What just happened? PETER whispered; eyes wide with confusion.

I'll explain, JUDE replied softly.

JCII stepped forward, addressing the group. *The Archon, Mr. Cross, has decided that each of you will be back in six months,* he said. *Same project, different agenda. Rest assured; he won't kill you—as long as you stick to this project with unwavering loyalty.*

He turned his attention back to the lab, his tone brisk. *Now, you have thirty minutes to clean this place up. It should look as though it was never touched. Meanwhile, we'll take care of...* he gestured at JAMES' body, his voice chillingly neutral. Then he pointed to JUDE. *You—get JOHN ready to leave.*

In the next thirty minutes, footsteps scrambled across the lab floor as everyone hurried to clean up every trace, leaving not even a crumpled paper behind. There was an unmistakable rush in the air—each person eager to leave, to reunite with their families, and to breathe in the outside world after nine long months. Though they wore balaclavas, smiles crept beneath each mask, evidence of the relief simmering under the surface.

Meanwhile, THO's men handled the final cleanup, working efficiently to dispose of JAMES' body. Three of them carried the body out while the others used chemicals to wipe away any remaining evidence.

17:45

Once their work was done, THO's men arrived to collect J. The team gathered around as J walked down the main hallway beside JUDE. BART noticed a change in him—the man who had been sobbing uncontrollably now seemed calm, even at peace. Just before leaving with THO's men, J turned back one last time. He hugged JUDE and, with a warm smile, simply said, *Thank you.* It was the only goodbye he offered, and with that, he stepped through the door with the men.

One of THO's operatives approached the group of eight remaining staff.

Cars have been arranged outside to take each of you home, he announced. *Please form a line, and as you're escorted out one by one, you'll be asked to return the bags you received at the start—make sure all items are intact. Your personal belongings will then be returned, and you'll be escorted to your car.*

Each person marched to their rooms, gathering their belongings with a jumble of relief, dread, and confusion. Meanwhile the four of them walked together, their thoughts heavy with unanswered questions.

I still can't believe JAMES saved us, BART muttered, shaking his head.

I don't know, PETER replied skeptically. *JAMES doesn't do anything unless there's something in it for him.*

And what would he gain from getting himself killed? ANDREA shot back.

That part…I still don't understand, replied PETER.

BART glanced over at JUDE, searching her expression for answers.

Well, whatever the case, we're finally going home, and that's all that matters, PETER said dismissively. *As for JAMES? He probably had it coming. End of story.* Without another word, he turned down the hall toward A34, while ANDREA marched off to A36, keeping her thoughts to herself.

Now, BART and JUDE were left standing outside their doors. BART glanced over and noticed JUDE struggling with her lock.

Do you want to talk about last night? he asked softly, a trace of concern in his voice.

JUDE paused, the door finally clicking open. *What about it?*

JAMES...didn't he come to your room?

No. Why?

BART hesitated, his words stumbling. *I—he...uh...Don't you want to ask about the bruises?*

JUDE smiled faintly, but there was something guarded in her eyes. *Didn't you take a fall?* she asked, the lightness in her tone clearly forced.

BART nodded, reading the unspoken message. She didn't want to talk about it. Not now, at least. *Yeah,* he muttered. *Big fall. Hurts like hell.*

18:10

With that, the four of them went to their respective rooms, packed their belongings, and then gathered again in the queue for exit. Each of them was silently grateful, a mix of relief and quiet thanks to whatever force had helped them navigate a situation that could've easily spiraled into something far worse. They stood in line, each of them taking a moment to reflect, to acknowledge the strange twist of fate that had allowed them to survive.

One by one, each name was called, and the members turned, offering a brief glance back at the others. A final wave, a quick nod, and then they walked through the door, up the stairs, and out into the world. PETER was the last to remain, standing at the end of the line, feeling the weight of everything that had just happened, yet strangely at peace.

A man suddenly called out his alias. PETER's heart gave a small flutter, but he straightened up and walked toward the stairs. He dropped the bag on the table in the centre of the hangar, removed his coat and balaclava, and placed them neatly inside. After retrieving his personal belongings, he was guided toward a white Honda City parked outside, waiting for him. The door opened, and after one last glance at the place that had held so many secrets, he was blindfolded once again, slid into the car, and the door clicked shut behind him.

The world outside seemed different now. And as the car began to drive off, the finality of it all hit him—the end of this chapter.

Their returns marked by the kind of joy that only familiar faces could bring. ANDREA was swallowed up by her family, the weight of their embrace comforting as tears blurred her vision. Her heart swelled with gratitude as she clung to them, unable to stop smiling through her tears.

PETER, was greeted with open arms. Nate, though unsteady, pushed through his struggle, his footsteps quickening as he reached his father. His wife stood close, tears of relief streaming down her cheeks, her arms reaching for him next. They all huddled together, an unspoken bond reaffirmed in the silence of their shared embrace.

BART, was met with a joyous reunion—his grandmother, her face lighting up with excitement, had baked him a cake to celebrate his return from the military program. She couldn't wait to hear every detail of his experience, bombarding him with questions. He grinned and responded, *it was a hoot and a half!*

As for JUDE, she returned to her empty apartment once again—a space filled only with the quiet companionship of her books. There were no warm welcomes here, no loved ones to greet her. Alone, she pulled out the crumpled note BART had given her while they stood in the queue back at the hangar basement. The scribbled phone number seemed out of place in her otherwise solitary world. Without hesitation, she texted the number, feeling a spark of something unfamiliar.

Hey Aarav, it's Samuela here!

Hey Samuela! If you don't mind, I'd love to take you out to the beach sometime... you know, as a date.

I'd love that! Our first official date!

XXVI

As JUDE stood in line behind BART, his alias was called up. Before he stepped forward, he quickly slipped a crumpled piece of paper into her hand.

See you soon, he whispered, flashing a brief, reassuring smile before heading off.

JUDE kept her hand closed tightly around the note, resisting the urge to look at it. She wouldn't risk drawing attention from one of the THO men; this little message could be their only way to communicate on the outside. She waited patiently, thoughts swirling about what lay ahead. She let herself daydream about her first night back in her apartment. After all, she wouldn't need to work for a while—this project had given her financial stability, a rare luxury. And then, there was her book. The thrill of finally being able to publish it brought a surge of excitement to her stomach, a feeling she hadn't experienced in so long it felt almost foreign.

JUDAS! one of the men called out. It was her turn.

Take care, JUDE, whispered PETER from behind, the last man left in line.

You too, she replied with a warm smile, then turned to leave, her heart racing with a strange mix of relief and anticipation.

The car sped swiftly down the street, but JUDE could sense only the darkness around her—the familiar darkness of the blindfold pressed over her eyes. This darkness had a way of triggering memories she'd rather forget, replaying fragments from the night before. Her pulse quickened as she relived those moments when JAMES had entered her room, latching the door behind him. Though she was now miles away, the memory still made her heart pound. JAMES moved closer, his face just inches from hers. His hand slipped around her waist, and his voice lingered in her mind, *ROMEO IS NOT COMING TO YOUR RESCUE TONIGHT.* As he leaned closer, his face mere centimetres away, she had struck, an intravenous needle. She plunged it into his neck, injecting a dose of Thiopental—the drug originally intended for the project until ANDREA pointed out its short duration in sustaining a coma. Now, in the car, her hands tightened into fists.

You fuckin' bitch! I'll make sure you stop breathing before this thing kicks in! JAMES's furious words echoed in her mind, his voice still sharp and venomous.

I had thirty seconds, JUDE recalled. If it had been Pentobarbital—the drug she'd been using on J for the past six months—it would have taken two minutes to kick in... more than enough time for JAMES to kill her. She replayed those tense moments in her mind; it could have gone either way. She remembered his large, unrelenting hands closing around her throat. Her vision had started to blur, her face reddening as she fought for air, her eyes rolling up, until the pressure finally began to ease. JAMES's body went slack, collapsing onto the bed. She stumbled backward, coughing hard, her eyes wet and raw as she gripped the headboard for support. For a moment, she just breathed, steadying herself. Then, she moved with purpose. Reaching into his pocket, she took his keys and headed to the inventory. She gathered spares of every piece of equipment needed to run a memory sequence.

Back in the room, JUDE set everything up in under ten minutes, moving quickly and efficiently. But as she worked, she knew the thiopental wouldn't keep him down for long. Once her setup was ready, she gave JAMES another shot, knowing each dose bought her only a narrow ten-minute window. Therefore, she hooked up a constant supply, just like in The Black Room, ensuring he'd stay unconscious long enough for her to complete what needed to be done. Everything was prepared, ready to be set in motion.

She recalled working on the memory sequence earlier that night, pretending to focus on the memory recollection program while, in reality, crafting a plan. She remembered swiftly connecting JAMES to the equipment, positioning the headcap, and then running the sequence she'd designed with careful intent. As she sat in the car now, recounting every detail, a quiet pride filled her. The sequence had done exactly what she intended—compelling JAMES to believe that the project could not move forward without the team, convincing him that only they held the key to its future. Even more, it erased every scrap of knowledge or memory that JAMES could have used against them, leading him to plead with CROSS on their behalf. A smile crept to her lips beneath the blindfold.

She savoured the memory of JAMES taking those bullets, replaying it in slow motion in her mind. Her thoughts turned to the conversations she'd had with J, and how, during those exchanges, she caught onto something crucial. Mentioning his company had triggered flashes of memories in him, just as seeing

JAMES's gun had sparked another set of recollections. She'd discovered a way to blur the lines between memory and reality, to plant a cue that could bridge the two worlds. The sequence she'd embedded—a subtle trigger—would activate a real-world response, seamlessly merging JAMES' memories with her intentions.

As she slipped out of A44 with J's call button, a sense of satisfaction welled up within her. That button was more than a simple device—it was now the trigger she'd embedded deep in JAMES' mind. She had designed the memory sequence with precision, compelling him to react to the same cue 330 times, each repetition reinforcing the reflex. By the end of those 330 repetitions, JAMES would draw his gun and take aim instinctively, without hesitation. She had crafted it so that his mind would respond automatically, unable to distinguish this learned reflex from genuine intention—a perfect response woven seamlessly between memory and reality.

And finally, she recalled that long-awaited moment with perfect clarity: she had knelt there, watching, her fingers hovering over the call button, waiting for the right moment. When it arrived, she pressed it—and for the 331st time, JAMES responded exactly as programmed. His hand instinctively drew the gun, took aim. She savoured the split-second that followed, reliving the chaos in slow motion: the eruption of gunfire, the thick smoke that filled the room, the resounding thud as JAMES' body hit the floor, face down. The calm after the storm......

THE END

Moonlight gently filters into the room through a gap in the curtains, casting a soft glow across the space. J lies in the midst of a deep slumber, completely detached from the world around him, wrapped in the warmth of his blanket, his senses lost in peaceful oblivion.

Suddenly, a weight settled on his legs, and as his vision cleared, he realized he wasn't just standing anywhere—he was standing in the exact same spot he had been before. His heart tightened, fear clawing at him. Was he trapped in the same loop again? Was this all a continuation of the nightmare he thought had ended—the lab, JUDE, JENESIS—had it all just been a detour? His pulse quickened as he glanced through the window. The street outside was dimly lit, the yellowish glow casting long shadows, and in the distance, the barking of dogs echoed. The scene felt eerily familiar, like time had folded in on itself, and he was stuck in a moment that should have passed long ago. He turned slowly, and there it was. Time read **22:10**, and yet again, there was a body lying motionless under the covers.

This was it. The nightmare he had fought so hard to escape had found him again. The familiar dread settled in his chest. He had given up—if this was his reality now, what reason was there to keep going? His eyes drifted to the door on his left. Another transition, another moment to briefly taste life. But this time, it wouldn't matter. He'd make it poetic—he'd take a knife, and with it, his life.

But as he moved, a shift in the bed caught his attention. Something moved beneath the covers, a subtle shift, a sign of life. His body froze, and in disbelief, he changed course, stepping toward the silhouette on the bed. With every step closer, the air around him seemed to shift. The unmistakable scent of fresh rain on a summer evening mingled with the sweet fragrance of jasmine and vanilla, and with it, a strange sense of calm washed over him. His heartbeat slowed, confusion giving way to something softer, more hopeful. The figure stirred again, and as the covers shifted, he saw her—the long hair, the soft features, the face he had only dreamed of seeing again. It was Meow. His breath caught in his throat as he dropped to his knees beside her, unable to tear his gaze away. He looked at her with a kind of reverence, as though seeing her for the first time, yet knowing in his bones that this was the moment he had been waiting for—everything else had been a blur, but now, in this quiet, fragile moment, everything was clear.

J flips on the lights, his hand trembling slightly as he gently brushes a lock of hair from her face. Her eyes flutter open, and she's awake now, meeting his gaze.

Are you alright, baby? she murmurs, her voice soft and soothing.

Yes... J replies, his voice thick with emotion. *I just—I missed you so much.*

What brought you awake in the middle of the night? she murmured, her voice soft with sleep. *Go back to bed, baby boy. We've got a road trip ahead of us tomorrow.*

J smiles, his heart swelling with happiness. This is all he ever wanted. In that moment, words seemed so inadequate. A million "thank yous" wouldn't even come close to expressing how content and at peace he felt.

When I'm far away, I realize just how much I miss your dumbass, he chuckles softly, his eyes twinkling with joy. *I can never get enough of you. I want you for the rest of my life. I love you so much.*

I love you too, she replies, her voice heavy with sleep.

J leaned in, a tender smile playing on his lips, and pressed a soft kiss to hers........The clock read **22:13**, marking the moment.

But as his heart soared, he missed the faint glow on his desk. His laptop screen remained on, quietly demanding attention.

In stark white letters against the dark, it displayed

> **..... Finally, he finds her again—the love he thought he'd lost forever. From a man drowning in emptiness to one who finds beauty even in the smallest of things, they rebuild what was broken. A family. A life. And in the quiet of their story's end, they live not just happily, but whole.**
>
> **Twenty-Two: Thirteen,**
>
> **- JUDE**

www.ingramcontent.com/pod-product-compliance
Lightning Source LLC
LaVergne TN
LVHW091658070526
838199LV00050B/2194